Pride Publishing books by M.C. Roth

Single Books
The Drumbeat of His Heart
A Song for His Heart

A SONG FOR HIS HEART

M.C. ROTH

A Song for His Heart
ISBN # 978-1-83943-744-1
©Copyright M.C. Roth 2021
Cover Art by Erin Dameron-Hill ©Copyright September 2021
Interior text design by Claire Siemaszkiewicz
Pride Publishing

This is a work of fiction. All characters, places and events are from the author's imagination and should not be confused with fact. Any resemblance to persons, living or dead, events or places is purely coincidental.

All rights reserved. No part of this publication may be reproduced in any material form, whether by printing, photocopying, scanning or otherwise without the written permission of the publisher, Pride Publishing.

Applications should be addressed in the first instance, in writing, to Pride Publishing. Unauthorised or restricted acts in relation to this publication may result in civil proceedings and/or criminal prosecution.

The author and illustrator have asserted their respective rights under the Copyright Designs and Patents Acts 1988 (as amended) to be identified as the author of this book and illustrator of the artwork.

Published in 2021 by Pride Publishing, United Kingdom.

No part of this book may be reproduced, scanned, or distributed in any printed or electronic form without permission. Please do not participate in or encourage piracy of copyrighted materials in violation of the authors' rights. Purchase only authorised copies.

Pride Publishing is an imprint of Totally Entwined Group Limited.

If you purchased this book without a cover you should be aware that this book is stolen property. It was reported as "unsold and destroyed" to the publisher and neither the author nor the publisher has received any payment for this "stripped book".

A SONG FOR HIS HEART

Dedication

For Q

Chapter One

The roar of the twin turbofan engines burst against Trent's ears like a koala calling for a mate. The sound was unexpected, coming from such a beautiful thing that seemed so innocent and sluggish. And while the plane was a lethargic beast on the ground, one that could hardly make a turn on its own without falling off the thick tarmac, it transformed into a serpent the moment the engines came to life.

Trent rocked back into the padded seat and clutched the armrest in a tight grip as his stomach dropped to the vicinity of his ankles. It was like the worst kind of roller coaster — one that he would ride fearlessly as a kid, only realizing later that its rusted parts were held together by bits of chewing gum.

He could hardly breathe as his ears pressurized, then popped, only to pressurize again. His mouth was dry, and his tongue was stiff with the need to hurl his light dinner all over the back of the seat that was tight against his knees. But the food couldn't make it past his throat with his stomach so low to the floor.

He glanced at the view through the tiny oval window that looked much too flimsy to handle the same forces that were battering his ears. There were two panes, and one had an actual hole in the bottom as if it were already prepared for the doom that awaited the passengers, himself included.

It was beautiful, though. The blinking lights of the city looked so similar to the stars, and they had started to meld together into one sphere of never-ending sky. The buildings that had looked so tall while standing on the ground now looked no higher than a sheet of Bristol board. The lake was lost, as were the stream of cars along blurred highways.

The moon was barely a sliver of light, but it was so bright that he had to blink to clear the spots from his vision. The silver beams illuminated a white fluff of clouds as they fluttered over the gleaming wing.

"See? It's not so bad," said Ian from the seat next to him. He moved his hand, so warm and comforting, to soothe Trent's. "That was a good take-off too. Nice and smooth." His smile was completely at ease and his grip soft as the plane trembled around them.

"I think I'm gonna puke." Trent gripped his stomach as the wing dipped again and they loomed sideways over the city of lights. *How are we even in the air at this angle?* He waited for gravity to grip them in a lasso and tear them back down to the earth.

"Smile," said Ian urgently as he leaned forward to rifle through the seat pouch. There were a few magazines that had probably been touched by hundreds of hands, as well as the day's newspaper, in the small elastic compartment. Ian found a slim white bag between the pages of one of the magazines.

"What?" Trent breathed deeply through his nose and forced his mouth shut as he slid his eyes closed. His mind whirled at the same speed as the plane as it continued to climb. Were they still sideways right now and slipping down to their doom? Maybe if they climbed high enough, he wouldn't feel it when they hit the inevitable bottom.

"T, baby, take a deep breath for me and smile," said Ian as he pressed his hand gently to Trent's chest at the level of his heart. It was enough to ground Trent into taking another breath, even as he quivered beneath the touch.

"If you smile, you can't gag, so you won't puke. Here." There was a shiver of sound as something slid beside him.

When he opened his eyes again with a forced grin on his face, the window shutter was thankfully closed. Without the dark blankness looking back at him, he could almost imagine being on a bus and not a massive plane that was soaring precariously in the sky. He could imagine that the tiny bumps were little potholes along the road, and the roar was a never-ending layer of slow strips carved into the asphalt.

Ian was right there, smiling and rubbing his chest until his warm palm rested over Trent's stomach. Ian's blue eyes were bright in the low light and his full lips were pulled back into a smile as he held the sick bag out to Trent. The ink carved into Ian's skull was blocked by the black baseball cap that he had insisted on wearing to the airport. The sight of Ian, so beautiful and familiar, settled something deep within Trent.

Trent grabbed the sick bag and slipped it back into the pouch between the layers of magazines, leaving a corner out so it would still be in reach if his stomach started to turn. When he leaned back, it lined his lips up perfectly with his new husband's, and he felt the steady tug that drew him in. Ian pulled back in surprise before their lips could meet, his gaze darting around the large compartment of passengers.

There was a child in the next row who was repeatedly kicking the seat ahead of him while playing with the touch screen that was built into the back of the headrest. It was a great idea to pass the time, but the way the child was hacking away at it was obviously driving the person in front insane. They looked back a few times, glancing at the father, who had his phone in his hand as he played what appeared to be a repetitive assassin game, while managing to stay completely oblivious to his son. There were others looking out of their windows or resting with their heads back with their eyes closed.

"Sorry." Trent smiled, not sorry at all. "I know you don't like PDA, but it's our honeymoon." Saying Ian didn't like it was an understatement. The man was simultaneously terrified and repulsed with the idea of PDA. It blew Trent's mind that this was the same man who had an exhibitionist streak that was larger than the aeroplane they were on.

"I love you. You know that," said Ian as he stumbled over his quiet words. "But when I kiss you, I want to do it right. I can't do it right with a kid staring at me." Ian cut his focus over to the little boy, who had given up smacking the touch screen and had started pushing the armrest up and down, his feet never stopping once.

"It didn't stop you in a public pool," said Trent with a smirk. "Or in the back seat of your rental when we parked at the baseball diamond." After renting a Hyundai on his first visit, Ian had learned his lesson and had stuck to large vehicles after that. It had taken a lot of convincing before Trent had found himself on his hands and knees in the back seat of a jeep.

"That was different." Ian crossed his arms before he leaned back in his chair. His long legs bumped the seat, so he splayed them wide, with one knee spilling out into the aisle and the other taking up a third of Trent's minimal space. "Why didn't you let me treat you to first class again? The leg room back here is atrocious."

Trent shifted in his seat and let Ian change the subject. His own knees were very firmly pressed into a cushioned backrest, while still being off to the side. It was a tight fit for him, and even worse for Ian, but there was no way that he could have allowed them to spend an extra two thousand dollars to get first-class tickets.

"If I really had my way, we would have driven. I may not own a car, but I can drive," said Trent as he tried again to get comfortable.

"And if I had my way, we would've done this months ago...before we got married," said Ian as he fiddled with the gold band on his finger. The metal was smooth and sleek, and it fit him perfectly. Trent had overestimated the size when he had bought it, and it had barely stayed on Ian's thumb without falling off. When Trent had found out that Ian had resized it, he had pretended to be furious, telling Ian that it was supposed to be a cock ring, not one for his finger.

"Are you excited?" asked Ian, turning in his seat as much as he could. He bounced one leg in the aisle and had started a steady beat against his thigh. His ring flashed in the artificial light with every movement.

"Yes, of course," said Trent as he swallowed the lump that had formed in his throat. "I'm super excited." Luckily, he managed to keep most of the terror out of his voice. Miami was huge, hot, hip and expensive. It was also everything that Trent wasn't.

He fiddled with his ring that matched Ian's. The skin under the band was faded and pale from months of being shaded from the sun. It had stayed on his finger from the day before Christmas, when Ian had proposed, until the morning of their wedding on August eighteenth. By then, he'd had to soap up his finger to even get the band to budge.

The wedding had been a small affair, with only Trent's closest family and his best friend, Candace. Ian had refused to invite anyone from his family, and Trent had wholeheartedly agreed to keep that rock buried as long as possible. It would have been next to impossible to get in touch with Ian's mother anyway, as she lived entirely off the grid. He had been a little bit surprised when Ian had refused to invite his fellow band members, but he'd explained that he didn't want them all to feel obligated to fly in for it. Trent's tiny town probably wouldn't have been able to handle them anyway.

The ceremony had been short and sweet, which had made it absolutely perfect in Trent's eyes. There was nothing worse than sitting through a two-hour wedding service that included an actual communion. There had been no speeches, no fancy photographer and no dancing afterwards, just a simple dinner at home. Ian had still insisted on carrying Trent over the threshold like some kind of creamy-thighed bridezilla, though.

"What is your house like?" Trent asked as he trailed his fingers along the arm rest. He'd seen pictures on Ian's phone of some of the different rooms, but it had compounded into a disarticulated checkerboard in his imagination.

Ian had talked about the house a lot, but his stories usually revolved around the infinity pool in the back yard, leading Trent to believe that the man spent most of his time in Miami swimming. Now that they were married, Ian was spending most of his time off work at Trent's, but the moment Trent had secured some vacation time for his honeymoon, they'd booked the flight.

"You are going to love it," said Ian, taking a deep breath before he dove in. "It's about four thousand square feet, I think, with three bedrooms and five bathrooms. There is a drum room in the basement that's pretty epic, and a theatre room for rainy days. I think you'll like the pool the best, though, and maybe the hot tub." A nostalgic look crossed Ian's face as he spoke about the house.

"Three bedrooms sounds like two bedrooms too many — or do you pick a different one to sleep in every other night?" Trent asked. The seatbelt sign clicked off above their heads, but the no smoking sign stayed glowing red and orange. He kept his belt pulled tight, even as Ian undid his and adjusted his seat back a few scant centimetres.

"Nah," said Ian as he looked up and down the aisle. "I hope they bring out drinks soon." He looked back to Trent and settled his hand over Trent's clenched one. "I've only slept in the one bedroom, actually, but I converted another into an office and the third into a library."

"But you don't read. I could hardly get you to sit still long enough to get through that magazine, and it was about cars." Trent crossed his arms and played with his wedding ring, spinning it endlessly.

"Not books, T…records. I told you about my record collection." Ian looked away as the hostess interrupted them, handing them two drinks after Ian's quick request. Trent took the cold plastic cup gratefully and sipped at the ginger ale. The bubbles flowed over his tongue and down his throat, making his mouth momentarily numb. He glanced at Ian's cup, hoping the same liquid was inside.

"Just cola, plain cola," said Ian as he caught the look. He tilted the cup back and gulped it down in three swallows. "I'm so thirsty, though. I should've finished that water before customs, but I got distracted pointing everything out to you." He placed the empty cup on the small plastic tray that folded down from the seat in front.

"I just couldn't figure it out." Trent shook his head. "Why would someone buy that many cigarettes and that much overpriced booze, just to take on a plane? Head to the closest box store and you'll pay half the price, and you still won't pay duty if you limit yourself." Although, strangely enough, after looking at the same neatly organized cigarette cartons for three hours, they had started to look downright delicious.

"A lot can happen if you get stuck in the airport for eighteen hours," said Ian as he waved down the stewardess for another drink, finishing that one too. "The first time I got stuck, there was a ten-hour layover. It was with the band, and I still drank back then. We just drank the entire time, and I got so wasted that I don't even remember the flight at all. I just fell asleep in Arizona and woke up in Buffalo." He slipped the newly emptied cup into the first one so that they were stacked neatly in the small circle on the tray.

"Then there was the England flight," Ian continued. "We spent a whole day in the airport because the plane had to be repaired. Twenty-four hours of sitting in a plastic chair and getting hit on by this random chick was enough to make me want to turn straight, just so I could fuck her and get her to shut up." He shuddered. "Man, I'm still thirsty. Maybe they can just give me a two-litre?"

Trent laughed, shaking his head as Ian caught the attention of the hostess for the third time. Her bright smile hadn't dimmed and a shimmer of recognition had floated over her face. Trent had seen the look before when someone realized who Ian was. Their eyes would widen just a fraction, and he would see the gears turning in their heads before they decided that yep, that was somebody famous.

Ian slipped her an American twenty, and she passed him a few cans without a second thought. She was about to step away when she paused and leaned back in.

"There are a few spots in first class that are open if you are interested in moving up. I'll see if there are two seats together." Her smile widened as Ian nodded more times than was strictly necessary.

"Yes, please get me out of these tiny seats," said Ian. "It's his fault anyway. He insisted on economy to get the full experience." He pointed an accusing thumb at Trent. Trent wilted in his chair as the stewardess chuckled.

"And how are you enjoying the experience?" Her smile lifted at one side, revealing her perfect white teeth. Trent took a second look at her, from her broad form to her strawberry hair that was pulled back into a perfect bun.

"It's, um…cosy." Trent tried to shrug, but his shoulders were pressed so close to Ian's that the movement hardly registered. He shifted in the seat, but his knee came up and struck the small plastic tray, sending the cups to the floor.

She laughed, a high tittering sound that sent a shiver down Trent's spine with how familiar it was. "I'll be right back." She disappeared up the aisle and ducked behind the grey curtain near the front of the plane.

A rumble of turbulence shook the plane with a burst of vibration and sound. Trent peered over Ian's shoulder to the window at the other side of the plane as he tried to see what could cause such a terrible noise on such a large bird. Through the thin pane of glass, he watched the wing bow and flex in a way that couldn't be natural for metal.

"Oh God," said Trent as he gripped the armrest hard. Ian held Trent's hand and pulled it to his chest. It was hard and hot and Trent could feel the slow and steady beat of Ian's heart under his palm. Trent's gaze snapped back to the magazines, where the corner of the bag was still visible. The bubbles from the ginger ale didn't feel so great in the pit of his stomach anymore.

"You're fine." Ian's low rumble was calm and soothing, but it did little to quench Trent's terror. "Clouds aren't as fluffy as they look, and the plane just has to work a little harder to get above them. Once we stop going up, it will be a lot smoother."

"We're still going up?" Trent looked around the cabin, but the rows looked totally flat to him. His stomach wasn't dropping anymore, and his ears had stopped popping, leaving his head filled with a steady pressure like he had a mild cold.

"Not for much longer. It will smooth out in a bit, I promise. I've taken this flight loads of times, and I'm always fine. You will be too." He brought Trent's hand to his lips in an uncharacteristic display of public affection.

The stewardess reappeared at the curtain and bustled over to them with a smile before she leaned close again. "Here... Just follow me. I'll grab your bags after we get you moved so no one will get jealous." Her voice was quiet enough that only they could hear.

Ian slipped out of his seat with a slight stagger as he tried to release his pinned left leg that had probably gone numb sometime during the ascent. Trent tried to follow, his arms flailing, only to realize that he still had his seatbelt strapped around his waist. He flushed as Ian smirked and the hostess let out a small laugh hidden behind her palm.

He grabbed Ian's soda cans that were between his legs, then pulled the buckle open and shimmied to his feet. His knees were completely numb and felt similar to the consistency of thick rice pudding that didn't have the bonus cinnamon. He took a step and nearly tumbled into Ian, who caught him with a hand on his elbow.

"It's like walking on a boat," said Ian as he let his hand fall so he could follow the stewardess, who was waiting at the curtain.

The floor was moving under Trent's feet in an alarming way. It wasn't anything like the gentle rock of his uncle's boat as the four-stroke engine cut through the waves of the Great Lakes on a calm day. This was more like walking in the back of a hay wagon as it tumbled along a weaving country road.

He braced his hand on the nearest seat and took a tentative step, pleasantly surprised when he didn't fall flat on his face. He made it down the aisle and through the curtain, barely, to where the other two were waiting behind the grandest set of plane seats that Trent could have imagined. They must've landed and gotten on another plane, because as the curtain slid shut behind him, he seemingly entered a whole new world.

This area was so much better, with enough leg room for two people, and seats that had extra padding and slid completely flat for anyone who wanted a nap. The built-in screens were bigger, and there was a bottle of champagne waiting for them in a bucket of ice. There were pillows, actual pillows, and not the ones that went flat the moment his head hit them.

"Here." Ian grabbed the bottle as he slid into his seat. He pulled a bill out of his pocket and presented it with the champagne to the stewardess. She took both with a slight nod of thanks.

"Just let me know if you need anything," she said as Trent slid the soda cans into the now-empty bucket of ice. She smoothed a hair back that had managed to slip away from her bun and turned away.

"Wait!" Trent called out, probably louder than he should've by the glance that was directed his way from across the expansive aisle.

"Yes?" The hostess looked back at him with a shy smile and a slight blush on her cheeks.

"Um, can I have your number?" Trent asked in a low voice. Ian spluttered beside him, choking on another cup of pop, and Trent flushed even hotter than the stewardess.

"It's not for me. It's for my friend. I just thought, if you were available, you two would get along." He sat back in his chair, suddenly wanting nothing more than to be right beside the flexing wing that might break off at any moment. Ian was still gasping and choking beside him, drawing every eye in first class.

The stewardess took a step back, and a bright flush passed over her cheeks as she chewed on her lower lip. She looked from Trent to Ian, then back to Trent.

"Oh, it's not for him. He's mine," said Trent, shaking his head as he pointed to Ian. Ian spluttered again, losing a second mouthful of pop as he tried to clear his throat. "It's for my friend Candace. Or I could give you her number and let her know that you might text her."

"I could take her number," said the stewardess as she nodded shyly and looked up and down the aisle, "if you show me a picture first."

Trent whipped out his phone and brought up the first picture of Candace that he had saved. It was a selfie of the two of them at Trent's wedding. She had been dressed beautifully, as always, in a strappy purple dress that left very little to the imagination, and her hair had been done up in a swirling up-do. She had smiled at the camera as if there had been no place in the world that she would've rather been.

At the stewardess's nod, Trent ripped off a corner of the newspaper in the seat pouch and used the pen she passed him to write down his friend's name and number. She slipped the paper into the pocket on her blouse before she nodded one last time and disappeared on the other side of the curtain.

"What the hell was that?" Ian hissed quietly. "I thought you were setting up a threesome—and don't get me wrong, I'm flattered, but we're gonna be tired after this flight." Ian let out a little laugh. "I definitely wouldn't mind. Not that I wouldn't prefer your ass, but I haven't been with a woman in so long—and it would be interesting to try with you."

"Not happening. I just have to keep up my reputation." Trent shook his head. He was still fascinatingly disgusted by breasts. "I have always been, and will always be, the best wingman ever."

A ding broke Ian's laughter, and the man fumbled with his pant pockets with a move that would not have been possible in the economy seats.

"Shit. I thought I'd turned this thing off. You can get in a lot of trouble for having your phone turned on in a plane." Ian flicked the screen open with a quick press of his fingertip to the back. His smile died and his brows drew together as he read whatever was on the glowing screen.

"Who is it?" asked Trent as he fluffed the pillow behind his head and reclined the chair a few degrees farther. It wasn't as good as his couch at home, but it was a definite improvement over the economy chairs.

"Mac wants to record the new tracks this week," said Ian as he clicked his phone off and shoved it back into his pocket. The seams strained as he nearly pushed the phone straight through the fabric.

"But it's our honeymoon," said Trent, unable to keep the whine of disbelief from his voice. He would support Ian's career in any way he could, but this crossed a few lines. He was so ready to get fucked through at least nine lives, and nothing was going to get in the way of that, not even Ian's best friend and manager.

"I'll take care of it, T," said Ian with a forced smile on his face as he reached for Trent's hand that had settled between them. "So, tell me again why we can't have a threesome?"

Trent snorted and turned away, squeezing Ian's hand once. This was going to be the best vacation of his life.

Chapter Two

Ian shifted in his seat for the third time in the last minute. He dragged his large feet against the thin carpet and ran his hand along the armrest before squeezing at the end. The seat crinkled as he shifted again, bumping his shoulder into Trent's, despite the large amount of room they were now sharing. Trent looked up from his movie and glared at his husband.

"What are you doing?" he asked too loudly over the sound that was blasting through the single earphone in his right ear. The movie was one of his favourites, but also one he'd never got to watch. It would last the entire flight and was the distraction he needed so he didn't keep thinking about the thousands of feet between the plane and the ground.

Ian looked at him and a bead of sweat on his smooth head dribbled over the crisp tattoo. He hunched his shoulders and locked his face into a grimace.

"Are you okay?" asked Trent, pulling the earbud from his ear. No one in the first-class cabin was looking their way, and even the stewardess had made herself scarce after delivering their bags to the cupboard above their heads.

"I have to pee so bad," said Ian as he shifted yet again. He moved his hand to Trent's knee and gripped hard as his own leg bounced against the ground.

"So go." Trent looked from Ian to the nearly empty pop cans with a raised eyebrow. The first-class bathroom was only about ten steps away and had been open for almost the entire flight. He turned back to his movie, but a tug on his shirt pulled his attention away again.

"I don't like peeing on planes. The suction is crazy powerful when you flush, and one of these days I'm going to flush and it'll suck my dick right out of my pants." Ian shook his head and his eyes glazed over. "I'll just hold it until Miami."

Trent glanced at his watch. They were an hour into a three-and-a-half-hour flight, and there was only so much space in one man's bladder. "Just go, Ian. I'll come and save you if your dick falls in." Resuming the musical, he plugged the earbud back into his ear as his husband rose from his seat.

He tried to keep his voice low as the words to the songs in the movie appeared on his lips. He was pretty sure that he had already made a few enemies in first class as he hummed along with the songs, but Ian had seemed to find it funny. He had just drummed along beside Trent, tapping his thigh to the sound of Trent's humming.

Trent looked up and stretched in the mysteriously comfortable chair, pulling himself out of the movie for a moment to look around. Three scenes later and the seat beside him was still empty. The little red light above the bathroom door still indicated that it was occupied, but there was someone waiting in line now. They tapped their foot before they let out a huff and headed to the other bathroom on the far side of the curtain.

He pulled the bud from his ear and tilted his head. Surely Ian would have screamed if he'd actually lost his dick in the toilet and Trent would've heard it over the movie. But there were also a large number of other things that could've gone wrong behind the flimsy doors. Ian did always have a bit of a weak stomach, and the airport burgers had been a bit red for Trent's taste. A medium-rare burger was not something that he ever wanted to experience, despite Ian's insistence.

He stood slowly from the padded seat, giving himself a moment to find his balance on the perpetually moving floor. The seats were far apart here and couldn't be used as a crutch like the economy chairs, so he had to move slowly. Luckily, the air had gotten smoother once they'd peaked above the clouds. Ian had been right about that.

He knocked quietly on the bathroom stall door and whispered through the hinged crack. "Ian, are you okay?" He pressed his ear against the door, feeling it bow under his weight.

There was no answer.

He knocked again, louder and more insistent as he called through the crack. No one looked up at his voice, and the disgruntled man from the line was already back in his seat with his arm tossed over his head as he seemingly caught a few minutes of rest. Trent's gut was starting to churn as worry set in. He shuddered as a picture formed in his mind of his dick-less husband waiting on the other side of the door.

The lock slid open and the light above Trent's head flipped green before the door started to move. It was barely cracked, when a familiar hand reached out to grab him. He didn't even have time to protest before he was pulled through the door into the bathroom and the lock clicked shut again.

"Took you long enough," said Ian as he released Trent and crossed his arms, leaning back against the small sink. His lips were curled up in a smirk and the sweat was long gone from his head. With the two of them standing in the small space, there was scarcely enough room to breathe.

Trent had never actually been in an aeroplane bathroom before, and he was very glad he had avoided the privilege up until that point. The toilet looked like something he could find in a port-a-potty at a park where homeless guys shot up. The sink was tiny, barely large enough to fit Ian's hands inside, and a small circular mirror was perched above it. There was a scrap of toilet paper balled up on the floor, and the whole room smelled like stale sewage with a hint of air freshener.

"I thought you'd lost your dick," said Trent as he flicked his eyes down to Ian's tented jeans. "So I was touring the plane looking for a new husband, but I couldn't find one hot enough, so I decided to just come and get you."

Trent's mouth went dry as Ian moved a hand down his own chest to the front of his jeans before he popped the button, revealing his hard cock that was already free from his boxers. He grabbed Trent by the shoulder with his other hand, pulling him even closer in the tight space.

"Since I was in here anyway, I thought that I might as well leave my mark," said Ian as he wrapped his arms around Trent's neck and lowered his mouth. Trent balked, his back striking the wall as he pulled away.

"I am not fucking you in an aeroplane!" Trent said through clenched teeth as he shook his head. He dropped his gaze to the bunched-up toilet paper, then around the small space. It was worse than the Hyundai. "It's not even possible anyway, because there is literally not enough room."

Trent tried to break Ian's grip, but the drummer held fast. Trent glared at the flimsy door and searched for the lock. There were people right on the other side of that door and it seemed thinner than a black-out curtain. He knew he couldn't keep quiet…not with Ian. And he did not want to smell sewage when he was getting fucked by the man he loved.

"Come on, T. Let's just fool around a little. I'll make you feel good. You know that." Ian leaned in, leaving Trent no room to move, let alone think, and he pressed his lips at the point behind Trent's ear that always made him moan.

A hand slapped over Trent's mouth as Ian nipped the same spot before sucking the skin. Trent's knees turned into jelly and he leaned hard on the thin door, distantly hoping that it could hold his weight. In his moment of weakness, Ian pulled him away from the door and toward the sink, before Ian flipped him around until he faced the mirror.

Trent's breath steamed up the glass and the edge of the sink cut a line across his groin. His face was already flushed, and his eyes were half-lidded with his pupils blown wide from the desire that suddenly rushed through his body. His lips were red and wet where Ian's palm had sealed the sound in. He already looked debauched, and he was only seconds away from giving in and letting Ian have his way. The man was insatiable, and he pushed Trent's limits constantly, but Trent could never deny him anything he wanted — not when a mind-blowing orgasm was dangling in front of him like a piñata.

Ian was already starting to kneel behind him, his legs going wide so he had the room in the small space. Trent heard the fabric of Ian's shirt catch against the opposite wall, so he shuffled forward as much as he could, pushing his belly hard into the rigid sink.

Ian wasted no time and pulled Trent's pants and boxers down together as he dropped. He grasped Trent's leg, helping him to slip one foot through the hole so he could force Trent to spread his legs wide. Trent was lucky he had taken his shoes off earlier in the flight or he didn't think he would've been able to pull the move off.

Trent's cock was already hard and peeking just below the tiny countertop, but he moved closer, leaning forward and going up on his toes until it was dangling into the sink. At least if he shot off, it would make for an easier clean up. His toes were just against the bottom of the door and the toilet seat, leaving little space for Ian to work.

Ian's mouth was on him without warning as he dipped his tongue straight to its goal and wiggled it against his rim. Trent was always a bit unsure each time Ian rimmed him. He had been sitting in the airport, then on the plane, and he had been sweating when he'd thought he was going to die. He bit his lip and gripped the sink as he tried to keep quiet.

After a moment of hesitation, he leaned back into the touch and let Ian go to work. His husband always knew exactly what he was doing and hadn't complained once. He knew Ian would lick him first, then spear him on his tongue before pushing his fingers inside one by one until Trent was stuffed and begging for more.

But this time, after a few licks, Ian moved away and stood up, scraping his back against the wall again. Trent's stomach dropped and he grimaced, but Ian was like a warm barricade of strength behind him, silencing his every negative thought. Ian tilted his head to the side and his neck cracked as the drummer stretched. Trent kept his *I told you so* to himself.

"I need you a little higher, baby. I can't quite reach," said Ian as he gripped Trent's hips and lifted him along the sink. Ian picked him up like Trent weighed positively nothing, and that did so many things for Trent on so many levels.

There was a moment of weightlessness when his toes left the ground, but then Trent gripped the side of the sink to steady himself. His legs were trapped between the counter and Ian, which held him secure enough that he wouldn't slide back down, but he would probably have bruises there in a minute. He had no idea how this was supposed to work once Ian started to move.

"Condom," Trent whispered as he tilted back for a kiss. Ian caught his lips, but the angle was too extreme and their teeth clacked uncomfortably. Ian lined his cock up with Trent's mostly unprepared entrance as it threatened to push inside.

"Already taken care of, T. I knew you wouldn't want the mess," said Ian before he started to grind forward.

Trent had expected a finger or two at the bare minimum before Ian went for the hole-in-one, but he must've been waiting longer than Trent thought. It usually took a lot for him to get pushy and lose his control, but then again, this was probably one of Ian's deepest fantasies. Trent bit his lip hard and took a breath to try to relax himself, hoping it was enough — but knowing it wouldn't be.

Ian stayed shallow at first, teasing Trent's entrance into compliance with the tip of his cock in the way he normally would with his fingers and tongue. Trent's body knew that cock so well, but it had been hours since it had been inside him. It was only a few soft thrusts before Ian was breaching him.

The condom was slick and so different from the usual heat of Ian's cock that it startled Trent as the head settled just past his rim. They never fucked with a condom anymore, trusting each other to be faithful. They'd both had negative test results, after all, and there was nothing like the heat of a bare cock sliding inside, with every ripple and vein rubbing against Trent's vulnerable rim.

"Oh Christ." Trent bit his lip hard enough that he tasted blood. It was a stretch to take Ian without any prep, no matter how many times he'd done it before. The man's cock was a multi-national treasure — at least, to those who had had the privilege in the past, in Trent's estimation.

"Wait, fuck, wait," said Trent as quietly as he could when Ian attempted to push himself deeper. His hold on the sink slipped as the ache suddenly went from tolerable to the wrong side of pain when Ian slid that extra inch. The condom tugged at his rim where skin would usually slide smoothly, and it fucking burned.

Ian stopped moving immediately, his body going taut from the tension.

"Sorry, T," said Ian as he nuzzled against Trent's neck while breathing hard. "I should've known better. You're always so tight for me." He swept his hands down Trent's sides to cup his ass, lifting him off his cock with a pop.

"Oh fuck." A wave of emptiness crashed over Trent and he strained back as he tried to fill it again, but Ian wasn't having it. He held Trent up and moved him back and forth over his cock so that the tip just kissed the surface but never sank inside.

"Please, I can take it," said Trent, gripping the sink and using it to force himself down that extra inch he needed. "I don't care if it hurts, just please fuck me." His cock throbbed, taking over every bit of self-preservation and shame.

"I'm not gonna hurt you, T." Ian pulled him right back up, so much stronger than Trent. "I'd never hurt you." Ian was shaking from exertion and need, but he obviously wasn't giving in.

Trent looked into the mirror, which had started to fog, and caught Ian's gaze. They were both breathing hard in the small space and Trent could see the strain it was having on Ian, but there was only one thing in his eyes, and it wasn't lust. It was love, pure and simple.

A knock at the door cut through the steamed haze between them and dumped a lake of ice water over Trent's head. Ian went tense as he slowly moved his hips back and lowered Trent to the floor before he tucked himself away once he'd pulled the condom off and stuffed it into the trash. Trent tried to follow suit as his heart fluttered, but he tripped over his tangled pants, falling back into Ian in the small space. Ian grunted as he caught his weight and they narrowly missed falling onto the toilet.

The knock came again, a loud *rat-a-tat*. Trent scrambled for his pants, pulling them up and buttoning the waist with breath-taking speed. Ian gave him a quick once-over before he turned the lock and opened the door just a crack. He used his body like a giant shield to keep Trent from view as Trent combed his hair with his hands and willed the flush from his face. His heart was beating faster than a hummingbird's and he couldn't seem to catch his breath. Even if he could get his breath back, he would just curse Ian anyway.

"Get out of there before my manager figures out what's going on." It was the stewardess on the other side of the door, speaking in a low voice. Her kind smile was gone, replaced by a raised eyebrow and a knowing look. She looked Ian up and down, before she peeked around him to see Trent still scrambling.

"I follow you on social media, and I get that this is your honeymoon, but I have to clean that bathroom. Not cool." She spied the crumpled toilet paper on the ground and her eyes narrowed.

"Sorry," Ian shrugged and slipped through the door, pulling it shut behind him and leaving Trent alone. Their voices drifted away, too low to be heard over the hum of the engines, and Trent was left alone with the staccato of his own heart.

Trent grabbed a wad of paper towel and wiped the lube and spit from between his ass cheeks with a grimace. There was a twinge as he made the pass with the rough paper, and he winced. The rest of the plane ride was not going to be fun. He grabbed the crumpled toilet paper off the ground and threw it into the trash, then washed his hands vigorously. He was not getting herpes from a plane bathroom.

He shuffled back to his seat, avoiding every gaze on the ten-step walk. He heard a few distant snores and saw one person typing on a silver laptop, but they didn't look up. Luckily, there was no one waiting in line either, but he knew that someone else had probably figured out what was happening and reported it to the stewardess.

Trent tried to think of how loud he had been when he'd got caught up in the moment and he shuddered. He was drawing the line at public washrooms in the future. He'd have to sanitize his junk where it had touched the countertop and sink. There was no knowing what else, and who else, had been there before him.

Ian was already in his seat with his legs stretched out and his chair tilted back, looking every ounce a man who'd just got laid. There was still a tent in his pants, though, even if Trent could only see it when he neared the seats, and his forehead was tinged with sweat again.

"I think that still counts," said Ian quietly as Trent shuffled past him to get to his seat next to the shuttered window. "I mean, technically, I was inside you, even if it was only for a second. So that means I am officially part of the mile-high club." He leaned back against his seat and smiled at Trent, who sat with a slight wince.

"You're an asshole," said Trent, looking away with a flush. His movie was still playing on the screen and he could just make out a whisper of sound through the abandoned earbud.

"I'm not the one who just gave the entire plane a show when I walked down the aisle with my fly open."

Ian laughed as Trent looked down at himself and found that, yes, his fly was completely open, and he could even see a bit of Little Trent poking through the slit in his boxers. He hadn't had time to go completely soft after all.

He scrambled with the zipper after carefully tucking himself back into the stretchy cotton, cursing as the teeth snagged the fabric.

"I'm getting a lock on any pants I wear in public," said Trent, huffing and leaning back into his chair. He winced as the new angle sent another shock up his spine. "And there's a new rule. No prep, no love."

"Did I hurt you?" Ian suddenly turned serious, all hints of joking pushed aside and replaced with concern. His gaze went dark at Trent's hum. "Shit, I'm so sorry, T. I guess I just got carried away."

"I didn't exactly try to stop you, either," Trent smiled, elbowing his husband. "You just have to keep in mind that you have a huge cock." He snickered as a passenger across the aisle opened their eyes and gave him a strange look. He lowered his voice until only Ian would hear him. "Just go easy on me. I want to last the whole honeymoon without my ass feeling like I just fucked a baseball bat."

"Is that a possibility?" Ian tried to ask seriously, but the spark in his eye gave away the joke. "Cause if you did that, then you would be ready to go all the time, no prep required ever again." A smile tugged at the edges of his lips and he let out a soft snort.

Trent smacked Ian on top of his head and turned to the window, lifting the shutter and peeking out into the black expanse. It still pulled at his soul, but he managed to shove the nausea to the side this time. There were no visible lights below them anymore, and the stars above were so bright that they outshone anything he'd seen.

The lights had dimmed in the plane as most people settled in and tried to sleep for the last hours of the flight. He could actually sleep if he wanted to. He wasn't sure if he should even try, for fear he would wake up in a free-fall. He pulled the shutter closed again.

"T?" Ian poked his side as he drew his brows together and started to bounce his legs on the floor. "I have to pee again."

"You are ridiculous." Trent closed his eyes and listened to the deep sound of the engines as they brought him closer to one of the most terrifying places on the planet.

Chapter Three

It was hot, so blindingly hot that Trent's T-shirt stuck to his back like a film of sticky cellophane. He'd thought he'd worn light enough clothes beneath his fall jacket, but apparently he'd underestimated just how different the Miami climate would be.

The humidity was enough to make his hair feel like it was standing on end, and his face felt gross after only a few seconds. It was also pitch black, but hot enough that it could be mistaken for mid-afternoon during a Canadian summer. It was one o'clock in the morning, but the pavement was still warm as if the sun continued to bake down from above. The breeze was steady and slow but did nothing to wipe away any sweat from his skin.

Ian sighed as they pushed through the glass doors that lined the exit. There were people milling around with haphazard piles of stacked luggage and sleepy expressions, which Trent was sure that he mirrored. He could hear planes taking off and landing in the distance, but the ground was completely solid beneath his feet. It was great to be able to walk normally again.

"It's so good to be back home," said Ian as he looked around the terminal, eyeing up different cabs and rideshares as they waited for passengers. "It's a touch warm for September, but you won't get better weather. No hurricanes in the forecast, either. That's something you have to watch for at this time of year." He raised his arm, hailing the nearest cab, before picking up all but one of the suitcases.

Trent was frozen. The soles of his sandals had melted into the sidewalk the moment that he'd heard the word *home* from Ian's lips. He'd never thought of this place as Ian's home. It was more of a place that was best left forgotten.

"You coming, T?" Ian's shout dragged his attention back to the thick, dark air of night. Ian was waiting for him behind a cab as if nothing were amiss in the world. His eyes were bright and his smile was wide, whereas Trent was aching to fall into the nearest pillow.

He dragged the last suitcase over to the idling cab and shoved it into the trunk with all the others that were stacked neatly like a Tetris game. He pushed against the lid then leaned his full weight on it before it finally snapped shut. His eyes felt grainy as he rubbed them then slid into the back seat next to Ian. The pressure in his ears hadn't quite equalized yet, and the night had a dream-like quality to it.

He'd taken a lot of cab rides in his life. Having no vehicle at home had forced his hand in that. When he did call the cab company, he had to bribe them to get them to come out of their normal area by offering them double the fares.

This cab was different from any he'd ever sat in, and it had him blinking to awareness as he looked around the interior. The driver smiled at them, smelling faintly of expensive aftershave that made his mouth water. The interior was clean too, with no tissues shoved into any available pocket and only a few speckles of dirt on the floor. He'd expected the stale smell of cigarettes, something that was illegal now in his home town but still managed to cling to the interior of older vehicles and their drivers. This cab was downright tasteful.

"It's too dark to see anything right now, but I'll take you out tomorrow in the Corvette and show you around town properly," said Ian as he looked through the dark windows. He still managed to look squished in the spacious back seat, with his knees pushed right against the base of the driver's spine.

"Sleep first." Trent let himself slide sideways until he was leaning on Ian's shoulder. The broad expanse would make the perfect pillow. The muscles tensed under his cheek and he peered up, wondering what was wrong. Ian was flushed while he looked between the driver and Trent.

Trent pulled away, feeling colder than the air-conditioned interior, and leaned against the window instead, letting his eyes droop. They'd come so far together, but sometimes it was the same as when they'd first met. Trent tried to blame it on Ian's background and the lack of support he'd had from friends and family, but sometimes he couldn't help but take things personally.

"Sorry," said Ian in a low voice as he reached out to grip Trent's hand. "Old habits, I guess." He squeezed once before letting Trent's fingers slip through his, bringing his hand back to rest on his lap. Trent grunted in response, trying to let the rebuke slide off him the way it used to. *Who am I kidding? It never slides off.*

Someone was shaking him moments later, and he batted them away with a flick of his wrist. He blinked, his eyes sticky and gritty as if he'd been asleep, although he couldn't remember dreaming. His neck was sore, though, so much so that he dreaded pushing himself upright.

He moved with a groan and winced as his shoulder suddenly came to life with numbness prickling his fingertips. There was a line of drool along the window that Trent quickly wiped away before anyone else could see.

The car had stopped moving at some point, but the engine was still running in a low idle that hardly made a noise. The seat next to him was empty, as was the driver's seat, but he could see the blur of people moving outside the dark windows. He pulled the door handle, pushing the door wide as he attempted to stumble out of the car. The belt forced him back into his seat.

"Oh, for fuck's sake," Trent grumbled under his breath. Ian was already laughing, a roaring noise that was much too loud for the early hour. Even the cabbie let out a small chuckle that made his round cheeks jiggle.

"That's two, T." Ian leaned in the door way, reaching across Trent and freeing him from the belt. "You get to three, and you get committed." It took Trent's brain a few seconds to realize that Ian was talking about a psychiatric ward.

"Don't get me started, Ian," said Trent, nudging his husband back so he could step out of the car. "How many times have you forgotten to turn the lights off? Or left the stove on? A lobotomy might be the way to go for you." He shook his leg out, tapping his sandaled heel against the pavement as he looked around.

It was still dark out, but there was enough light from streetlamps and house that it looked similar to dusk. There was a thick sidewalk on either side of the two-lane road that was paved to utter perfection. It looked like every twenty feet or so there was a palm tree on the thin grassy boulevard that was mowed and vibrant green, even in the dark. Beyond that were stone fences and wrought-iron gates that lined the opposite sides of the sidewalks. It was as if he had awoken in some sort of apocalyptic universe where everyone had built up walls to keep the zombies out.

Ian was dragging his large bundle of suitcases to the nearest gate. This gate had stone pillars on either side and a black iron fence that spanned an area that was wide enough for three cars to pass side by side. The lane was a cobbled driveway of every shade of beige and grey that was lit with lanterns that glowed a mellow yellow colour. There was an outline of a house beyond, but it was shrouded by darkness. At least, Trent thought it was a house. It looked more like a mansion from this distance.

"Come on, T. There is a California King that's calling our names," said Ian as he stopped at the gate and punched a code into a small box that Trent hadn't noticed. "The code is 49248 if you ever get locked out." There were a few consecutive beeps, then a click before the gate slide smoothly sideways, leaving a yawning maw for them to walk through.

The cabbie was already back in his car, patiently waiting for Trent to remove the last suitcase and close the trunk so he could carry on. Trent could only assume that Ian had already paid the man and hopefully left a tip behind too.

"What the hell is a California King?" Trent asked as he grabbed the heavy case and slammed the trunk shut.

He gave a little wave through the back window and the cabbie accelerated slowly down the winding street.

Trent rushed to follow Ian through the gate before it could snap shut on his heels. It looked heavy enough to break him in two if he were unlucky enough to get caught in it.

"It's like a king bed, only bigger and more awesome." Ian dropped his cases and pulled Trent into a hug, leaning down to place a kiss on his lips. "It's so good to finally have you here." His smile broadened under the dim lights.

As they approached the house, it grew from the shadow of a mansion into an actual one. The stone drive was crescent-shaped around a green circular garden that stood at the front of the house. In the middle of the garden was a palm tree that shaded a bunch of colourful shrubs underneath. It was all maintained and neatly trimmed, even though Ian hadn't been there in weeks.

It was about a one-hundred-foot walk before they finally made it to the front door, and by that time, Trent was thoroughly intimidated. The imperial measurements that Ian always insisted on were clogging his over-tired brain.

Ian produced a key from the pocket of his carry-on case and fiddled with the door, entering a second code as he turned the lock. The lights flickered on in the front hall as the door finally opened.

Trent's mind was too tired to come up with any description beside the word 'massive.' The foyer itself, with its grand staircase leading up to a second floor, was bigger than half of his house back in Canada. The floors were some kind of material that shimmered under the bright lights, although they transitioned to a more traditional wood through the doorways on either side. The ceiling was at least twelve feet high and lined with pot lights that kept any shadows at bay.

"How the hell do you change the lightbulbs?" Trent murmured to himself as Ian busied himself with dragging the luggage through the door. All Trent had to do at home was stand on a chair to change his lightbulbs, which were maybe a measly eight feet up.

The door clicked shut behind them, and there was a clunk as the lock engaged automatically. Ian moved past him and up the stairs, leaving all but one suitcase behind.

"Are there zombies here?" Trent asked as he stared back at the door. With the gate along the road, why the hell would Ian need such an intense lock on the front door? Or maybe there were vampires. *Sexy zombie vampires. I'm way too tired.*

"Just a few gators, but I haven't had one close to the house in a few years, so we shouldn't have to worry," said Ian as he looked back over his shoulder. "They aren't any worse than that raccoon you tried to fence with."

'Fence' was a generous word for what had actually happened. Trent had only been in his boxers when he'd seen a raccoon in the backyard, snarling and circling. He had grabbed a tea towel, which was the closest thing on hand, and the broom at the back door, hoping to scare the thing off with some waving and shouting. He hadn't expected it to turn on him with razor-sharp teeth that were dripping with likely infected saliva. He had pinned the raccoon to the ground by its snarling head, and they had circled each other as Ian laughed in the doorway and ignored Trent's frantic pleas to call animal control. Luckily, one of his neighbours was a trapper and had rushed over after hearing Trent's screams. He'd laughed too when he saw the scene, but he had stepped in to help with the animal shortly after.

"Well, I hope I get to see you fend off a gator with nothing but a pool noodle," said Trent as he climbed the stairs after his husband. From the middle of the stairs, he couldn't actually reach the banister on either side. What if he suddenly lost his balance and fell? There would be no way to catch himself until he hit the bottom. His staircase at home was narrow, steep and led to the dungeon of his tiny basement, complete with a cracked floor and the occasional mouse.

They turned down a hall that was lined with doors that were mostly shut. The floors were a deep, rich wood and the walls were an unfortunate beige. They passed a small bathroom that was filled with black fixtures, gleaming porcelain and a different shade of beige on the walls. *Fifty shades of beige and not a spot of colour to be seen.*

"It's all bedrooms and stuff up here, so it's pretty closed in, but downstairs is mostly open-concept," said Ian as he finally pushed open the door to their destination.

The room was utterly massive, with a ceiling that peaked to a skylight that currently showed a thin shimmer of stars that had managed to cut through the city lights. The room was bigger than any bedroom he'd ever been in, and in the middle was the largest bed he had ever had the pleasure of seeing. The sheets were stark white with a fluffy comforter on top, and the room was so cool that it sent a shiver up his spine. His shirt had long since dried in the cab, but the air conditioning here was really pushing it.

"I ordered a side stand for you before we came, and it looks like they got it in here okay," Ian said as he motioned to what Trent could only presume was his side of the bed, where a dark wooden side table sat. It was completely bare except for an unopened box of tissues that someone had placed there. A matching stand, heaped with a clock, a lamp, a watch, a charging cable and a few music magazines, sat on the other side.

Ian was moving to yet another door, which opened to reveal a walk-in closet that was filled to the brim with neatly hung clothing. Trent dropped his bag and crossed the room, grasping the handle on the remaining door and pulling it open to reveal a glistening bathroom.

"How is everything so clean? You've been gone for months." Trent ran his finger along the pristine marble countertop. The shower in the room was the second largest he'd ever seen, the largest being at a hotel in Toronto that he had visited the previous year for Ian's concert.

"Lisa comes in every week and keeps it spiffy while I'm away, and she's on call for stuff like deliveries. When I'm in town, she usually comes every day."

His voice drew closer, and suddenly Ian had closed in behind Trent, wrapping his arms around his shoulders and pulling him back against his chest. Trent leaned back into Ian's warm bulk and played with one of Ian's thick wrists. His fingertips didn't come close to touching when he wrapped them around it.

"You have a cleaning lady?" asked Trent. He could hear the awe in his voice, as if he had just discovered that Ian was a prince. He knew how much money Ian had, and it was upwards of the multi-millions, but the number rarely glared at him.

"Well, it used to be a guy named Steve who did it, but then he moved out of Miami, so the service sent Lisa instead. I just have to let them know when I'm coming and going, and they take care of the rest." He mouthed against Trent's neck. "Now, am I missing something, or did you not see the bed? You were supposed to dive right into those sheets." He moved lower to suck a bruise along the junction between Trent's neck and shoulder. It was just below the small bruise he had left on the plane, and it turned Trent's knees soft in the same way.

"Mmm, back rub first," said Trent as he rolled his shoulders and stiff neck. Ian could be rather vigorous, and in his current condition, he could actually pull a muscle—or worse. "You give the best back rubs, and I love it when you fuck me when I'm all loose and gooey."

"Deal." Ian pulled at Trent's pants, flicking the button open and unzipping the fly with one hand as he pulled Trent's shirt up with the other. He dragged his fingertips over Trent's pierced nipple on the way up, sending a zing of pleasure down to his belly. In moments, Trent was completely naked, and Ian was guiding him to the bed and dropping him on bedding that was softer than chinchilla fur.

Trent groaned and rolled in the sheets as he let them touch every inch of his body, which was slowly starting to heat in the cool air. The mattress was so soft that he melted into it like warm chocolate, and the thread count of the sheets had to be higher than Ian's libido.

Trent watched through heavy eyelids as Ian undressed slowly, pulling his shirt over his head in a way that made his arms bulge. The drummer knew how to show off every line in his body so that he looked like the sex symbol he could be. And Trent was the only one to reap the benefits.

Ian's pants were next, revealing his cock that was already half-hard and nestled against trimmed dark-blond hairs. Even at half-mast, the size was still impressive, matching some of the average guys Trent had been with. But of course, none of them had ever been inside him. Ian was the only one to do that to him.

"Roll over," said Ian as he dropped his last bit of clothing to the floor. He moved close, like a prowling predator, and Trent loved that he was the prey.

Trent rolled, moving up until he could grab one of the pillows at the top of the bed and bring it under his head. It was so soft and the perfect support, so he just let himself melt. Three-and-a-half hours in the air and a sleepless night of anticipation were catching up to him quickly.

A warm hand at his side made him jolt, but as Ian grasped the muscles there and kneaded, he let out a long groan. He relaxed into the bed farther as Ian went to work on his back, rubbing hard and pulling every bit of tension from his muscles. Being ambidextrous, Ian could do completely different things with each hand at the same time, and one of the things he was best at was taking Trent apart.

Ian leaned over and the pot lights flickered off, plunging them into darkness. He could barely see the outline of his hand on the sheets, let alone anything else in the room. The sky above had clouded over, dimming any light that could have shone down through the skylight from the moon.

Heat soaked into his muscles from Ian's palms, and slowly each knot unwound as it was massaged into utter submission. He drifted his eyes shut as he allowed himself to feel every sensation in the dark. Groans and whimpers forced their way through his mouth without restraint. A few times, Ian shifted over him, and his cock would drag along Trent's body as he worked his way down. It was hot and hard against him, slipping against his sensitive skin as pre-cum dripped from the head.

He fell deeper as it went on and on, until he was thinking only of Ian. A dream fluttered behind his eyes, even though he could still feel Ian's hands on him. He was awake and not at the same time, so utterly relaxed that he never wanted to move again.

He jolted as something pressed against his rim, warm and slick and pushing inside. The dream wavered, but his limbs stayed locked beneath a layer of sleep.

"Wha?" Trent asked, his voice slurred with exhaustion. The strange feeling between his cheeks retreated and he nuzzled back into his pillow.

"Shit, are you asleep? Ah man, I'm like rock-fucking-hard here," Ian mumbled and Trent felt the bed shift as he pulled back.

Trent tried to answer and tell Ian that it was fine and he could do whatever he wanted, but all that came out was a tiny snore. The pillow was so comfortable and getting better with each minute that passed.

"It's okay, T, just sleep for me, honey. I'll still be hard for you in the morning," said Ian as he kissed the back of Trent's exposed neck before pulling the blankets over both of them. He moved in close, and Trent found the strength to release the pillow to attach himself to Ian's neck, so he could rest his head against the sound of Ian's heart. Trent settled his leg between Ian's and brushed something hard, hot and damp.

"Shit," said Ian as he let out a gasp and rocked his hips into the warm touch. "Christ, T, you are so hot, even when you're drooling on me." Ian gripped Trent's leg and pulled it up so it was tossed over his hip and no longer grazing his groin. "But I'm not gonna take advantage of you when you aren't even awake. Sleep tight, T." He pressed one last kiss to Trent's forehead, and it was the last thing Trent remembered before he was drifting off to sleep.

Chapter Four

Trent woke slowly in a room that was not his own. It was bright, as if the sun itself had peeked through the bricks and mortar to settle on a shelf above his head. It was chilly too, but much more comfortable than he would normally have his house set for this time of year—at least, not unless he wanted to pay a couple hundred bucks in utilities every month.

He blinked and his vision was immediately filled with a brilliant sun that was shining through the massive skylight in the ceiling. There was a sliver of crystal blue within the light, and the fluttering wisps of a few distant clouds that rolled lazily across the sky. As the spots faded before his eyes, it changed into something beautiful. He could see the appeal, despite the wake-up call.

He rolled over and pulled the blankets high up to his shoulders before wiggling his toes to try to get some warmth back in them. Ian was slack-jawed beside him, with his eyes scrunched up and a tiny snore coming from his mouth. Ian grumbled something in his sleep before he rolled and planted his face directly into the pillow.

The tattoo on his side stood out, still black and bright against tanned skin. The scar was pink and brighter than usual in the natural light, looking almost painful as it stretched over his ribs. Ian rubbed the spot in his sleep before he flopped his hand back to the bed and let out another muffled snore.

Trent crept out of bed, shivering as he relieved himself in the bathroom that looked like something out of a magazine. The double sink was an invention that should have been mandatory in every house, but the shower was the stunning centrepiece. There were matching towels in another shade of beige that made him shudder, but that was the only thing that was mildly off-putting about the room.

He peeked back around the corner, but Ian was still planted into the pillow as he attempted to smother himself. He ducked back into the bathroom and shut the door quietly before he flicked on the shower.

It took a while for the hot water to finally burn away the cold, but once it did, it nearly scalded the skin off his back. He cranked it down and stepped back into the spray, letting the water fall down him in a rush of warmth. It tasted a bit different as it slipped into his mouth and over his tongue, and the smell of it was just a tad strange. It was nothing bad, just another reminder that he was far from home.

He perused the copious amount of different body washes and shampoos, most of them feeling almost full when he lifted them from the shelf. He opened each cap and took a whiff, looking for the smell that was so distinctively Ian. The sandalwood with shea butter was close, but still off the mark.

He settled on a body wash that smelled almost like his regular kind, with just a tad of citrus blended in. The moment it touched him, he instantly felt more expensive. It lathered differently from the trusty name brand that he'd been using since high school, and when he rinsed it away, it left him feeling polished and new.

Ian was still asleep when Trent crept back into bed with his hair damp and the heat of the shower clinging to his skin. Ian was on his front with his legs spread wide below the sheets, utterly naked beneath. His head was tilted to the side and his snores had faded to deep relaxed breaths while Trent had been away. The position hid his cock from Trent, even as Trent gently pulled the sheets down to reveal firm buttocks.

Something was reachable though, something that Trent hardly ever thought to pay any attention to. He was always so focused on the great beast that was Ian's cock that he hardly ever had the time or energy to look elsewhere. He had taken Ian's sac into his mouth and licked along the seam, but he'd never dipped lower to what lay hidden beneath. That hidden part was now bare to him—a tight furl that drew him in with a sudden fascination.

He ran his fingertip over the surface with a slow, gentle slide, and it clenched beneath his touch. His mouth watered as he suddenly longed to taste it. He'd rimmed others before, but never Ian, even though Ian delighted in doing it to him at every opportunity. And Ian loved to be woken up by a blow job, so a rim job would probably make his day.

Trent leaned down until his face was just above the hairless stretch of skin, before he stuck his tongue out and licked. It was smooth and soft and tasted of Ian, only deeper and darker, with a hint of sweat from the previous day. The muscle twitched against his tongue before it relaxed and let the tip glance inside the very centre.

He circled the rim, pressing with every slow round. With each revolution, the furl softened beneath his touch and opened a bit. He dipped inside and sank into the warmth that was Ian. It was better than cocaine.

Ian gasped beneath him and his body flinched as he came awake all at once. He flipped over, ripping Trent's mouth away from him with a powerful move that left a hard cock hovering where a hole had been moments before.

Trent didn't wait or even look up to check in with Ian before he sank down on that cock until he choked as it hit the back of his throat and pushed beyond. It stretched his throat even wider as he swallowed around it, doing his best to supress his automatic gag — and mostly succeeding.

"Fuck, T." Ian bucked up as he lost control, sinking another inch into Trent's throat. His hands gripped Trent's hair and pulled the strands hard enough to hurt.

Trent gagged in earnest and pulled back with a gasp. Drool seeped from the corner of his mouth, and he wiped it away with a smile before he dove back in. Only then, with his lips stretched wide, did he look up at Ian. The man looked like an incubus getting ready to feast. His pupils were blown wide, and his face was flushed red with desire as his chest heaved.

Trent slid his tongue around the base of Ian's cock and licked up and down the broad vein that pulsed as he stroked it. He dropped his hand down, past Ian's sac, to the wet entrance hidden behind it. He let his finger graze over the hole that was still loose and soft, before he dipped the tip inside.

"Shit, T, stop," said Ian as he tugged hard at Trent's hair.

Trent pulled back, his mouth and hands coming away with an obscene pop. His naked ass hit his heels as he sat back, wiping his mouth with the back of his arm. Ian's face closed off in a way that had never happened during sex, and his brows were scrunched together in something akin to pain.

"Sorry, Ian. Did I hurt you?" asked Trent in dawning horror. He had tried to keep his teeth well behind his lips, but it wouldn't be the first time that he'd accidentally grazed Ian's cock with a sharp incisor as he got a bit over-zealous.

"It's okay, just not here," said Ian as he blushed and looked away. His shoulders hunched and he looked farther away than Canada.

"You don't want me to suck your cock?" Trent's jaw dropped as he glanced at the two balls nestled in Ian's sac. Yep, they were still there. Ian hadn't lost them in the aeroplane bathroom on the way to Miami.

"No, you can suck my cock all day if you want. That's not what I meant." Ian shook his head and grabbed Trent's hand before putting it back onto his slick shaft. It was barely half-hard. "Just not my ass." He flushed brighter as he said it.

"O-kay," Trent stuttered, completely shocked. Never in any of their times together had Ian ever said anything that would hint that he had a problem with that. "Sorry?" Trent wasn't sure what else to say, so as a true Canadian, he went for his default.

"I'm just not a big fan of it—not on me, I mean," said Ian as he let Trent's hand fall away from his now soft cock. "I just—." He paused, swallowing whatever he was going to say before tilting his head back and looking out through the skylight as if it would hold the answers.

"It's okay, Ian. You don't have to explain it to me if it makes you uncomfortable. I just wish you would have told me before I had the chance to fuck up," said Trent as he reached for Ian's hand and stroked the palm tenderly. "I get it, though. There's stuff I don't like too, and there's nothing wrong with that." He shifted back so Ian could close his thighs. They were pushing Trent from his position in between them. Ian slammed his legs shut as soon as Trent backed away.

The dreams of topping Ian fluttered away in ashes, but Trent only felt a distant sense of loss. Trent was good at topping and loved to take someone apart, but he would also do anything to stay with his husband.

"What's something you don't like?" Ian asked, as if he'd never considered it before. He crossed his arms and shifted back until he could lean against the massive live-edge headboard.

Trent turned away and pushed off the bed before he started looking around for his suitcase. The room was large enough that he could probably lose a body in it, but at least there was no clutter. Beside the stuffed closet and Ian's bedside table, it looked like a hotel room and not a home. He found the suitcase just inside the closet door and reached for the zipper to reveal his clothing. The house was too chilly to be walking around naked.

"T?" Ian asked again from his position on the bed. He hadn't moved, but his eyes tracked Trent's every movement.

"I just don't want you to be upset," said Trent as he pulled a fresh pair of boxers over his legs, followed by a pair of jeans that Candace had bought for him. They were snug, but comfortable, and caused only minor muffin top. At least his ass would look good.

"I'm not going to be upset, T. We're in the same boat, remember, and I don't want to do something that bothers you." Ian looked like he was really starting to get worried now. He had drawn his legs up to his chest and wrapped his arms around them to pull them tighter.

"I don't like fucking in public," said Trent with a sigh as he pulled his shirt on, doing anything to avoid looking at Ian. "Saying I don't like it probably isn't strong enough. I hate it. The thought of someone else walking in on us when we're together gives me the shivers—and not in a good way. It's a vulnerable moment for me and I don't want to share that with anyone except the person I love." He snapped his mouth shut before he could say another word. He'd already said too much, and Ian's mouth was hanging wide in shock.

"Oh." Ian's brows drew together. "But I—"

"How about we drop this terribly awkward conversation and go get some breakfast? The last thing I ate was that creepy-ass sandwich at the airport, and I'm starving. I'm surprised I didn't get food poisoning, actually. Who puts pickles and tomatoes on a tuna melt?" He shuddered. The texture had been off from the start and the bread had been soggy, as if the cucumbers had melted into the stale crust days before. The taste hadn't been bad, but he was being generous. He'd had to eat something after he'd turned down the rare burger.

Ian smiled softly and pulled himself from the bed. "Sounds like something I might do." Well, he was the one who had ordered the sandwich for Trent. Ian shook his head once before he bent over and gave Trent a quick kiss. He paused, looking at Trent for a few long seconds before he headed into the closet to grab an outfit that Trent had never seen before.

"Did you want to eat in or out for breakfast?" Ian asked as he pulled a black shirt over his head that was two sizes too small for his arms. It fit him perfectly across the chest and waist, though. The shorts that followed fit much better, leaving ample space for his thick thighs.

"In," replied Trent. He was not too keen on an eggy muffin from a greasy restaurant first thing in the morning. "I can make French toast if you want."

"I don't think I have the stuff to make that. I don't usually order much for groceries when I'm here, because I just end up ordering in. There's a service where you can order from any restaurant and they bring it to your door or gate," Ian explained slowly as he started down the stairs, sticking to the right side so he could skim his hand along the banister.

The deep, rich wood was smooth under Trent's hand as he followed. The hall looked even better than what he remembered in his sleep-dulled memory from the night before. He counted twenty pot lights in the ceiling before he shook his head and gave up on calculating the electric bill.

They moved to the kitchen, where another set of automatic lights flicked on overhead as they entered. The kitchen wasn't as modern as Trent had expected, but it was certainly high-end and had decent character. The wooden cupboards stretched from floor to ceiling, with enough space for every pot and pan in a Boxing Day flyer. There was also a hefty stainless-steel stove and a fridge that could fit at least two bodies alongside a roast turkey.

"Sounds neat." Trent knew he had that kind of thing in Canada too, but not in the boondocks where he lived. "Just order me whatever, but no tomatoes or cucumbers, please." He wouldn't be eating those two things for a while.

Ian ordered, and in a surprisingly short amount of time, there was a buzz at the gate as it arrived. Ian let them in with a setting on his phone, as if he were some kind of security guard, and met the delivery person at the door.

It was tastier than Trent had expected and still steaming hot. It wasn't an eggy muffin either, but instead an omelette stuffed with too many toppings to count and a glass of orange juice. An artistic muffin was in a little baggie on the side, looking far too exotic to eat and somehow tasting even better when he found the courage. By the time he was finished, he regretted his choice of jeans and was thinking about the pair of baggy shorts that he'd packed.

They toured the rest of the house, Ian walking ahead animatedly as he then paused at the doorway to each room. The soundproof drum room, the theatre room, the record library, a placid-looking living room and so many others that Trent started to lose himself in the maze of too many square feet. *So many rooms and so many things for one person alone.*

The last stop, of course, was the back yard, where the pool from Trent's dreams was dug out of the hard earth. The heat from the sun struck Trent as soon as he stepped out of the sliding glass doors, and his bare feet brushed the concrete pad that created the walkway to and around the pool. Beyond that was green grass that was so full and lush that it looked like it might be from a magazine.

The pool was a massive, glistening stretch of water with a diving board on one end that stretched over the water like a lost limb. The lining wasn't blue like Trent had expected, but dark, which gave the illusion of looking into a mirror. The bottom was hidden beneath the tiny waves that rippled under the breeze, but it looked too deep to be able to touch.

He knelt beside the edge and braced his hands on the concrete so he could lift his leg out over the water. He expected the water to be as cold as the colour, but as he dipped his toe beneath the surface, it was shockingly warm. He sank up to his ankle, and there was hardly a goosebump raised on his leg.

"Oh, that's hot," said Ian as he bent over and dipped his hand into the water. "I'll dial it down a bit. Mac must've crashed here or something and messed with the settings." He flung the water off his fingertips and dug for his phone, adjusting the temperature with a few clicks.

Before Trent's eyes, the water began to move.

"That's the infinity setting so you can swim in one direction and never hit the end," said Ian as he looked up from his phone.

"It's fast," said Trent as he dipped his foot back under the stream. It moved over his toes, almost as if a river to nowhere had suddenly sprung up in the middle of the backyard. The only noise was the quiet lapping of water over his foot and against the far wall. Ian clicked something on his phone and the water stilled again.

"If you ever want to adjust anything, just let me know and I can get you set up on the app. It connects to the hot tub too." Ian motioned off to the end of the pool, where a second pit of water was carved out of the concrete pad. It was much smaller and the water didn't look nearly as deep. "Did you want to go for a dip?"

"Sure." Trent nodded before he stood and turned back to the door. "I think I can find my way back to the bedroom. I'll get my swim trunks." And he would finally have an excuse to rid himself of the jeans that were giving him swamp ass. Candace knew clothing, but she obviously didn't know Miami in September.

Trent was almost at the door when there was a touch on his elbow. Ian gripped him gently and pulled him back, forcing him to spin around. He was shaking his head, his eyes drawn and serious.

"Sorry... No clothes allowed in the pool," said Ian, loosening his grip and trailing his hand down Trent's arm. The sun reflected off his bald head and Trent had to squint against the bright light. At least he wasn't the only one who was sweating.

"I know. Let me go change," said Trent, trying and failing to retrieve his arm. Ian's grip tightened and a smirk broke over his face.

Ian slid his phone away, grabbing Trent with both hands and lifting him off the ground to spin him around. Trent squeaked as his feet left the floor and he flailed his arms and legs as Ian spun him, chuckling the whole time. As terrifying as it was to get spun around as if he weighed nothing, it also made him harder than he was willing to admit.

"No clothes, T, not even swimming clothes." Ian whispered into Trent's ear as he set him back on his feet. Ian's breath fluttered against his neck, sending a line of shudders down Trent's spine.

"Oh," said Trent. He looked down and fiddled with the edge of his shirt as Ian suddenly withdrew his hands and took a step back. The back yard was so open, like a freaking football field, but they were surrounded on all sides by fencing. There were trees beyond that, and although Trent could see the neighbouring homes poking through the shrubbery, he didn't see any windows.

"Is that okay, T? I don't want to push you after what we just talked about," said Ian, all playfulness dropping away, replaced by concern. There was evidence of Ian's arousal, but the man apparently still managed to keep his head.

Trent's belly bloomed with warmth and he broke out in a wide smile. For all the regret and fear he'd felt when he'd thought about telling Ian that he didn't like sex in public places, he was finally glad that he'd managed to have enough courage. It seemed to be one of Ian's favourite things, but just the fact that he was checking in with Trent made his heart swell.

"It's your house, after all," said Trent, pulling his shirt over his head. "We have to christen every surface, and we might as well start with your favourite spot." His smile widened as Ian's eyes went suddenly dark and tracked to Trent's pierced nipple.

Two piles of clothes fluttered to the ground, then Ian was diving into the pool. His long body stretched out and carved through the water as if he was built for living there amongst the artificial waves. It was the second time Trent had seen Ian in the water, and it still took his breath away.

Trent, being a normal and sane person, circled around until he found a ladder at the side of the pool. He lowered himself onto the first rung before he glanced back over his shoulder to try to track his husband. The warmth lapped at his ankles, completely harmless and inviting.

"Don't you drag me in," Trent called across the water to where Ian was treading ever closer. He had to pause just to watch the man's muscles ripple beneath the waves. He was a work of art, like the Mona Lisa, only male, sexy and naked.

"Nah, I learned my lesson last time," said Ian. "And you can't touch the bottom either, so I don't want to play too rough." He moved close until he was right behind Trent as he lowered himself to the second rung. "Doesn't mean I don't get to play around, though." He pressed a hand against Trent's exposed ass cheek.

Trent shrieked as the water sucked the heat from his skin as it dried in the breeze. It wasn't even that cold and the air was even warmer, but it was like stepping out of a hot shower into a cold bathroom—the worst part of getting clean.

"Ah, Ian, stop. It's cold." Trent flung one hand towards his husband, who laughed and ducked just out of reach. The next touch was at Trent's hip, then the middle of his back, sending every goosebump on high alert.

"Come in, T. The water's nice and warm for you," said Ian as the top of his chest glanced against Trent's lower back. Ian gripped the ladder with his hands resting on it under Trent's, before he lifted himself with a strong jerk. Ian kissed the back of Trent's neck at the same time as the cold water pressed against his back.

Trent shrieked again and let go.

Ian was strong enough to lift him when he was limp from too much sex and to catch Trent with one arm and swing him around. But his weight was completely unexpected this time. Ian's wet hands slipped on the railings as Trent's full weight fell against his chest, then they were both falling back into the dark water.

It was nothing like jumping into a lake, where every ice crystal from the previous winter would sneak into his swim trunks and turn his balls into raisins. It was warm, but the water was so unexpected that it made his body tingle all at once, and he let out a shiver beneath the surface.

Ian broke through first, pulling a bedraggled Trent up a second later. Trent took a second to find his rhythm of kicks and paddles before he was able to swim back over to the side of the pool, throwing his arm over the edge. It was strange to have his junk floating around so freely as he kicked in the deep water, especially since Ian's presence was affecting him already.

"Sorry," Trent mumbled as Ian laughed in the centre of the pool, treading water as if it were the easiest thing in the world. "Why is the pool so deep?" He looked down into the dark water, but he still couldn't see the bottom. The filter below must've been black as well to blend in so seamlessly.

"To keep people the fuck out of it," said Ian with a smirk as he sent a splash Trent's way. "When somebody gets a place with a pool, everybody is suddenly their best friend. They start showing up to eat your snacks, drink your beer and piss in your pool—or they bring their girls back here and see if they can get lucky in the water. You can't do any of that when the pool is so deep that you can't touch the bottom." He chuckled darkly. "Keeps the fuckers out of my pool."

"And Mac?" Trent asked as he let go of the side to float back over to Ian. The sun beat down on his back as he paddled closer, and he could predict the terrible sunburn he would have shortly. "You said he uses your pool when you're away. He doesn't bring his wife here, does he?" Trent looked around, wondering if he could see pussy juice floating around. There was a leaf at the far end that looked highly suspect, but other than that, the pool was clean.

"Nah, he comes to work out in the pool with the infinity jets," said Ian as he pulled Trent to him. "Everybody in the band has a key and knows the codes, so they can use the pool when they want. No one else, though."

Now that they were both drenched, Trent could feel nothing but heat from Ian. That, and the semi-hard cock that pushed into his thigh as he stilled his kicking legs. He had to be careful to avoid kneeing Ian in the balls.

"No chance of getting lucky in the pool then?" Trent asked as he pulled himself up, using Ian's neck as a handle, and trusting Ian to support both of them in the water. Their lips met in a slide of heat and moisture that never seemed to get old. Every time Trent kissed Ian, it was like kissing him for the first time when he had still been a type of virgin, wet and shivering against his bedsheets. And Ian kissed the way he fucked — a never-ending onslaught that completely consumed both of them.

Trent had to pull away and gasp for breath when he felt the water rise and lap against his chin. He kicked his legs as Ian's pace stuttered and they sank even farther.

"I can make it work, T," said Ian. He gripped Trent by the hand and pulled him through the water with powerful strokes until they were back at the same ladder. Trent reached out automatically and gripped it with one hand, holding them up as Ian's kicks stilled.

"You keep holding that, T, and I won't stop. If you need a break, just let go," said Ian, leaning in to cover Trent's mouth again. He sealed his lips over Trent's and swept his tongue into his mouth, sucking and fucking in the best way possible.

Trent had to focus hard so that his hand stayed gripped on the metal surface and didn't relax the same way that the rest of his body did. It wasn't that it was too much to hold them up, but it was difficult to focus when Ian was doing that with his tongue.

Ian gripped Trent's arm and lifted himself up, sucking what would surely be a line of light bruises along Trent's throat that would fade in a few minutes. He pressed his teeth like a threat against Trent's skin, bringing Trent's cock to life beneath the water. Trent rocked his hips as he wrapped his legs around Ian, pulling him up and flush until their groins were rubbing against each other.

Grinding in the water was strange. The usually molten heat was dulled by the cooler water, and the slickness wasn't as smooth as their pre-cum would have been. It was like trying to grind into Ian while he was still wearing pants but feeling completely exposed the entire time.

"I want you inside me, Ian," he said into Ian's mouth as the man came back for another kiss. "I want you to get out of this water and lay back on the ground so I can ride you. I love it when your cock pushes so deep that I think I'm gonna fall apart. And when you keep going until I come but you push me through it, and past it, until I'm begging you to come inside me."

"Fuck," said Ian as he nipped at Trent's lips, groaning aloud. He wanted to grip Ian's shoulders and feel along those muscles as Ian took him apart, but he was still holding the ladder and holding on for both of them.

"Or maybe you want to take me from behind and pound into me as hard as you can. Like you're unleashed, but you can't get enough because I'm just so tight for you. No matter how many times you take me, I always squeeze you just right." Trent let his head fall back as Ian attacked his throat, but he didn't stop talking.

"But there's no lube, and we can't make it to the bedroom, so I would force your cock down my throat instead. I'd take you so deep until I couldn't fit another inch, and you'd fuck my mouth like I was made for you." Trent groaned as Ian flicked the piercing through his nipple. Ian moved his other hand back around to his hole, pressing the tip of one finger inside. The intrusion was small enough that it didn't burn, even with the drag of the water, so Trent was able to relax around it. He knew Ian would take care of him.

"Get the fuck out of the water, T," Ian growled, dipping his finger just a little bit deeper before he pulled it away.

Trent spun around to face the ladder, flipping his hands and heaving himself up to the bottom step. His body was suddenly so much heavier than it had ever been, and he struggled to overcome gravity as the water dropped away to just below his buttocks.

"Stop," said Ian, as he gripped Trent's hips hard enough to leave an imprint of his hands. Without another word, he was spreading Trent's cheeks wide and dipping his tongue along the crack until the tip flicked inside Trent's rim.

"Shit," Trent groaned as his hands slipped, pushing his ass back against Ian, who took it all in stride. A finger slid in alongside Ian's tongue and pushed in all the way in one slick thrust, before it tapped along Trent's prostate like a mandolin.

"More," said Trent as he pushed his hips back. He wasn't sore anymore from the lack of prep on the aeroplane, and he was so empty that it nearly ached. "Come on, Ian. I can take it."

"I know you can," said Ian as he moved back to sink his teeth into one of Trent's cheeks. "And you're gonna keep taking it until I tell you that you're ready." When he pulled back, his single finger disappeared, only to be replaced by two. They pulled Trent wide so that Ian's tongue could push in between them, flicking at his rim as he spread them.

"So good for me, T. Look at you stretching so wide as you get ready for my cock. Not yet, though. I don't think that you're ready for me yet. You aren't begging." He licked his way back in with an earnest devotion that Trent envied. Everything that Ian did, he did well — drumming, writing songs and fucking.

"Please, Ian," Trent begged a moment later, too far gone to stop himself. His dick was jumping and twitching above the water every time Ian grazed his prostate, and little dribbles of pre-cum were dropping down, only to swirl away.

Ian grunted as he pulled out and gripped the ladder rail to heft himself up. He was shockingly cool as he pressed to Trent's back and Trent let out a whimper. It was too much, but so far away from being enough that he wanted to scream.

Trent heard Ian spit. It wasn't as good as lube, but desperate times called for desperate slick.

"Can you hold me, T?" Ian asked, his voice strained as his wet cock rubbed between Trent's cheeks, so much hotter than the rest of him.

Trent nodded, too far gone to speak, but clenching his hands down on the handles in response. Ian shifted in the water again before dropping one hand away, presumably to guide his cock, and the other went to Trent's hip to brace himself. Ian's added weight had Trent's arms shaking. He didn't know what would happen when he came, but for now, he was okay.

"You're so tight, T," said Ian as he finally steered his cock to Trent's entrance.

His tight ring had drawn closed as Trent strained to hold both of their weights. The head of Ian's cock pressed and pressed until the ring of muscle finally gave way and he was slipping inside, hilting himself in a single thrust.

Trent' shut his eyes as every nerve in his body lit up when he was stretched over unyielding flesh. Ian's cock was hot, hard and so big that it made him ache, but it was the ache that he craved every minute that Ian wasn't inside him. There was that little bit of masochism in Trent that wanted to make Ian keep thrusting, not giving Trent any chance at recovering, but Ian was right. He was tight, too tight for Ian to move.

"Ian, what the fuck?" A yell bounced across the yard and Trent's eyes snapped back open as he tightened around the cock inside him.

Just outside the glass patio door stood someone Trent didn't recognize through the blurred haze of arousal that was suddenly crashing down. Their arms were crossed as they blatantly stared with a curious mixture of humour and surprise on their face.

Trent's stomach plummeted as Ian froze behind him, his hand gripping hard into Trent's hip as they hovered precariously over the water. There was nowhere to hide as they were laid before the stranger like a bunch of risqué eye candy.

Trent did the only thing he could think of. He let go of the railing, sending them both plunging back into the water.

Chapter Five

Ian was forcibly ripped from Trent's body as they plummeted into the dark depths, and a gasp pushed through Trent's lips as the water closed in over his head. His shoulder struck Ian's hard chest, and they became a tangle of shocked limbs in a mass of dark water. There was a moment of pure panic when Trent was certain that he was going to die without having one last orgasm.

The side of the pool was out of reach, and every time he kicked, his limbs seemed to flail uselessly, pushing him farther away from Ian until he was alone beneath the surface. The bottom looked so far out of reach that he knew he would run out of air before he reached it.

Then he opened his eyes through the sting of chlorine and saw the wavering sun straight above him, filtering through a few inches of water. He thrust toward the surface with all of his strength and gasped as be breached it.

A shiver ran through his body that had nothing to do with the water temperature as he paddled the foot and a half over to the ladder. Water had settled into the back of his throat, and he hacked as he tried to clear it. Trent clung to the ladder with both hands and watched as Ian surfaced a few feet away. The sound of laughter grew louder as the stranger approached.

"What the fuck, Brian? What are you doing here?" Ian spluttered as he treaded along the top of the water, looking no worse for wear after the unexpected dunk.

The dots slowly connected in Trent's mind as he gripped the rung tighter. The name was familiar because he had heard it many times from Ian. The stranger looked familiar too, after Trent managed to blink the water from his eyes. Brian was the bassist in Ian's band, and one of Ian's good friends.

"You cut me deep, Ian," said Brian as he stopped on the edge of the cement pad. His dark black hair that dangled down to his shoulders looked almost blue in the sunlight as he shook his head. He was broad like Ian but at least a foot shorter, and his skin a tad darker beneath the tattoos that were curling up his arms.

"No sex in the pool, man," said Brian as he looked between Ian and Trent with a frown. "That's your rule. But to think all this time, I could've been bringing chicks back here for some fun. Bros before—" He trailed off as his gaze settled on Trent. "Bros before bros? I dunno." He rubbed the back of his head in a move that was so similar to Ian that it made Trent blink. There was a layer of muscle beneath his tanned and inked skin, but he was closer to Trent's build than Ian's.

"We weren't technically in the pool." The words were out of Trent's mouth before he could stop them. "All the action was at least a foot above the waterline."

There was a pause, when Trent worried that he might have overstepped, before Brian burst out laughing. Ian chuckled behind him and splashed a handful of water at his back. Trent turned, beaming as his husband swam closer and looped a loose arm around his waist. There was no heat behind the touch, but it was still a possessive gesture that made Trent want to continue their activities, despite the interruption.

"Brian, this Trent. T, this is Brian, the bane of my existence." He nodded between the two of them before placing a quick kiss on Trent's cheek. He grasped the railing and pulled himself out in a waterfall of tiny droplets, completely shameless about his nudity.

Trent flushed from the kiss that was so unlike Ian, who usually dreaded all forms of PDA. Or the flush could have been from the view of a very nice, very tanned ass wiggling right in front of his face.

Brain had looked off into the distance as Ian pulled himself from the water. His gaze was clouded, and he was biting the edge of his lip as his brows drew together in concentration. His attention suddenly snapped back faster than a chihuahua on Ritalin.

"I got it. Bros before Joes. That's awesome." He nodded to himself and a smile pulled over his perfectly white teeth. He could have been attractive if he wasn't the polar opposite of Trent's type.

Trent scrunched up his face and shook his head. "As a fan, I am very glad that Ian is the one who writes the lyrics and not you. That was just awful." Ian's lyrics were like poetry on steroids, and he always seemed to know exactly how to manipulate them so Mac could use his voice to the fullest extent.

Brian burst out laughing a second time, glancing back over his shoulder at Ian, who was bending over as he reached for his clothes. Not that Trent was watching

Ian… He just loved the picture that Ian's sac made from behind as it peeked through his parted thighs.

"Why am I just meeting you now, Trent? We should've met ages ago," said Brian as he offered his hand to Trent, who, after a quick glance down to make sure everything was in order, accepted the help.

As he landed on his feet on the concrete, he realized that he was actually quite a bit taller than Brian and almost as broad. It was only the man's short stature that made him appear burlier than he actually was. Brian made an even stranger picture with his long, straight hair, but Trent wasn't one to judge, especially when he probably resembled a drowned rat at the moment.

"Good to meet you, Trent," said Brian as he turned the hand grip into a shake. "And thanks for getting with this guy and finally taking him off the streets. He was starting to look like a stray cat out there—all mangy and everything." His eyes crinkled at the corners as his smile broadened. He looked like a person who spent most of his time smiling.

"Keep it up and I'll toss you in," said Ian from where he was pulling his boxers up his legs.

Trent chuckled as his boxers hit him in the face a second later. He pulled them over his legs, grimacing as wet skin tugged at the fabric. He looked at his jeans that were pooled on the concrete and promptly decided against even attempting it. Anything that Candace bought him would fit like a second skin, which also meant that if he put them on wet, he would have to amputate his legs at the hip if he was ever going to get them off again.

"What are you even doing here, Brian? Not that it's not good to see you… I just wasn't expecting you so soon," said Ian. He looked at the remainder of his clothes, seeming to have the same train of thought as Trent. His boxers looked normal and not a tad extra-full like Trent's still did.

"Mac sent me," Brian shrugged, his humour dropping away. "And I did text you like fifteen minutes ago. At least now I know why you didn't answer." He looked Trent up and down again and his smile quickly made a reappearance. "If I were gay, I would understand the appeal."

Trent flushed as Ian raised his hand and swatted his friend across his shoulder. "That's my husband you're eyeing, so back off before I dunk you in the pool." He looked immensely intimidating, even though he was almost naked.

"You wouldn't, Ian!" Brian backed away from Trent with his hands raised in defence. "Bros before Joes, you know that. And I've got my phone on me." He pulled his phone from his back pocket, dangling it in front of himself like a shield as he continued to back away. "It's a business phone, Ian, and you can't mess with it."

Ian stalked forward, matching every step that Brian took back, looking like a large, nearly naked predator. He grabbed the phone from Brian's fingertips with a great swiping paw before he tossed it onto the soft grass a few feet away. It rolled end over end a few times before it settled on the blades with its blank screen reflecting the sun.

"Oops," said Ian as the phone tumbled away, unharmed. "Guess you're free game now." He feinted to the right and Brian yelled before he turned and booked it back to the sliding glass door. He ducked behind it, pulling it almost all the way shut so he could peer through the crack, as if the glass alone would protect him.

"Tell Mac that if he wants something, he can come here and introduce himself properly to my husband. If he isn't mature enough to do that, then he can do the next tour without me." Ian shouted across the lawn before he shook his head and started toward Trent.

Trent wasn't completely sure what to do with himself. He was lost somewhere between giggling and goading the two of them on as if they were a bunch of drunk teenagers who had snuck into a college party. The way Ian was throwing his weight around definitely wasn't helping the situation with Little Trent, though.

"Okay, sounds good, Ian. Great to meet you, Trent. I'll see you tomorrow at dinner," said Brian as he darted back onto the lawn, giving Ian a wide berth. It was surprising how fast he could run as his short legs carried him over the grass before he grabbed his phone and darted back into the house.

"Sorry about that, T," said Ian as he moved close enough to place a kiss on Trent's lips. Trent wrapped his arms around Ian's neck and pulled him closer, like he always did. He loved to feel that column of muscle flexing beneath his hands.

"Mm-m, it's okay," Trent pulled back and licked his lips. "I wanted to meet everyone anyway, but not while I'm naked and you're balls deep." The sun had dried Ian almost completely and his skin was hot to the touch.

"Did I hurt you, T?" Ian smoothed his hand along Trent's arm. "I know I pulled out pretty suddenly there, and it kinda stung. If it hurt me, it was probably way worse for you." He dropped his other hand to Trent's ass, and Trent let out a gasp as Ian kneaded the hard globe.

"It was the opposite of fantastic, but you'll just have to make it up to me later. But first" — Trent placed a kiss on Ian's lips—"you owe me a ride in the Corvette with the top down and the music blaring. I've been daydreaming about that for weeks." The mere thought of driving in that car made him hard, and he wasn't opposed to a little bit of patience and edging, as long as it paid off in the end.

Ian reluctantly pulled away and Trent dragged them up to the bedroom before he tossed his too-tight jeans on top of his suitcase. Ian disappeared into the bathroom and the water flicked on in the shower. His gut ached with the need to follow Ian, but he knew that if he did, he would never get to see Miami.

He grabbed a new pair of loose shorts and pulled on the same T-shirt that he had worn for breakfast. His skin had the deep scent of chlorine, but he actually didn't mind it. It never made him itchy, and his skin would be super soft for the rest of the day.

He waited for Ian to burst from the steam that was filtering through the bathroom door and watched him dress in his usual ensemble. Ian gripped Trent's hand in a warm, meaty paw before he dragged him down the stairs to the garage. It was one of the rooms that they hadn't toured, but it was one of the most beautiful in Trent's eyes. It wasn't the high ceilings or the stark white paint along the walls that drew him in, but the two vehicles sitting in the centre of the space.

"Can we take this one next time?" Trent asked as he sidled next to a red BMW. It wasn't a convertible, but it was sleek, and the paint shone with a newness that could never be replicated by a simple wash. The seats were black leather with silver thread binding, and it was a stick shift. Trent had to wipe a dribble of drool from his lips. It was so close to his literal dream car. If it had been sky blue, then it would have hit it dead centre.

"Do you even have your licence?" Ian called from across the garage where he was lowering himself into the seat of a very familiar Corvette. It was the same car that had almost hit Trent on the day they'd first met.

"Hey, girlie," said Trent as he strolled to the front corner, rubbing his hand along the bumper that had looked like an accordion the last time he saw it. "I owe you a lot, you know. Thank you." He smiled over at Ian, who rolled his eyes.

Trent was about to walk to the passenger side when he noticed something on the hood. The corner was bent about a centimetre out of place, with the yellow paint slightly smudged. It looked out of place amongst the rest of the polished and repaired frame. He pushed his fingers into the divot and stroked the rough edge.

"I thought I would keep that part, just for me," said Ian as he pulled himself out of the car and moved in behind Trent, reaching for the same place. "It reminds me of the day that I met the love of my life, the most beautiful person I've ever known."

"Such a romantic." Trent swallowed the lump that formed in his throat and blinked back the tears of happiness that threatened to flow. Sometimes the things that Ian said would hit him straight in the heart. It was no wonder that the man could churn out lyrics like he did. Most of the fans credited Mac for them, but hardly anyone knew the master behind the words.

"Well, the garage had a different opinion when I told them that." Ian kissed Trent before he pulled back and chuckled. "They insisted that it was just going to rust, and if I wanted the love to last, I would replace the hood." He moved away and lowered himself back into the car, starting it with the push of a button.

Trent followed suit as the roof folded back into a concealed compartment behind them. He searched for the belt, which was higher up than he'd expected. The seat was stiff beneath him, as if it hadn't really been worn in properly yet. He could imagine that he was probably one of the first ones to sit in it next to Ian.

"You ready to hear this baby purr?" Ian asked as the garage door opened and he flicked the car into reverse.

Trent had never been more ready for anything in his life. Vibrations from the bridled engine shot through the floor and up his feet before going straight to his cock. Heat pressed down on him as they left the air conditioning, but then the gate opened wide, and they were out on the street, roaring down the concrete.

The street looked completely different in the daylight, more like a sturdy gated community instead of a bunch of zombie fortresses. It was beautiful, though. Each house was different, as if an architect had individually designed every single one with the utmost attention to detail. They probably had. They weren't the cookie-cutter houses that Trent was used to seeing or the grand, grey buildings he saw on top of hills in the country. These were stylish pieces of art that were loved and enjoyed by those who lived there. They were also massive, none of them looking an inch under four thousand square feet. Trent vaguely wondered if any of them were compensating for something. He knew Ian certainly wasn't.

"This is my favourite place to drive," Ian shouted over the wind that battered the tops of their heads. Trent was grateful that he'd managed to fit in the last-minute haircut before the wedding. He had been starting to go downright shaggy, but it was out of his eyes now, even though he knew that by the end of the ride it was going to be an absolute mess.

Despite their speed—which had to be exactly the posted limit—and the exotic body of the car, no one looked up as they whipped by. They were either used to it, or they didn't even care to look at the car. The farther they wound down the road, the more Trent understood why nobody cared about a smoking hot man whipping past in his beast of a car.

The other cars on the road were ones that he'd seen in his wet dreams. He'd seen them online or in a movie, but he had never thought he would be close enough to hear their engines roar and smell the taint of their exhaust. An actual McLaren had him cutting off a groan and whipping his head around to keep his eyes on it. It was baby blue and could melt into the Miami sky if it were given the chance.

"You okay, T?" Ian shouted as his hands gripped the wheel. Every movement was under tight and powerful control, and his eyes never left the road. The car shifted seamlessly with the paddle shift next to the steering wheel. It was safe, and so utterly boring that it made Trent want to gag. He didn't want a purr. He wanted a fucking roar.

"One day I'm gonna drive one of those," said Trent dreamily as he looked back again, sighing when the McLaren was already out of sight.

"You think you could handle it?" Ian slowed as they approached an intersection where a blonde lady was crossing with a dog that was about half the size of most house cats. Ian watched them carefully, as if the dog might run at the car and squish itself under one of the tires.

"Pull over," said Trent, crossing his arms and trying to keep the pout off his face. His words fell on deaf ears and the engine rumbled as Ian touched the gas and shifted seamlessly from first to second. Trent grabbed Ian's shoulder hard and leaned close to yell in his ear. "Pull over and I'll show you."

Ian looked at him, knitting his brows together, but he slowed and steered right until the tires dragged along the edge of the kerb. He gripped the steering wheel even as they came to a complete stop with the hazard lights flashing.

"What?" asked Ian, but Trent was already moving.

The belt came away with a slip of the button and a solid tug, but the door resisted until Trent hit the button to unlock them. He poured out of the passenger side, very aware that he was at least partially hard in his pants and that his shorts would do nothing to hide the evidence.

"Out," said Trent, poking Ian in the shoulder and pointing behind his back with his thumb. There was a full minute of bleak hesitation before Ian followed his directions and landed in the passenger seat. Trent smacked Ian's hands away when he reached over to turn off the hazard lights.

"I can do this, Ian. I'm not an idiot," said Trent through gritted teeth. He didn't have a car, true, but that didn't make him an invalid.

"It has a lot more horsepower than you probably think," said Ian as Trent pulled the buckle across his chest. "It's not like driving a Toyota."

"I've never driven a Toyota," said Trent as he adjusted his seat, mirrors and steering wheel so he fit better in the space that had been set for a fucking giant. He glanced around the cabin, memorizing where every button was before he went to push the start. He eyed the paddle gearshift.

"I'll admit I've never actually used a paddle gearshift," said Trent. He glanced over at Ian, who looked even more worried, "but I'm sure I'll figure it out. I won't hurt your baby."

"You're my baby too, ya know," said Ian as he gripped his shorts at the sound of the engine roaring back to life.

Trent put the car into gear and slowly pulled out into the lane once it was clear. Only one car had passed them in the time they'd been sitting — a Lamborghini that was white and had the angles of a polytetrahedron.

The steering wheel was coated in leather too and gripped perfectly under his hands. The tiniest movement sent the car left and right with unerring accuracy, and the engine responded to the lightest touch on the pedal. Trent went rock hard.

"I don't know if I ever told you," said Trent as he pulled his lips back to reveal his teeth, "but I'm a bit of a car buff." He hit the gas and the engine roared. It wasn't the most powerful car that Trent had driven, not by far, but it still took his breath away as it accelerated. It had been so long since he'd had that kind of power under the hood, and almost ten years since he'd even driven something that wasn't his mother's car, but it came rushing back in an instant. His reflexes heightened until he could see and feel everything as they whipped faster down the road. The rumble just made it that much better as the world began to blur.

Ian gripped the middle console so hard that Trent swore he could hear the leather creak over the wind, and he scrabbled with the open window, obviously looking for anything to hold on to. Trent let out a laugh as he pulled out and passed the Lambo that had sped past them when they had been stopped.

"Do you trust me, Ian?" Trent yelled over the sound of the wind and the beating of his heart. There was a smile on his lips that he couldn't get rid of, and Ian was looking more terrified by the second. Ian nodded stiffly, his face going pale as the engine hummed higher.

Trent did a quick check of his surroundings, making sure that there were no bumps in the road that would interfere, before he downshifted violently, letting the engine growl. He hit the emergency brake, turning the wheel at the same time and not letting go of the gas for a moment. Rubber streaked along the pavement, leaving a permanent mark of their presence as the tail end of the car spun around in a U-turn. As they slid into place in the opposite direction, Trent disengaged the e-brake and the car burst ahead.

"Holy fuck," Ian whimpered beside him — actually fucking whimpered. Trent glanced over at his husband and let off the accelerator until they coasted to a more reasonable speed. Ian's skin was pale and his lips were pulled tight over his grimace.

"You okay?" Trent asked, slightly worried when Ian took a few deep breaths before answering.

"You don't even have a car," said Ian with a shake of his head. "Where did that even come from? This was not covered when we talked about hidden talents." He burst out laughing a moment later as the colour finally returned to his cheeks. "That was pretty awesome, though, even though I thought I was gonna die."

Trent put his foot back down, letting the car surge ahead but keeping it well under control. He dropped one hand on his lap and braced his other at the top of the wheel. The speedometer was reading a very high number, but he wasn't sure if he was looking at miles or kilometres per hour. If it were miles, he didn't think he would ever go soft again.

"I had a fling with a mechanic in college. It only lasted a month, but I drove the shit out of every fancy car that came through that shop before I bent him over the hood and fucked him into it." Trent cleared his throat. He'd never really talked about his previous relationships, because if Ian was anything like him, a giant green monster would definitely make itself known.

"Anyway, he had a high-end shop and had mostly customs, higher models and a few super cars thrown in. He told me I was a natural the first time I got behind the wheel, and I was in college, so I had no survival instinct." Trent continued with a shrug, remembering the time fondly. It had been a stretch of summer days where the roads were hot enough to melt rubber and there hadn't been a single rain cloud in the forecast. It had made for a perfect chance to put his life on the line.

"So, to be clear, I wouldn't be averse to you bending me over the hood of that BMW I saw in your garage," said Trent. "As long as the gate is locked to everyone and the door is closed. No interruptions this time." His words made him throb painfully and he was sure there was a damp spot in his shorts. At least they were black.

With Ian being gone for weeks or months at a time, Trent usually spent the first few days of Ian's return with nothing more than a robe on. Half the time the robe didn't even make it off, and instead Ian just pushed it up and aside before he sank back into Trent's inviting heat.

Before the Miami trip, Ian had arrived in Canada by plane, insisting that he fly with Trent on his first trip in the air. Before that, he'd been finishing up the European portion of his tour, and he'd landed in Canada the night before their flight to Miami. It had given them hardly any time to be intimate, and Trent was about to bust a nut.

"I would love to do that now, but I promised to show you around," said Ian. "And I'm still in shock, so you'll have to give my dick a bit to catch up." Ian glanced down at Trent's lap and let out a laugh when he saw Trent's situation.

"Deal." Trent pushed his wrist down on his throbbing erection and shoved it into submission as he pulled over to the side of the road. He still had to walk with a bit of a limp, but he was doing much better by the time he slid back into the passenger side. Seeing Ian at the controls again had his cock threatening to surge, but it was dampened by the way Ian drove like an old lady on her way to church.

Ian drove endlessly along the twisting roads that were starting to look very similar. There were a few places that caught Trent's eye and had him straining to look as they passed by at the posted limit. Some places even looked like home, before he realized that he was looking at the garage of a freaking mansion. And the garage was still bigger than Trent's actual house.

They passed a few parks and what looked like a zoo, although Trent didn't actually see any animals except for those on the entrance sign. Ian kept on driving and telling him about different hot spots, like where the best coffee shop was and the best place to get a quick burger. A few stories popped up as he twisted through one of the city centres where people were milling about. A few of them actually looked up as the gleaming yellow car caught the light.

By the time they finally stopped at one of the numerous restaurants, Trent was starving and his bladder was ready to burst. He rushed ahead of Ian, leaving his husband to order while he relieved himself. He caught one person staring at Ian as Trent made his way back to the table, and although they snapped a picture with their phone, they didn't look like they were going to approach him.

Ian looked completely oblivious to the attention, instead staring out of the window as he waited for Trent to return. He was swirling a glass of cola around with his straw as Trent approached, and he greeted Trent with a brilliant smile. Trent kept his hands to himself, wondering if he would have to sit on them to keep from grabbing Ian and planting a kiss on his beautiful lips.

"Does that happen a lot?" asked Trent as he tilted his head in the direction of a second flash of light. If they were trying to be incognito, they could at least turn their flash off.

"Hmm," said Ian as his lips curled back in a smile that was much too false for his face. It was the first time that Trent had seen Ian's media-face in person, and the difference was startling. This Ian was cold, calculated and ready to please, as if his warmth and personality had drained away to leave a fan favourite that was nothing more than sex and drums.

"Mac gets it a lot worse than me," said Ian as he shook his head and looked back out of the window, letting his smile drop away. "People see him sing, and they fall in love. I'm just a guy hidden behind a bunch of drums." He gave a self-deprecating laugh.

"What did you order for me?" Trent asked, stalling Ian in his tracks as he started to spiral. For such a large man, he was so terribly sensitive that it made Trent want to wrap him in a bundle of bubble wrap so that nothing would ever hurt him again.

"Burger, but not just any burger," said Ian as an actual smile lit up his face. The false Ian melted away, and the real thing shone before Trent's eyes like a beacon.

"Is it a bison burger? Cause one of these days, I'm gonna eat a buffalo," said Trent, shutting out the rest of the restaurant and focusing solely on his husband. He twirled his ring around his finger and let the warmth of it spread through his limbs.

"Do buffalo still exist, though? I thought they were all hunted to extinction," said Ian, his eyes going wide.

"There is a buffalo farm just outside of town at home," said Trent. "I'll take you out there some time. The things are so huge that they scared the crap out of me the first time I saw them. Fuzzy too, and the babies are so cute you just wanna snuggle with them." Trent wrapped his arms around his torso as if he were snuggling a tiny bison that was still wobbly on its legs.

"But you want to eat them?" asked Ian, tilting his head to the side.

"They are supposed to be delicious," said Trent with a nod, hoping that explained everything. All animals were cute to him, and he was a firm believer in ethical care for livestock, but he also loved meat.

"Well, I got you a regular beef burger made of cows," Ian deadpanned, letting out a small chuckle as he continued. "But it has literally everything on it, including onion rings and sweet potato fries. And the sauce is like mayonnaise died, went to hell and learned

all of the devil's tricks, then exploded in your mouth."
Ian wiped the corner of his mouth as the tiniest bit of
drool escaped.

"Fries on a burger," said Trent with a grin. "Sign me
up."

The food was great, although Trent may have
dislocated his jaw trying to take the first bite. He
shrugged, rubbing it and writing it off as *practice for Ian.*
The waiter seemed to know Ian too, as more than just a
fan, and had their order to them faster than seemed
possible. And luckily, by the time the food arrived, the
fan had departed the restaurant with one last
suppressed squeal and too-bright flash.

"What is it?" Ian asked as he caught Trent's smile.
Ian finished his plate off, including the smear of
ketchup that he scooped up with his spoon and
plopped into his mouth.

"It's just different than I expected," said Trent as he
pushed his plate away and leaned back in his chair. "I
was expecting another planet where everything
someone eats is some kind of artisanal special, and
everyone had fancy cars, fancy dogs and wives with tits
that are size double M. People here are just normal." He
looked to where a young couple was feeding their
squirming toddler bits of their burgers. The woman
was smoking hot, and the man looked like he'd just
stepped out of a photo shoot, but they were still doing
normal activities.

"Yeah, it's not so bad here," said Ian as he sighed
and leaned back in his chair. "I first came here after we
had our big break and I could finally afford the real
estate. I fell in love with the people, the parks and the
sun. I can't really imagine living anywhere else right
now." He patted his stomach once and lifted out of his

chair, grabbing his wallet and heading to the counter to pay.

Despite the good food and the warm feeling in his chest, Trent's stomach sank. He could see why Ian was in love with this place, because Trent already found himself warming up to it, and it hadn't been twenty-four hours yet. His home wasn't sunny like this, and there were no places to eat out, unless a person wanted to survive on stale sandwiches from the coffee shop.

"Ready to go?" Ian came back, his face relaxed and soft in a way that Trent rarely saw it. Trent downed the rest of his drink before he nodded and lifted himself up. It wasn't time to worry about something that might never be an issue.

As they stepped outside, Trent stifled a yawn behind his palm. The air was so fresh and the sun so bright that it had melted his brain into a sleepy goo. And now that he was full of beef, he was about two seconds away from napping.

"How about we head back and I show you the home theatre system? We can order dinner when it gets late." Ian studied Trent, who was fading fast. Ian looked wide awake and so genuinely happy that Trent had to smile. "Don't forget about dinner with the guys tomorrow, though," said Ian as they reached the car. The doors were locked, which was ridiculous because the top was still down. Trent shook his head with a small laugh.

"Where are we going for it?" Trent asked as he buckled himself into the seat and leaned his head back against the leather rest. Translation… *What the hell do I wear?* Candace wasn't there to dress him this time, and he always managed to fuck it up on his own. Ian wasn't any help either, always replying with *'you look great, T.'*

"A sushi place. Mac picked it," said Ian, "but it's a good place with lots of variety. We usually just let him book all the spots for us because he always does a great job. Is that okay?" He looked up when Trent didn't answer at first.

"Sure," said Trent with a shrug, his sleepiness fading fast. "They have to have something cooked on the menu. I'm not a big fan of the whole raw fish thing, but I'm sure it will be great." There was no way he was going to complain about it and ruin his first official meeting with Ian's band members. Brian seemed like a great guy, but Mac had left something to be desired on their first meeting.

The drive was short as Ian took a different and faster route back to his home. The noise of the city and airports faded away to the hum of quiet streets with the occasional car. Trent whooped when he spotted a Honda amongst the glimmer. *At least somebody in this town has the sense to buy a practical car.*

After they parked next to the BMW in the garage and the automatic gate and garage door had slid shut, Trent followed Ian to a room that he had only been in briefly. It was a few hundred square feet, with no windows and only one door. Along one side were theatre-type chairs that looked more comfortable than his La-Z-Boy at home. They faced a massive projector screen that took up the entire far wall. The speakers were relatively small but high end, so the sound was clear as Ian cranked the volume and started the first movie in the queue.

Trent picked a seat next to Ian, leaning back and relaxing into the padded leather. It reclined completely, had adjustable lumbar support and even had a massaging setting that could be either independent or tied into the action of the movie. There was one thing that was missing amongst the expensive get-up, however.

The chairs were completely separate, with two arm rests and one cup holder on each. It meant that Ian was about two feet away from him in the closest chair. What Trent really wanted to do was snuggle into a soft couch and put his ear to Ian's chest, just to hear his heartbeat. But like this, he could only just touch Ian's hand. That, and there was no way he was going to be able to drift off with that amount of sound and vibration.

"You okay, T?" Ian asked as he paused the movie, the sound cutting off abruptly like a microphone falling under water.

Trent rolled on his side to face Ian in his chair, unable to wipe the pout off his face. "I just want to snuggle for a bit. That's all." For a comfortable chair, it was awfully uncomfortable to be alone in.

"Come sit with me then," said Ian as he patted his lap, leaning back so there was more room. If Trent hadn't been six inches shorter than Ian, the prospect probably wouldn't have been nearly as terrifying. Sitting on someone's lap was left for people under five-foot-five, or toddlers with Santa. He was a grown-ass man.

"Come on, T," said Ian as he patted his lap again. He tapped his fingers on the arm rest and glanced at the remote that was well within reach.

Trent pulled himself up and stumbled over to Ian before he very gingerly sat back against him. It took a minute of adjustments before he didn't feel like he was going to slide straight off and onto the ground.

He tried to hold himself aloft, conscious of every pound on his six-foot frame. He wasn't chubby by any means, but he certainly wasn't skinny, either, and although Ian was strong, there was a point where his lap could only hold so much. Trent shifted as he tried to get comfortable, a leg digging into the bones of his ass and Ian's collar bone pressing a line into his back. He was pretty sure that Ian was now looking at his shoulder instead of the movie screen too. And were those car keys in Ian's pocket, or something more interesting?

Sweat gathered between them as Trent's back started to ache from keeping himself partially upright. He tried to sag back, just a bit, but Ian's breath stuttered for a moment as they made contact. It wasn't a good stutter of arousal, but closer to the one that Trent made when Ian let his weight slam down after he came.

Then Ian shifted, with the buckle of his belt digging into Trent's lower back like a pry-bar at the base of his spine. Something else hard and sharp, which honestly felt like a hunting knife, poked a bruise on the back of his thigh. Every breath was a tense and slowly building heat.

"I don't think this is gonna work," Ian finally admitted with a groan, whispering into Trent's ear over the sound of the restarted movie. Trent was off him in a second, fanning the sweat on the back of his clinging shirt, and stretching out his legs. Ian was rubbing the tops of his thighs with a grimace before he reached up and grabbed the remote.

"I'll add a couch onto the grocery list," said Ian. "I'm not saying you're too heavy, but you have a bony ass." He wiggled his toes, which looked slightly pale from lack of circulation.

"I do not," said Trent, crossing his arms. "You were just trying to get frisky with me. Between that belt buckle and your keys, I was worried for my health."

"I don't have any keys in my pocket," said Ian. He managed to keep a straight face for two seconds before he started laughing. "I'm just happy to see you is all."

"I knew it," said Trent as he rubbed his back where *something* had left a round bruise. His shoulders sagged as he looked back at the movie, which had started up again. Ian's eyes flashed to the screen as someone was murdered in full view of the camera. A head spun, and eerie eyes floated in the darkness. It was a typical horror movie—unrealistic, hilarious and fucking terrifying.

Trent glanced between Ian and the screen, but his husband didn't look back up as he was swept away to another reality. Trent shrugged and snuck to the doorway, opening it just enough for him to pass through. He had to blink the spots from his vision as he stepped out of the darkness.

He glanced at a clock on the way upstairs and saw that it was already late and nearing dinner time. His stomach was still full from their late lunch, and he didn't think he would be able to eat anything else.

He made his way up the stairs to the massive bed with the expensive sheets. After grabbing a T-shirt from Ian's closet and a pair of boxers, he changed in the bathroom then brushed his teeth. He flicked off the light then slipped into the bed, tossing until he found a spot that he could bury his toes to keep from getting too cold. He would have to remember to ask Ian to turn the AC warmer before he came down with hypothermia.

He drifted off to sleep as the exhaustion of travel and dread finally caught up with him. He only stirred for a moment when the bed dipped beside him hours later and a kiss was pressed to his forehead.

"Love you, T. Good night."

Chapter Six

"Give me your honest opinion, Ian. How do I look?" Trent asked as he twisted in the mirror again. He had pulled on a pair of black jeans, a gift from Candace that felt designer but definitely wasn't, and a blue button-up top. His problem was with the button-up. It was fine for work, and he'd worn something similar many times, but it was something that could be found in the front window of a tractor shop.

"Looks good to me, T," said Ian, as he sighed and sat back on the bed. He'd dressed in his usual default of black everything, which always looked good. Then again, anything Ian wore always transformed as soon as it stretched over his shoulders.

"Do I look like a farmer? It's terrible, isn't it?" Trent pulled the shirt back off, ripping one of the buttons off in his haste. It rolled away, pattering like the footsteps of a mouse.

"Just wear one of my shirts," said Ian, now lying completely back on the bed. "We have to be there in like thirty minutes, and it's a twenty-five-minute drive, T."

He glanced down at his watch, where the large square glowed bright with the time.

"I can't wear one of your shirts, Ian. I'll be swimming in it." Trent grabbed his suitcase and upended the rest of the contents. There were colourful T-shirts, tan shorts and a random quarter that had found its way in there at some point. It rolled away to join the button. "I need to make a good impression so your friends will like me." There was nothing appropriate in the pile, and to be honest, there probably wasn't an outfit that would match his demands in his dresser back home either.

"Brian likes you, and you were naked when you met him," said Ian as he shrugged one shoulder, crinkling the sheets. "Just pick something, anything, or we are going to be late." He lifted himself off the bed and started toward the door.

"I know Mac already hates me, but what about the other two?" Trent asked as he threw the crumpled clothes back into his bag, refusing to leave a mess for the housekeeper. Someone had made their bed twice now, and everything had mysteriously remained dust-free, but Trent had yet to meet the one responsible. It was actually getting a little bit spooky.

"Mac doesn't hate you." Ian paused in the doorway and looked back in confusion. "Why would you think that?" The drummer blinked slowly as if the thought had never occurred to him.

"You're kidding, right?" Trent looked up from the mess, shaking his head at the look on Ian's face. "Just ask him sometime, and he'll tell you. If he's a good friend, he'll be honest." Panic shot his stomach higher into his throat as he spied the time on Ian's wrist. They were officially going to be late. "Just go start the car and I'll be down in a second."

He dove into Ian's closet, going straight to the back. The back of a walk-in closet was where clothing went to die—that was, if a walk-in closet was anything like the bottom drawer of his dresser. Ian always seemed to pick clothes from the front few hangers, which were primarily black and grey. Far at the back, there were a few more colourful options that looked like they hadn't been touched in years. Trent even found the tags on a few of them, which he forced himself not to read after the first one nearly gave him an asthma attack.

He searched for a tag that said XL, instead of Ian's ridiculous size. Finally, near the very back and partially buried beneath a blue jacket, was something that would fit him. It was hideous in a way that made him love it instantly—like his one and only knick-knack that was a tiny jester mouse complete with the iconic hat in rainbow colours.

He jumped into the Corvette and buckled his seatbelt, still breathing hard from the run down the stairs. He expected the car to race off as soon as he hit the seat, but Ian hadn't even put it into gear. Instead, Ian's mouth was hanging open and his eyebrows were high on his naked head.

"It's fucking orange," said Ian as he stared, and his mouth opened and closed a few times. His bright gaze swept over every line of the sweater as if the secrets of the universe were laid out along the seams.

"Do you want me to go back and find something else?" Trent's cheeks burned in embarrassment and anger. He should have gone with the farmer shirt after all. At least he knew what to expect with that.

"Hell no. You look awesome in this one," said Ian as he hit the gas and they flung out of the garage. He slowed down at the gate, waiting for it to open, before the car hummed back to life as they cleared it.

Trent's stomach warmed and his anger fizzled out as quickly as it had come. In truth, he probably looked like he belonged in a pumpkin patch, but the sweater was nice. It was soft and clung to all the bits he wanted it to, while leaving softer bits to the imagination. When he looked down, he could see the small bump where his nipple piercing was, and felt a zing of satisfaction. He wasn't a farmer boy. He was married to a rock star.

They made it to the restaurant in twenty-three minutes, which was approximately thirty seconds before their reservation. Ian had actually managed to go a few miles above the speed limit this time, and at one point, he drove with a single hand. Trent had given him a little clap and got a scowl in return.

The waitress recognized Ian on sight and led them to their table with only a swift curious glance in Trent's direction. A few of the others in the packed restaurant looked up as they passed as well, but they quickly returned to their meals. Trent only heard one rushed whisper of Ian's name as they rounded a corner near a birthday party, complete with three massive helium balloons at the table.

The atmosphere grew progressively quieter and the lights lower as they were led through the depths of the building. Finally, when Trent was sure that they were about to hit the far wall, they turned a corner to reveal a private room with six chairs set along a long table. Three of the chairs were already filled, but only one face was familiar.

"I'd ask you why you were late, but I've already had my fair share of the details of your honeymoon," said Brian as they approached. Trent flushed as Ian rubbed the back of his neck.

"I couldn't find my shirt," Trent blurted out, realizing a moment too late that that could be taken the wrong way too. Brian chuckled and shook his head.

Trent's gaze snapped to two identical mops of curly blond hair. He'd seen them on stage playing the lead and rhythm guitars before, but they'd blurred into the background when Trent caught sight of Ian. One thing he hadn't realized was that they were twins — identical twins. Their smiles were identical too, although one sat back in his chair with his head down and the other leaned forward with a hand outstretched over the table.

"I'm Max," said the blond who had offered his hand. Trent rushed forward to shake it, realizing a moment too late that his hands were still sweating from the heat of the Miami outdoors. Max's hand was firm and callused, and he shook with the perfect amount of pressure before he let Trent's hand fall away.

"This guy here is Devon." He slapped the shoulder of the blond who was sitting back against the chair with his head down. "Shake his hand, you idiot stick." Devon snapped up his hand a second later to vigorously shake Trent's before he snatched it back and slumped down in his seat. Trent shook out his numb fingers and tried not to grimace.

"Don't mind him," Max continued before he gave his brother a sideways glance and a nod. "Devon is on the spectrum so he's not usually a fan of eye or physical contact."

"Oh, I'm sorry." Trent pulled his hand back and rubbed along the knuckles as he glanced at Devon, trying not to look, but looking all the same. The blond appeared to be completely normal except for his downcast eyes.

"Spoken like a true Canadian," Brian cut in, and suddenly the tension was gone. Ian was already pulling a chair back and taking a seat at the far end, and Trent scrambled into the middle chair. There was one chair left open on the other side of Trent, leaving only one space for the only member who hadn't shown up yet.

"Where's Mac?" Ian asked as he looked around the table, seemingly noticing his best friend's absence for the first time. "He's usually the first one here."

And there it was again. The tension that had lifted from Trent's shoulders came crashing down with the force of a tsunami. The carpet under his feet was suddenly the most interesting thing that he had ever seen, complete with his sandal print and something red and tacky that pulled the fibres together near his toes. If Ian needed another morsel of proof that Mac hated him, it was kicking him in the face right now.

Brian grimaced and shrugged. "I don't know, Ian. He's been out of sorts since you guys had that fight." The bassist sorted his silverware and placed his fabric napkin over his lap.

Ian stiffened beside him, his whole body going tight and his fists clenching in his lap. Trent kept his mouth sealed shut. If Ian hadn't told him about a fight, then there was probably a good reason.

"I didn't think you guys heard that," said Ian softly, before he reached out to fiddle with his own silky napkin.

"I think everyone in England heard that one, Ian," said Brian. "What were you guys even fighting about?"

"Nothing," said Ian. His gaze told Trent what his words didn't. For just a moment Ian looked at him before he moved back to the white tablecloth. Now was not the time to say *I told you so*.

Luckily, the conversation was interrupted as the waiter approached them. Trent perused the fancy menu that had prices so high that they made his eyes water. Everything on it made his stomach want to wilt away to nothingness. He didn't know what onigiri was, but it looked terrifying. Seaweed belonged in the sea, and not on his plate.

"Do you like calamari?" Ian asked as he finally started to notice Trent's panic. "That's fried and usually battered squid." He pointed to a picture that looked vaguely like onion rings, only smaller.

"Calamari." Trent took a second look at the picture, bringing the menu up close so that he could see it in the low light. "Isn't that foreskins?" It was exactly what the picture looked like. Battered and fried foreskins.

A few drops of beer hit Trent's cheek as Brian spluttered across the table. The twins burst out laughing, one roaring and one quiet, and Trent flushed to the tips of his ears. Ian dropped his menu and smacked his palm across his forehead before rubbing his eyes with a groan.

"Well, for ice breakers, that has to take the cake," said Max as he recovered. Brian was still choking, but there was a light glimmering in his eyes that had Trent smiling.

"How many foreskins have you tasted before? They can't be better than calamari with a spicy chili sauce," said Brian as he wiped his napkin over his face. Max snorted and buried himself in his beer.

"I dunno," said Trent, looking to the ceiling as he thought back to his college days. "Like ten, I guess, but never with hot sauce. Not as many guys are cut these days."

Ian groaned, bringing his menu over his head to hide beneath it as his friends laughed. Trent patted the drummer on the shoulder, more relieved than he could express with words. There were a lot of people who Trent accidentally offended as soon as he opened his mouth, but Ian's bandmates seemed like normal people who wouldn't judge him too harshly.

"He told us that you were the sweetest person he'd ever met," said Brian as he pointed at Ian, who was still trying to shrivel away. "I was expecting some tiny little thing who tried to hug everybody and would refuse to eat meat."

"But meat is delicious," said Trent, figuring that he might as well keep going, because he couldn't dig himself any deeper at this point. "As long as it's cooked and not wrapped in plants — unless that plant is bacon." He turned to Ian with a shake of his head. "I can't be the sweetest person you've ever met." Ian had met so many people that Trent was only a tiny red dot on the map of his world.

"You are definitely the sweetest person I've ever met — and the kindest, and the most beautiful," replied Ian, locking eyes with Trent.

Butterflies swept into Trent's stomach as the restaurant faded away until it was just the two of the sitting next to each other with hardly any space between them at all. Ian's gaze dipped to Trent's lips as he swept his tongue over them. There was a moment of regret when Trent remembered that he had told Ian he hated sex in public places. He'd fuck Ian in the middle of the decorative fish tank right now if he could get away with it.

"Okay, enough of the squishy stuff," said Brian, completely ruining the moment and drawing their attention back to the table. Brian steered the conversation back to safe territory. He asked Trent about his family, where he'd grown up and how he'd met Ian. By the time their food had arrived, Trent was finally relaxed and feeling brave enough to try a deep-fried baby octopus along with his foreskins.

"Oh my God, these are so good," said Trent as he dipped another cephalopod in thick sauce and pushed it into his mouth. "So much better than that." He pointed to the mystery roll on the edge of Ian's plate. Trent had tried one bit of the sticky, slimy, salty mess and had instantly vowed off sushi for the rest of his life.

After his first glass of water, he'd ordered a beer. He didn't usually partake, especially around Ian, but the taller man had encouraged him, vowing that it was just fine if Trent had a few, even if he couldn't. One beer turned into two, and Trent was feeling the buzz by the time he downed his last drink. When the waiter offered him another, Trent politely refused.

"It's okay, T. I don't care, and I'm driving." Ian ducked down to speak close to Trent's ear so he could be heard over the loud conversation of his band mates.

Trent shook his head, even as he looked around at the empty glasses on the table. "I can't keep up my sweet reputation if I get wasted on the first date." He laughed and swallowed a belch that made its way up his throat. "And besides, I'm a lightweight. Any more and I won't be able to get it up tonight."

Ian laughed, and a bit of tension eased from his shoulders. He nodded to himself, happy that he finally seemed to hit something on target. "And I am definitely getting it up tonight. We've been practically celibate for the last three days, and it's our honeymoon."

Devon shot him a strange, shadowed look and Trent cut himself off. "Sorry." He dropped his voice. Perhaps he'd already had too much to drink if he was speaking loud enough for the others to hear.

After a little bit of begging, Trent finally convinced them all to get a massive dessert concoction that was made up of a triangle of puff pastries surrounded by a layer of chocolate cheesecake at the bottom. They were struggling to get down the last few bites when Trent saw movement out of the corner of his eye.

There was a hand on the back of the chair that had remained empty throughout the entire dinner. At first, Trent had kept looking over his shoulder as he'd waited for Mac to appear, but well into dinner, he had given up and let himself relax. Now, looking up to the thin and short singer, every bit of nervousness came rushing back.

Trent had only met him once before, in a hotel just after a concert, and his first impression had been an absolute disaster. Mac had grown his hair out from what he remembered, now short instead of buzzed at the sides, but he was still slim, with every line in his body taunt with strength. He was lean everywhere Ian was bulky, but he still looked so fucking strong.

"You guys started without me?" Mac asked as he gripped the back of the chair, his knuckles bleeding white from the pressure. Trent could see a line of pink scars across the surface from the repeated scrapes that Ian had told him about. Ian had said that there wasn't a fight out there that Mac wouldn't start and finish.

"And finished. Where the hell were you?" Ian asked as he crossed his arms and turned to his best friend as the rest of the table went silent. Trent wanted to slip down in the chair and slide out from under the table to get away. He didn't care that he would have to crawl over the dollop of chili sauce that he'd dropped.

"I was busy talking to the studio and lining up our next recording session. You could've at least waited for me." Mac gripped harder, and Trent swore he heard the chair creak. "You can't wait a bit while I'm out there making sure we all get paid?" His voice went from angry to downright furious.

"We got here two and a half hours ago, Mac, not just a couple of minutes," said Ian. "You're the one who made the fucking reservations. You knew exactly when you needed to be here." No one else said a word, either used to the interaction or too afraid to interfere.

"So, I have to come running every time it suits your fancy, when I'm fuck'n working, but you can take off for eight weeks in the middle of recording and it's fine?" asked Mac, shaking his head. His fair face had started to flush red, making every faint freckle stand out.

"We talked about this, Mac, and all of us agreed to the changes. Not all of us can keep working forever without a break. Something had to give." Ian let out a sigh and abruptly stood. "But this isn't the time or the place for that conversation. What's up, really? Don't give me a bullshit answer."

Mac's eyes flickered around the table as if he were seeing the others for the first time. Then his gaze snapped down and Trent felt them burning into the top of his head. He looked up, catching that gaze that was full of nothing but loathing. How could Ian miss this?

And what the hell had Trent done to deserve that kind of reaction? He'd met Mac once, briefly, and it hadn't been warm and fuzzy — but it wasn't that bad.

"Sorry I missed dinner, guys. Next time," said Mac. The loathing was gone, wiped away as if it had never been there, and he nodded grimly. The only evidence of his recent outburst was the flush that had spread down his neck and into the collar of his dark shirt. He turned and walked out of the room, leaving silence behind him.

Trent's stomach ached from more than just the overload of food, and for a second, he thought he might throw up. It didn't help that Ian was looking so confused and helpless as he gazed after his best friend.

"Can we go back to your place?" Trent asked quietly. Ian nodded, but didn't even turn to look at him, his eyes still trained on the door.

"I'll take care of the bill, guys. You can take off," said Brian as he shifted in his seat. "Trent, it was great meeting you again. Take care of this big guy." Devon had faded back into his seat as if he could melt into the cushioned backrest, but Max was watching Ian with a dark look.

Trent nodded, nearly shaking as he tried to stand. He gave a weak smile, thanking everyone while effectively avoiding their gazes, before he touched Ian's elbow to get his attention. Ian flinched, before he seemed to remember himself and turned to Trent.

"You ready to go?" asked Ian. He gave Trent a weak smile before he turned to lead them out of the door.

Trent slipped his hand ahead and tried to grasp Ian's palm. He wanted to stop the drummer and pull him close, letting Ian cry on his shoulder as Trent made everything okay again. He traced Ian's palm, then slipped through his fingers like Ian hadn't even noticed the attempt. Trent snatched his hand back and kept his eyes locked firmly on the carpet. He could hear whispers from the tables around them, and he knew that they must've heard the altercation, and they'd definitely seen his rejection.

The drive home passed silently except for the stray sound of a car alarm and the steady whirl of wind through Trent's hair. The sun had set, leaving a different Miami behind as the moon's glow cut through a stray cloud. There were still people on the streets as they walked under the streetlamps, but some of the warmth had been sucked out of the landscape. The green grass was dark and ominous under the coat of night, and alligators could be lurking literally anywhere.

The gate scraped open as they turned in the driveway, and Ian still hadn't said a word. The wheels popped as they rode over the uneven cobbles, and the sound of the engine bounced back from the trees that lined the property.

Trent led the way inside, not willing to be brushed aside by Ian yet again. There were only so many rejections he could take in one day before it broke his heart. It was hard to love someone and downright painful most days, and sometimes he needed reassurance so that he knew that it was at least worth it.

Miami had been a mistake. The people were nice, and everything was so rich and beautiful, but Ian was different here. Trent wanted the Ian who would sit in the backyard and chew on the end of a dandelion as he worked on beats and lyrics for the band's next hit. He wanted the Ian who would wake up at three a.m. and leave a voicemail on Mac's phone as he tapped out a beat that had come to him in his dreams.

Trent took one step through the door, his mind already preparing himself for the worst, when something grabbed him.

Chapter Seven

Trent's scream was high and shrill, like something out of a horror movie, as a cold hand gripped his arm in a tight embrace. His heart leapt as he cursed himself for not turning on the lights or waiting for Ian to follow him. Mostly he cursed himself for getting trapped in his head long enough to let someone sneak up on him.

"Jesus, T, you scared the crap out of me," a voice chuckled into his ear. "If I knew you were so easily frightened, I would've taken advantage of it before now." Ian's breath was hot against the shell of Trent's ear and smelled of salt and raw fish.

Ian pulled him back a step until he was pressed into his broad chest. The voice was Ian's, low and familiar, but so unexpected that his heart was still beating fast. Trent thought the drummer had still been in the car, lost in thought. He'd heard the door slam shut after him too, but Ian must've squirrelled his way in behind him somehow.

"Your hand is freezing," said Trent with his teeth chattering in his skull. He reached up to place a hand over Ian's, and the heat was sucked out of him like a winter storm.

"Let me warm it up for you." He gripped both hands around Trent's waist, chilled even through the layer of his orange sweater. One dipped low, playing with the hem, before thrusting under Trent's shirt and splaying over his back.

He shrieked again, trying to wiggle away from the freezing grip, but Ian held on tight. It was worse than jumping into a pool that sucked every bit of heat from his body.

"I love it when you scream for me," Ian whispered against the shell of his ear before he soothed along the lobe with his tongue. "You gonna scream for me tonight, T?"

Trent paused as he tried to catch up. The drummer was hard against his ass, and his voice was teasing and light. Mr. Brooding and Miserable had disappeared. Trent hoped it wasn't a mask, because he didn't want one on his account.

Trent snapped his jaw shut with a click and shook his head back and forth. "You have to earn another scream, Ian. And I don't think you have it in you."

"You know I like a challenge, T." He dropped his cold hands and settled them on Trent's hips. Suddenly, Trent was being lifted. He laughed as Ian literally tossed him over his shoulder in a fireman's carry. His first instinct was to flail, but he really didn't want to get dropped on his ass on flooring that was probably more expensive than a new hip.

Ian walked past the stairs and into the living room. Trent had only seen it in passing, and it was one of the blander rooms in the house. It had a normal-sized television along one wall, and a fancy couch that looked like it was more for aesthetics than actual sitting. There was a white shag rug in the middle of the floor that Trent had skimmed around before, not wanting to stain it with his footprints.

"Perfect," said Ian as he lowered Trent to the couch. Ian was breathing hard after the workout, but his pupils were blown wide as Trent sprawled back onto the cushion. Trent expected to sink into the grey seat of the sectional as he threw his head back. Instead, it felt like he hit a brick wall. No, a brick wall was too generous. This couch had to be made of a tectonic plate.

"Ow." He rubbed the back of his head and looked around to see if he'd hit the arm by accident. He was still a foot away from it. "I'm pretty sure this couch is made of concrete. It's got the right colour, anyway." It was the exact same grey as most fresh sidewalks, only it lacked the jagged ridges that made it more comfortable to face plant on.

"I've honestly never sat on it before," said Ian as he rubbed the back of his head, flushing pink across the bridge of his nose. "I got it as a gift about a year ago, and it looked nice, so I put it in here." He looked around the living room and shrugged. "I usually watch television in bed or in the theatre room. We can go to the bed if you want instead."

"Nuh-uh," Trent pushed himself up until he could sit on the rock-hard padding. "You promised me that we would christen every room in this house, and so far, we are zero for twenty. We have to start somewhere. And you are *not* carrying me up those stairs."

"Fair enough, T." Ian leaned in close, but Trent stopped him with a hand on his shoulder and a shake of his head.

Trent slid to his knees, using the couch as an extra-firm back rest as he fumbled with the buckle on Ian's pants. "I wanna try something," he said as he caught the zipper. The teeth were stuck on something, but whether it was Ian's straining length or the little strip of fabric under the zipper, Trent wasn't sure. It hovered in and out of view as he tried to look closer, and he gave one last tug before he was able to wrench it open.

"Are you drunk?" Ian took a step back and he settled his hands over Trent's. "We aren't doing anything if you're drunk, T. I know you're into it, but you still can't consent like that."

"You've got to be kidding me," said Trent as a pulse of anger glowed hot in his gut. "You're my husband and I consent, so let me try to deep-throat you." He cut off his glare before he hummed and grabbed for Ian, but Ian simply took another step back out of reach.

"How many drinks did you have tonight, T? I think it was five or six, wasn't it? I don't want you to get hurt because you don't have control right now." Ian pulled his zipper back up, despite the resisting bulge, and turned to face away. "Don't fight me on this one, T, not about this." His voice went quiet as he stared out of the glass window to the pool beyond. There was more in his voice than refusal. There was an echo of sharp pain there too.

Trent thought back to the slight blur of dinner and tried to count the drinks he'd had. He'd thought he'd stopped when he had just been starting to feel a bit of a buzz. The pressure and the need to fit in had driven him to drink more than he normally would, especially since he was a lightweight at heart.

"As angry as I am right now, that's actually kind of sweet of you," said Trent as he leaned back against the couch, finally giving up. "I think it was five, but I don't remember for sure. I don't think you understand how much I want you right now, though." Trent sighed and let his head fall back. His groin ached with the need to be free from his pants, but Ian was pushing him away...again.

An idea struck him with the delay of every single sip of alcohol that he'd taken. "I get that I can't touch you and you can't touch me, but I bet you won't stop me," said Trent as he grasped the clasp on his own pants. He struggled with the button that had somehow grown in the hole, before pulling the zipper down and dipping his hand inside. Ian's eyes went dark and his mouth dropped open as Trent let out a long groan at the contact.

It was exactly what he needed. His shaft was squished awkwardly inside his pants and getting sweatier with each passing throb. He pulled it out of its bend to slap against his belly and the soft padding of carefully trimmed hair that was there. The head was already tinted purple, and there was a smear of pre-cum quickly drying on his palm. It wasn't enough to slick the way, but Trent had done more with less.

"What..." Ian stumbled over the word before he flopped his mouth open again.

Trent stroked himself once from tip to base, letting his hand drag along the sensitive skin before he gripped the base hard enough to feel the throb. The veins stood out in purples and blues when he didn't let up the pressure. He had never touched himself in front of Ian, but there was something so intimate and erotic about Ian watching as he took himself apart.

"I think we need to change spots, Ian," said Trent as he pulled his hand away and pushed himself to his feet.

The rest of the drying pre-cum on his hand had smeared on the couch, leaving an obvious stain beneath his palm. His cock caught at the edge of his zipper as he stood, and he winced before tugging his pants down a few inches.

He pointed to the couch. "You sit there and enjoy the view." Ian stepped to the couch and lowered himself as ordered, grimacing as he struck the hard seat. Trent made his way to the blank television screen, turning to face Ian with a flourish that made his head spin.

"Can you put on some music for me? Something I can dance to," said Trent, suddenly feeling awkward in the silence with Ian looking at nothing but him.

"You gonna dance for me, T?" asked Ian, looking like he was trying not to pout. He knew as well as Trent that Trent couldn't dance for anything. Bouncing and shifting from side to side was the highlight of Trent's ability. Ian reached for the remote regardless and tuned to a music channel with a slight smirk.

"Country music, *blah*. You wound me, Ian," said Trent as the sound of an acoustic guitar filtered through the expensive speakers that were dotted around the room. "Easier than rap, I guess." He laughed and gave an awkward shrug as Ian's gaze settled on him with full attention.

Trent did what he knew how to do, which wasn't dancing in any sense. He shoved his hand back into his pants and wrapped it around his cock while still keeping himself somewhat hidden behind the fabric of his boxers. He gripped the shaft with the perfect pressure while he moved his thumb to the head and flicked the piercing there. It sent a zing of sensation down his shaft and straight to his gut, and he humped the air in response. He moved his other hand under the edge of his sweater and pulled at his nipple piercing harsher than Ian ever would.

"Can I see?" asked Ian as he shifted on the seat before palming at his groin. His legs were splayed wide as if he could relieve the pressure behind the zipped seam.

Trent shook his head along with the music as he gave himself another tug and tilted his head back until he could see the black-and-silver light fixture above his head. It wasn't as good as Ian's hand, and he was convinced nothing ever would be, but it was a pretty close second.

"I don't want to upset you," said Trent as he made eye contact again. Ian's free hand clenched so hard on the chair that his knuckles went white, but his lips curled up in a smirk.

"You want to drive me crazy until I'm begging to see you, T?" asked Ian. "It's not gonna happen. I'm just an innocent bystander who's enjoying the show."

Trent snorted. Yeah, an innocent bystander with a dick like a porn star that could currently cut diamonds. Trent couldn't see it fully beneath the denim, but from what he'd felt earlier, Ian was struggling to hold on to his control. He honestly felt for the drummer. If Trent had a dick that big, he would probably dedicate his life to keeping it wet.

"I hope I don't blind your delicate sensibilities, then," said Trent as he let go of his piercings and started to shimmy his jeans from his hips. The tent in his boxers was downright obscene, despite the attempt that his sweater made to cover it. He grasped the hem and pulled the soft material over his head so he was almost naked before Ian's eyes. Just one piece of clothing left.

"You should go get me some lube, Ian." Trent rocked his hips into the air as he fondled himself through the cotton. "I don't know about you, but I'm ready to go all the way." There was a spreading wet spot on his boxers that got bigger with each pass of his hand. If he had been sober, he probably would've come already.

Ian launched himself out of the chair, stumbling a few painful steps before he adjusted himself and ran out of the room.

"At least I know how to keep you motivated," Trent shouted at Ian's retreating form before he grabbed the remote and changed the music to something that didn't make him quite so depressed.

He pulled an armchair to the middle of the carpet and grabbed a towel from the closet beside the deck door where the pool towels were kept. He flung the towel over the chair and settled back onto it, knowing that he wasn't careful enough on his own to keep from smearing lube and cum onto the fabric. He could still see the stain he'd left on the couch as it started to crust, and he didn't want to ruin every piece of furniture in the house.

He flipped one leg over each of the arms, testing the strength of the chair and the limits of his flexibility. The pose left him completely exposed but still covered by his cotton boxers. He deliberated for a moment before he stood, slipped his boxers off, then took the same pose, this time covering himself with a stiff pillow that matched the sectional. It scraped against his cock in the most uncomfortable way.

Ian paused as he entered the room, raising his brows and his mouth dropping open again as he looked at Trent, so openly displayed. Trent shifted and pushed down the embarrassment that threatened. Ian had seen it all before, and more, but there was something different about this. This wasn't handing the reins over and letting Ian take him apart. This was him taking control of himself and blatantly putting himself on display. The look Ian was giving him just barely made the tightness in his stomach worth it.

"Catch," said Ian as he tossed two items to Trent at the same time. Trent cursed Ian's ambidextrous ass that could make it look so effortless and so sexy at the same time.

Trent squeaked, releasing the pillow as he tried to catch them. The pillow hit the ground with an actual thud, as if were made of rock and not polyester.

One of the items smacked him in the stomach, a mere inch above his precious commodities. It rolled and jammed in the seam of his hip, while the other item hit his palm.

"Meanie," said Trent with a huff, as he settled back and grabbed the thing that had hit him in the gut. His mouth fell open as he brought it up and held it out at arm's length.

It was a bright pink dildo, and so life-like that he half-expected it to be warm. There were veins, divots and even a slight arch off to one side that was more realistic than any dildo he'd ever seen before. It was soft in his hands, with a texture almost like skin and nowhere near silicone. The size was perfect. It was just on the side of too big with a length that made him shudder in anticipation.

"Wait," said Trent as he tilted the dildo into the light and brought it closer to his face. "Is this your cock?" The ridges were familiar, and the curve to the left was exactly the same as Ian.

"Yep." Ian nodded, crossing his arms and leaning back on the couch. "I finally took Candace's advice and got a copy made of the real thing." His face was tilted upwards, as if he was daring Trent to call him out.

"It's pink." Trent turned it over in his hand again. The details were right on the mark. He could even see the faint impression of the little freckle that Ian had right down near the base. He loved flicking that freckle with his tongue and listening to Ian moan as he played with the ultra-sensitive flesh.

"The one I sent her was blue, if that helps," said Ian with a shrug and a raised brow.

"You sent my best friend a carbon-copy of your dick?" Trent nearly dropped the dildo. His best friend had his husband's cock for her perusal and pleasure. And she would probably use it on the stewardess from the plane, if they decided to hook up. Candace had seen Ian's package up close and personal before, but this was a whole different level.

"She's a collector. Can't have her missing out on the star." A smirk stretched across his face. "But she's not the reason that I took Viagra and sat in a chair with a mould on my dick. I did that for you."

Trent's dick twitched, even as he pictured Ian sitting in a salon chair with a magazine in his hands and a groin full of plaster. And the fact that Ian had to take Viagra to keep it up long enough was downright hilarious. That would've been an interesting conversation with his doctor. *Oh hey, I need some blue pills so I can get a mould of my cock made for my horny husband.*

"You want to fuck me even when you can't," said Trent with sudden realization. Something about that made his toes curl and his legs open wider.

He pulled the fake cock up to his lips before snaking his tongue out to lick at the head. It was spongy, just the way Ian's cock was, but the temperature was all wrong and it tasted like plastic. It was soft against his teeth as he dragged them gently over the crown before teasing at the shallow divot with his tongue. It was slick, and getting slicker, but there was still something missing. There was a reason that he didn't like sex toys, but Ian hadn't left him much of a choice. It was this or nothing, and his cock chose the former in less than a heartbeat.

"Mmm-m, I think I like the real thing better, but I'll keep trying." He dropped his lips over the head and stretched his mouth to let it inside. The plastic taste overwhelmed his palate, but it was no worse than giving head with a condom. He pushed past the taste until the cock tapped the back of his throat, then a little bit beyond. It tickled his gag reflex and he pulled back with a small cough and watering eyes. In his imagination, he could take Ian's whole cock in his mouth or his ass like a champ, but reality was cruel.

"If I practice hard enough, I'll be able to take the whole thing," said Trent through heavy-lidded eyes. He stared at Ian as he dropped low again and groped himself through his pants. There was hardly any blue left in his dark eyes.

When he reached the same spot, he forced himself to swallow and take it even farther. He turned his lips up just a hair to try and supress his gag reflex. There was a tense moment when he thought it just wouldn't work. It was too big, too wide and too hard to fit down his throat. All his efforts at home alone, preparing for Ian, were shot to hell when the real thing was in his mouth.

But then it was sliding deeper and deeper until his lips touched his fingers that were grasped around the base. The stretch was alarming, and his first thought was utter shock. He was so full and he couldn't breathe. He could scarcely even move.

He drew back with a gasp and licked the drool from his lips. "I am such a quick learner." He praised himself as if Ian weren't even in the room. He would've let out the little cheer that was bubbling under the surface, but then he would've looked even more ridiculous than he already did.

"I wonder if I can multitask just as well." He popped open the cap of the lube that Ian had tossed at him and spread it over the fingers of his left hand. He moved it down, past his cock, to his tight entrance. It was always so tight when he touched himself, and this time wasn't any different. It didn't matter how many times Ian fucked him—or for how long Trent tried to finger himself. He always snapped back shut, as if he were a permanent virgin.

At least with Ian, he could relax as the man pushed inside. Trent knew Ian would make it so good for him, whether it was with his cock or his hands. It made the discomfort worth it, and the sting a mere nuisance.

He shook his head and tried to ground himself. He wasn't alone as he traced his finger around the rim, spreading slick and dipping in. He could do this, and imagine that it was just Ian inside, and not his own short stubby fingers that were utterly useless on his body. He gave himself one breath to get used to the feeling before he took the fake cock back into his mouth. He needed something, anything, to distract him from the pressure of being breached.

It was like patting his head and rubbing his belly at the same time. He could only focus his mind on one thing, no matter how distracting each was. There was a stutter and a stumble before a rhythm slowly built under his hands. He would withdraw his finger from his ass as he pressed the cock into his mouth. He didn't go deep enough to gag himself again, but instead sucked it in noisily, swirling with his tongue. Then, as he pulled back for air, he would push his finger deep. Soon he used a second finger to spread himself wide.

Ian watched the entire thing in utter silence, as if he were afraid that any sound might startle Trent and still his hands. The drummer wasn't still, though. He ground his palm down on his cock before he finally gave in and pulled it out into the air. He gripped the couch hard, as if it were the only thing holding him back from getting up and throwing Trent down onto the floor.

"I can't reach, Ian," said Trent as he whined and pulled the dildo from his mouth before setting it on his belly. He arched his back and brought his leg up high so he could curl his fingers deep, but he still couldn't reach. He was so close that it made him ache, but his fingers were just too short. They were always too short, and the angle was all wrong. Every other man he'd fingered, he could always reach their spot, no problem, but he was useless when it came to his own body.

"Ian, please, I need you now. Make me come." Trent groaned and pushed down onto his fingers, but it was no use. He needed more, but he was so tight. His rim ached as he clenched hard, as if he could draw himself in deeper and reach that spot that was flaring like the worst itch. He could try another finger, but he could barely fit two, even as he jammed them deep as hard as he could. There was no pleasure, only tightness and ache.

"I'm right there, T. Fuck yourself on me and I'll make you come so good," said Ian, his words slurred with heat, oblivious to Trent's struggle. "You're gonna push me in there in one go and I'll stretch you so wide that you'll be feeling it for days. I'll slide right across your spot, just the way you like it, then harder so you won't be able to do anything but take it."

"Please, I want you now. Just fuck me." Trent was lost in his head and in utter longing for his husband, but no matter how hard he begged, Ian didn't stand up.

"Get the lube, T, and pour some over my cock so you can take me." Ian gripped himself hard at the base with a cut-off moan as Trent followed his directions. "That's good. Now fuck yourself, baby. Fuck yourself until you can't anymore."

Trent pressed the slick head to his entrance and paused. It was warm from his mouth, and the texture was almost perfect. It did feel like it was Ian there and not just a replica. And Ian told him to push it all in at once. That sounded like the best idea he'd ever heard. It would feel so much better once Ian was inside.

He pushed the dildo hard and it popped inside with a harsh thrust that broke through any resistance with a jolt of shock and pain. He let out a whine as he clamped down and his body protested at the sudden intrusion. It wasn't like Ian at all. It was too much, too fast. There were no hands on him that soothed his muscles into submission and no lips on his that would take his pain away.

"Ease up for me, T. It's just me. I know you can take it. You were made for me," said Ian, flinching as Trent let out another high whine.

Ian's voice helped, but it was so far away that he might as well have been across the world. It was too much, and exactly the same as any other time Trent had experimented with toys. He could make someone come twice before he pushed inside them, sweet and slow, and brought them to another peak, but he couldn't seem to do that with himself. He knew he should be able to make himself relax, but it was like his body rejected anyone or anything that wasn't Ian. He needed Ian's hands on him and the salt of his sweat along his tongue for his body to unwind. He need that voice in his ear, not from across the room, and he needed that real cock splitting him wide. Everything else was just a game — a game that he was bound to lose.

"Hurts." A tear fell from the corner of Trent's eyes as the ache peaked. He still wasn't ready to give up, though, not when Ian had given him such a gift. Ian wanted this and wanted him, and there was no other way.

He pushed harder, seating the cock even deeper inside, and pushing through any remaining resistance that his body had to offer. He clenched along the base and adjusted his grip.

"T, stop," said Ian, dropping his hands to the couch. His smirk was gone, and the blush of arousal had disappeared from his face.

"I want to, for you, Ian, but..." Trent cut himself off as he bottomed the toy out with a final push. It was so deep, too deep, and it fucking hurt.

"T, stop *now*." Ian's voice rose and he pushed off the couch. The pillow thudded against the wall as it was tossed out of the way. Ian knelt in front of Trent and gripped the base of the toy and tried to pull it out, but Trent held tight.

"You won't fuck me for real, but I want you so bad," Trent whined as Ian clamped over his wrist and forced him away. The toy pulled out slowly, leaving Trent so empty that it almost hurt worse. He had failed again and Ian still wouldn't touch him. Even now, his hands were gentle, scarcely a tickle, as if he didn't want to linger.

"T, what are you doing to yourself, huh? You don't have to hurt yourself just to try to make me happy," said Ian as he finally gave in and touched Trent. "I don't think you tore anything, but you're really red down there. I want you to be happy, and besides, we have all the time in the world." He wrapped his arms around Trent and lifted him from the chair, bringing them back to the uncomfortable couch. He pulled Trent close with trembling hands.

Trent melted into the embrace, realizing that he was shaking too. He didn't know what had happened in his mind. He had wanted so badly to please Ian, and he was so horny that he just couldn't stop himself. It still didn't make sense, and neither did the tears falling down his face to drip on his chest.

It was cold with the air conditioning cranked against the evening warmth of Miami, and Ian's arms weren't enough to keep it away. The emptiness was fading fast, leaving a vivid ache that was worse than anything he'd felt before. Another shiver streaked up his spine and he let out a shuddering breath. He had ruined everything, but there was one way that he could fix it.

He grabbed Ian's chin and brought their lips together. The heat of the kiss spread from his mouth and stilled the trembling of his limbs. He could taste the soda that Ian had had at dinner. There was more, but the unique flavour of his husband overwhelmed it. He dipped his tongue inside and moaned as he plunged deep, taking Ian exactly how he wanted to be taken.

Ian went rock-stiff against Trent before he let out a sound that had Trent arching up into him. That noise was pure sin with a side dish of flattery, and it came from deep within Ian's chest.

"You taste so fucking good," Ian pulled back enough to say against his lips before he threaded his hands into Trent's hair and flipped them so Trent's back was pressed into the stone-coloured couch. Ian was harsh, almost brutal, as he tore the control away from Trent and left him spinning and wanting.

The kiss wasn't sweet or sexy in any sense. It was consuming. It sucked every bit of Trent out of his body and into Ian's like the kiss of an incubus. Ian gripped tighter until Trent could feel the strands of his hair barely clinging on. He was pinned to the couch as Ian feasted upon him. He could barely breathe, let alone think.

And Ian didn't stop. If anything, he pushed harder until Trent's lips bruised under the touch. It was as arousing as it was terrifying, to feel Ian lose complete control. Trent's cock throbbed against Ian, and suddenly his legs were being pried wide around Ian's bulk. He groaned and rocked up in an enthusiastic agreement.

A blunt head brushed against his entrance in a flash of pain as Ian kissed him harder, sucking Trent's tongue into his mouth. Ian let out a broken, desperate moan before Trent felt wetness seep against him as Ian's hips stuttered.

The dampness spread along his crack and dripped down to the couch in a near-torrent as the drummer continued to come. The man who had an iron-clad control and who never came before Trent, had just defied both things.

Trent's head swam and he drew in a gasping breath as Ian finally retreated. There was a pool of wetness on Trent's belly from an orgasm that he'd never felt, and his lips were numb and swollen. He gripped the couch with one hand, and fisted Ian's shirt with the other as the world spun for a moment before he settled at last on his husband.

Ian's eyes were so wide that there was more white than colour in his gaze. His lips were scarlet and swollen, with one roughened edge from where their teeth must've pinched it. He took fast, shallow breaths as he gripped Trent as if he would somehow try to run from his pinned position.

"Fuck!" Ian jerked off the couch as if he'd been hit with a taser. Three long strides and he was across the room, dropping his head into his hands as his back hit the wall. "Fuck, T," he said again, clawing at his temples violently and leaving red streaks where his nails dug into the sensitive flesh.

"What? What did I do?" Trent's head buzzed as he wiped his lips with the back of his hand. There was a tiny bit of blood that rubbed over his knuckles, but it probably looked worse than it actually was. There were no bruises, other than the red marks where Ian's hands had dug in—and a crap-ton of cum dripping on the couch. "Oops, sorry about your sofa. I didn't like it anyway, to be honest," said Trent as he tried to calm his husband, who sounded close to hyperventilation. Ian bent in half as he gripped his head like his hands could carve away his innermost thoughts. "Or I can try steam cleaning it first if you're attached to it. Ian?" He would need more steam than a train, but he was willing to try. The couch did match the décor, but it wasn't that difficult to match with beige, so it really wasn't something to get worked up about.

Trent's thoughts came to a sudden halt. They had both been worked up, and Trent had literally begged Ian, even though he'd flat-out refused him more than once. Maybe Ian thought he had pushed too far when he'd lost control? Even though he'd hardly even touched Trent except for a kiss and a bit of a grind.

It may have been the sound of his name or the tremor in Trent's breath that finally caught Ian's attention. He dropped his hands from his head to hang limply at his sides. There were ten red imprints that looked close to bleeding where Ian's nails had pressed into his flesh. He was still hanging out of his pants, opened, exposed and completely forgotten.

"You taste—." Ian shook his head and cut himself off with a shudder that travelled through his entire body before he took a deep breath and straightened. "I'm sorry, T. I hope I didn't hurt you. Can we just go to bed?" He rubbed along the grooves in his skull, grimacing at the bruises they would probably become.

It took a moment before Trent could reply. It was as if a switch had been flipped, and Ian's panicked and terrified demeanour had shattered into quiet regret.

"Sure... Let me just clean up and I'll meet you upstairs." Trent had barely finished speaking before Ian was disappearing from the room and walking away without looking back.

Trent brought his hand to his mouth and dipped the tip of his finger inside. His taste? He'd eaten the dessert last, so he probably tasted mostly like chocolate, but Ian had never reacted like that before.

He cupped his palm over his mouth and nose so he could breathe in the scent of his breath. *Whiskey.*

Chapter Eight

Four days later, Trent finally woke up with someone beside him in the bed. Over the three previous days, by the time the sun peeked through the skylight, the sheets were cold except for his own warmth. Ever since Ian had lost control of himself, Trent had hardly seen him at all.

Ian would leave the house long before Trent woke, and he wouldn't return until the air had grown thick with humidity and the crickets were calling to each other. Trent had waited up for him on the first day, despite the way his eyelids had drooped as he read in bed.

On the first morning, Trent had wandered the house, expecting Ian to be behind one of the doors, still moping about the previous evening. Trent had been ready to show Ian that he was completely fine. Sure, his rim had been tender and sore, but no more than it would have been after a good fucking. His head had pounded fiercely as he'd wandered the house, but he had guzzled water and the feeling had soon disappeared. He had been fine. At least he'd kept telling himself that. And the tightness in his chest had probably just been heartburn.

But behind every door, there'd been nothing more than neat rooms with dust-free ornaments that looked like they'd been chosen by someone else. The only room that looked anything like a home was the drum room, but even it'd been empty.

Trent sent out the first message after he gave up his search and grabbed his phone. It had been simple.

Where are you?

Three hours later, after a breakfast of stale cereal, suspect milk and worry that deepened from concern to downright fear, he finally got a reply.

At studio recording.

There was nothing more for the entire day. It was a promise broken and a honeymoon shattered in three simple words.

Ian had returned near midnight looking empty and exhausted, and Trent hadn't had the heart to tell him how furious he had been to be left alone in an unfamiliar house, in an unfamiliar place, with nothing but take-out menus and a credit card that was getting closer to its limit each day. He'd had a card from Ian, one that probably didn't have a limit, but somehow it hadn't felt right using it. If they were both eating together it seemed fine, almost natural, for Ian to pay, but when Trent was dining for one, he was paying for his own meals — even if he didn't really have a budget for it.

"We're recording right now, and you know how much that takes out of me," Ian had said after the second straight day of Trent wandering an empty house. *"I can't get out of it. This is my career we are talking about here."* It had been close to midnight when the gate had moved back and the yellow Corvette had pulled into the garage.

During the day, Trent had amenities at his disposal that had never been an option before, except in hotels. His muscles ached from so much time spent in the water, as he'd tried in vain to beat the infinity jets, and his skin had gone crispy and red on his back where he'd fallen asleep on a lounge chair next to the water. He'd had a car at his disposal, and not just any car, but the car of his dreams. He'd put in several hours racing around town, then thirty minutes just sitting in the car before he could walk straight.

The weather had been perfect, and the sun bright and powerful. The people had been friendly too, and so open and easy with him. When he'd gotten turned around on the road and hadn't been able to find his way back, more than one person had helped point him in the right direction. Every day he'd set out in a different direction, sometimes getting deliberately lost just so he could strike up a conversation with a stranger. It had been almost sad.

More than one woman had hit on him, even after they'd seen his ring. It had definitely been flattering when they'd been perfect tens and had doted on him.

One afternoon, he'd treated himself to cooked seafood at a restaurant that was close enough to the water to smell the salt on the breeze. Trent had waited for his order, admiring the neat cursive on the hand-written *Help Wanted* sign in the front window, when a woman had slid across from him in the booth. She'd flirted for a few minutes before she'd tried to give him her number with her perfectly manicured nails brushing over the back of his hand. When he'd declined and explained that he was married and one hundred percent gay, then she'd just shrugged and disappeared.

Less than a minute later, a man had slid across from Trent. The guy had been built of wet dreams with hair so black that it looked blue and a perfect complexion matched with a five-o'clock shadow that was completely deliberate. He had been slim, witty and stunning, and he'd literally taken Trent's breath away. When he'd made a pass at Trent, Trent had actually considered it for half a second, before he'd realized that first, this guy was a one hundred percent bottom and two, he was the other lady's brother.

So, when the light dribbled into the bedroom and he reached next to him and hit solid warmth, he broke out in a smile fuelled by gallons of relief. Here was the only person he really wanted to hit on him, and the only one he wanted to ask for directions.

He pulled himself across the short expanse that separated them on the massive bed and laid his head down on Ian's chest. Ian stirred at the movement, before he snorted and groaned as he came awake. He stretched out, before collapsing back into the pillow top.

"You're here," said Trent without lifting his head. His anger and loneliness were soothed by the sheer heat of his husband. Things could still be salvaged. Ian's chest moved under his head as he chuckled, the sound reverberating around his ribcage.

"I should be here for the rest of the honeymoon, T," said Ian as he trailed his hand down Trent's back.

"We're all finished for now. I crammed in every bit so I could come back to you. What did you get up to?" He shifted in the bed and tugged the sheets down over their bodies as the warmth started to rise. It was as if there was nothing between them except love — no worry, no doubt and only iron-clad control. The terrible evening and Ian's disappearance lay as distant memories that would never be brought up again.

"Mmm-m, drove your car around. Got lost. Got a sunburn. Ate way too much food." Trent snorted and pushed himself up on his elbows. "I still didn't see the maid, but I know she must've been here at some point. Someone keeps doing the laundry — and it's not me." At one point he'd actually considered picking up security cameras so he could try to catch her in the act. He just wanted to thank her for her hard work, after all. Then he realized that he couldn't put cameras up in a house that didn't really belong to him. That would just be weird.

Trent chewed his lip as his gaze dropped down Ian's chest, over his slightly round pecs to the small pink nipples. The tattoo rose was the most faded of all of his tattoos and looked nothing like the flag on the side of his head. There was the perfect amount of light, almost-blond hair that grew between his pecs, and it was soft and curly instead of coarse and wiry.

He moved his focus lower to the scar across Ian's ribcage. When they'd first met, it had been bright, nearly red and still sensitive when Trent had reached out to touch it. The lettering along it was still crisp, but the scar had faded to a soft pink now. Sometimes at night, Ian would rub it in his sleep and Trent would watch as the line flared bright. It would take days sometimes, but it would always return to the same pink as his nipples.

"Will you tell me how you got this?" asked Trent, as he skimmed his fingers slowly over the scar. He usually avoided the spot with his hands or his tongue, afraid that he would somehow harm Ian. He wanted to say more to fill in the silence that had settled between them, but he held back. He didn't need to revisit the other night, but he needed to know more about the man he was married to. There were things that Ian had never told him, but Trent didn't want Ian to be afraid to share himself if he was ready.

"It was an accident," said Ian as he let out a deep sigh, his voice still heavy with sleep. His eyes were bright, though, and he blinked a few times as he answered, as if trying to push his sleepiness away.

"Will you tell me what happened?" Trent urged softly as he dipped lower to the lettering. *Never again.* He waited as Ian took another deep breath before he started to speak.

"This was from a piece of glass," said Ian as he dipped his hand low and followed the movement of Trent's fingers. "It was from another car. It went straight through the windshield and hit me here. An inch to the side and…" His voice waivered as he paused and licked his lips.

For the first time, Trent noticed the ragged edges on the scar that he could scarcely see through the knotted tissue. It was big, stretching down the side of Ian's ribs and rolling over the small bumps that the bones made underneath. If it had hit a few inches to the side, it could have caught on the bone and twisted straight into Ian's lung.

"I hit another car going sixty miles an hour. I was lucky that it was so late and that I was driving slower than I used to back then. I was drunk…really fucking drunk. I'd been drunk for four days straight by that point, because I was celebrating being in the top ten with our new release." Ian shook his head at the memory and his lips quirked. "I don't even remember what song it was now.

"The other car was fine and the people too, but my car was totalled, and I'm lucky to be alive with only a bit of a scar. It finally shook something loose in my head and I hit rehab the same day I got out of the hospital. I took a cab straight there and I never looked back." Ian gripped Trent's hand that was splayed across his pec and brought it to his lips. "The guys were supportive and helped me through my recovery. Hell, they still help me with it all the time."

"When did you get this?" Trent ran his fingers over the tattoo. *Never again* marked permanently into Ian's side. It still looked so fresh, as if the ink had never really dried.

"About six months after the accident. I hated a lot of things about myself back then, but I didn't want to be that person ever again. I'm not a nice drunk, T," said Ian, running his hand down Trent's back. "Sometimes I was so fucking awful, and I remember every little thing I said and did. I remember it, but I couldn't stop it—and I couldn't stop drinking either. It was like candy." His dark eyes caught Trent's. "What do you taste when you have a drink of hard liquor, T?"

Trent shifted on the bed and thought back to his drinks from the other night. They had been top shelf and probably some of the best he'd ever had. "Sour, bitter and a bit of fire, but not in a bad way, I guess. I've never thought about it before." Drinking had always seemed like part of the ritual at some events, while remaining taboo at others. He could get plastered at a birthday party, as long as it wasn't his niece's. Out at the bar, he would order something cheap just so he could avoid the awkward pause if he turned a free drink down from someone else. He didn't really like it, but he didn't really want to go without it, either.

"Not me, T," he shook his head, his eyes going distant. "It was the best thing I've ever tasted. I could drink it all day, every day and I'd never get enough. The way it rolled down my throat and burned the whole way was fucking perfect. But it made me mean, and I didn't take no for an answer…not for anything."

Trent let that sit in his stomach as he thought it over. "Did you ever…?" He trailed off, unable to ask the question. *If I'd said no, would Ian have been able to stop himself?* He drew meaningless letters on Ian's belly instead of thinking about it. The hard muscles rolled just beneath the surface, so ready and strong.

"Almost. I was lucky that I passed out before I could do anything, but yeah. I didn't stop, even when someone said no." Ian' gripped Trent's hip and squeezed. "I can never drink again, T, 'cause I'd never be able to stop. The other night was too close. When I tasted it on you, I just lost myself. I can't let that happen—not when I've got you. I love you so much, T, and I never want to let that go." His eyes shimmered in the bright light as the sun started to peek through the glass overhead.

"I love you too, Ian. Thank you for telling me." Trent leaned forward and pressed a kiss to Ian's sternum. Ian's heart beat frantically beneath his lips like a sparrow fluttering against a windowpane.

It made sense now — the loss of control and the way Ian had devoured him. There was no other word to describe what had happened between them. And Trent could imagine that if Ian hadn't come so soon or if he'd actually been drunk, nothing would have stopped him. Trent didn't know if he'd ever tell his husband 'no', but he'd never had to before.

"Do you think less of me because of it?" asked Ian as he clenched his eyes shut and turned his head away from Trent. Trent grabbed his chin and forced his husband to meet his gaze.

"No. Never. We all do shit that we aren't proud of, but it shapes the people that we are today," said Trent, watching a look of relief pass over Ian's face. "I mean, I've never tried to rape someone, but I did some pretty bad shit in my college days." Even the memory of some of his darker days made his gut clench.

"My perfect husband," Ian' pulled his lips up into a small smile and his tone turned teasing, "I refuse to believe that you could do anything as bad as that." He looped his arms around Trent and pulled him closer until he was right on top of Ian and settled between his wide-spread legs.

"I was once in a high-speed chase with the cops. They never caught me, and I didn't turn myself in," Trent grudgingly admitted. Ian's mouth fell wide. "See? I'm a terrible person." Trent groaned and rolled off Ian with a small laugh. Ian followed him through the sheets and placed a hand on Trent's chest to push him back into the blankets.

"Is it bad that I find that a little bit hot?" asked Ian as he leaned in for a kiss, licking into Trent's mouth before he pulled back.

"Why do you think I was driving so fast?" asked Trent. "My dick was so hard that I couldn't reach for the brake without creaming my pants." He laughed, letting the darkness flutter away as Ian joined him.

"Can I ask you something, T?" Ian's laughter fell away. "Do you like Miami so far?" The look of vulnerability that crossed Ian's face broke Trent's heart. It was obvious that Ian was in love with the city, even if he hadn't really made it his home yet. Some parts, like the empty beige rooms, were downright sterile.

"Of course I do," said Trent honestly. "The weather is awesome, and the people are super nice. I love the pool too, but the sunburn I could live without." Trent smiled as Ian suddenly relaxed.

"Will you stay here with me?" asked Ian, his strong voice booming in the suddenly silent room.

The question was the equivalent to driving into a stack of sandbags at one hundred kilometres per hour. Not only would it hurt like fuck and probably demolish the car, but the mess would explode all over the road. They would have to bring in entire crews just to sweep the sand up. Trent's stomach went through a very similar experience, but he wasn't quite sure if it was from the car's perspective, or the sandbag's.

"Umm-m." It was the only thing that would come out of Trent's mouth. He flapped his lips and tried to force air through his mouth, but it didn't work. Panic rose in his throat as the seconds of silence ticked by. Ian was waiting for an answer, and every second that went by, Trent's panic thickened.

"No." Trent finally forced the single word out that was at the forefront of all his thoughts. *No. No. No.* He could say it a hundred times and it wouldn't quite express the finality of that word.

"What? Why? You said you loved it," said Ian, sitting up suddenly and leaning back against the headboard. All hints of sleepiness were gone.

"No, I said I liked it. Let's see here, Ian." Trent rolled out of bed and stared down at Ian. "Since we've been here, I've spent most of my time alone. Your friends don't want me here, especially Mac. I have a job waiting for me back home, and a house, and the ladies and my friends and family." He counted off on his fingers as he got louder with each point.

"So, it's okay for me to fly to you every eight weeks and stay in your shitty house with your shitty bed and no fucking hot water, but you won't live in a fucking mansion with me?" Ian yelled right back. "I've made so many sacrifices for you, T, but you never want to return the favour." Ian crossed his arms, and his eyes went dark.

"Being happy isn't about a big house, Ian. What the hell would I do if I were here all the time? Where would I get a job?" Trent threw his hands up in exasperation. His house was tiny, but it certainly wasn't shitty.

"You don't need to get a job, Trent." Ian's arms bulged as he clenched his fists, but Trent refused to get distracted by the sight.

"I'll stop you right fucking there." Trent's vision blurred. "I'm not some sugar baby looking for a Daddy. I've earned my own way in this world, and I'm not going to waste my life sitting here, waiting for you to finish up with the boys and come home." He watched as Ian withdrew into an impenetrable shell. "I'm not trying to be an asshole, Ian. Since we've been here, we've hardly spent any time together and it's like you don't want to even be around me. It's supposed to be our honeymoon, but you've barely touched me. Why would I want that for us every day? It might be good for your career, but it wouldn't be good for us."

"Fine." The word was final and absolute. Ian stormed out of bed and into the closet, pulling the closest shirt out and pulling it over his head. It was one that had shrunk in the wash, and it rode an inch up Ian's belly, exposing his treasure trail beneath.

"Are you just going to leave again?" Trent asked. His throat clogged as Ian nodded and grabbed for a pair of pants without even looking at him. "I guess I can find my way to the airport then. I'll take a taxi so you won't have to worry about picking up the car." Trent couldn't stop the tears from blurring his vision, but he could keep them from falling down his cheeks.

Ian froze and finally turned to Trent. "You're just going to leave?" His voice was flat.

Trent shrugged and looked to his open suitcase on the ground. He was already packed, as if he'd never been in the house in the first place. He realized that he'd never moved a single article out of the suitcase and into the house. His toothbrush was still in there, along with his hairbrush. He returned them after each use, like a library book. "I don't want to spend another day here by myself, Ian. If I'm going to be alone, I might as well be at home."

Trent wasn't sure what he expected. Maybe Ian would stop dressing and apologize. Maybe he would just stay instead. Trent didn't need the apology, after all. It wasn't a deal breaker. What he didn't expect was exactly what happened.

Ian nodded once as he straightened his shirt and tugged his pants up to hide the exposed seam of his belly. He walked out of the closet, through the door and didn't look back once.

Chapter Nine

Trent lowered himself back to the bed as he heard the front door slam shut on the lower level. The sound crept through the halls and into his ears, hitting his heart like a perfectly aimed arrow. Ian had left. Even after everything, Ian had still left. He hadn't even hesitated.

It had been their first fight, at least their first fight that had any real substance to it. There had always been misunderstandings in the past, but that couldn't be avoided when they were worlds away from each other for the majority of their time. But Ian had been standing right there this time — and he'd just left.

Trent looked back to the door, as if Ian would suddenly appear in the frame if he stared long enough. He didn't. Trent had no friends in Miami that he could call, and nowhere to go that wasn't Ian's house or some fancy restaurant that he couldn't afford.

He grabbed his phone from where it lay buried within his suitcase. He'd texted Candace about the stewardess, but he hadn't heard back from her yet. It wasn't strange for her to go a week without texting him if she hadn't actually seen him in person. *Out of sight, out of mind.* The only other messages were the short replies from Ian when he had spent the days away. Trent didn't expect one today, and there wasn't one now.

He pulled up his banking app to check how much money was left in his dwindling chequing account. What he'd said to Ian had been completely true. He paid his own way in the world with the paycheque he cashed every other week. He still paid for his mortgage, utilities and anything else he needed around the house. Of course, he didn't complain if Ian showed up with a housewarming gift when he visited. So far, he'd received a second side table for the bedroom and living room, as well as a larger television that made his old one look like a box of tissues.

His account was low, dismally low. Ian had paid for their flights, and Trent had assumed he would pay for their return flight together, but now it sounded like he would be the only one going back.

An unexpected trip would wipe his account out — and then some. There would be the flight, then taxes and of course the taxi ride to the airport, which couldn't be cheap. He would have to eat at some point, and airport food was expensive as hell. Then, of course, there would be the taxi ride when he got home. He couldn't expect Candace to pick him up from the airport with no notice, especially when he hadn't planned on returning home for weeks.

He could put it all on his credit card, but then he would be paying interest for months until he managed to pay off the balance. And that would destroy his credit and his chances of renewing his mortgage.

There were no other options. He was stuck in a place where he wasn't wanted, and he couldn't escape either.

He shook his head and let out a long sigh. The pillow top was so comfortable beneath him that he wanted nothing more than to collapse back into it and sleep the day away. He could try to convince himself that this was just a nightmare and that he'd wake up soon enough. But sleep would get him nowhere right now. He needed a very long walk before he could figure out what to do next.

He paced through the rooms as he looked from detail to detail, trying to find something that he hadn't noticed before. There was no draw to the modern set-up, and no character to speak of. It was just room after room of sterile luxury. He searched for a picture of Ian or his family along the walls—or even a picture of himself.

The only picture he found was of the band. It was perched in the sound-proofed studio where Ian's massive drum kit sprawled across the floor. On the far side of the room were recording equipment and a few massive computers. The walls were smeared with splashes of colour and random posters, to the point where it neared chaos. It was messy, terrible but absolutely Ian. It was also the only room that had a heartbeat of its own. If the whole house had been like the soundproofed studio, Trent could see himself staying—after some reorganizing of course.

The picture was stained, with curled corners that were attached to the solid wall with different-coloured thumbtacks. The people in the photograph all looked so young and thin. Even Ian was so skinny that he was almost gangly, with hands that were much too big for his long arms. Mac was the only one who looked the same, with his arm slung over Ian's shoulder and a smile on his face.

That smile was something that Trent had never seen in person before. The pictures on the internet really didn't do Mac justice, but neither did meeting him. This loose, relaxed, grinning singer looked like a man who was just entering his prime, with his best friend at his side. Ian looked the same way, with his smile so wide that all his teeth were showing.

Trent made his way back into the living room then out through the patio doors by the pool. He left them open, knowing that it would only be a moment before the elements drove him back inside. It was hot for so early in the morning, and the sun was trapped behind a thick screen of clouds that made the air feel even hotter. The wind was still and too quiet to even toss a palm frond.

He dipped his toe in the pool before he sat down on the edge of the concrete and hung his legs over the sides, skimming his toes across the surface. The tiny wrinkles disappeared before they reached the ledge.

"What to do," he said to no one but himself. The lawn was cut, and the windows were polished to a transparent sparkle. Even the dusting above eye level was done, which made him shudder at the mere idea. He could see why Ian worked all the time when he was here or spent most of his time out and about. It was pretty for a prison, but it was still a prison.

He lay back against the concrete and his spine cracked against the rigid surface. The sky was starting to clear above his head, and a hint of sun peeked through the blanket of clouds like a piercing eye. The air was getting steadily hotter, but the concrete was cool, along with the water against his ankles.

He tossed his arm over his face to shield himself from the worst of the light. His thoughts whirled as he tossed different possibilities around. It was too bad that he didn't have Brian's number. He had a feeling that the man would be happy to help him in his situation, even if he was Ian's friend first.

* * * *

He didn't realize that he'd fallen asleep until he was suddenly awake again. There had been no dreams, just the gentle whirling of his constant thoughts. The heat had disappeared from his skin except for a line across his face where his arm lay.

It took him a moment to realize why his clothes were suddenly clinging to his skin. At first, he was mildly terrified that he had fallen into the pool and was on his way to drowning, but as he pulled his arm away and shifted, he realized that he was still on the hard concrete.

The cold stone had seeped into his muscles and bones, and pulled forth every ache until he felt more like a tree limb than a person. He also realized that it had started to rain some time before. The rain was soft and hardly made a sound against the water, but it was enough to soak him completely. It was also creeping inside the door where he'd left it open.

He cursed when he saw the puddle on the wrong side of the glass. Ian's flooring was top-quality, which probably meant that a sneeze would make the edges curl. There had to be litres of water in there already and more slipping in by the second.

He had meant to take a stroll along the grass to cool his head before he went back inside. It hadn't seemed necessary to put the extra effort in to close the heavy glass door when he would only be a minute. The last few mornings he'd peeked outside, then darted back upstairs for his swim trunks anyway. But who knew how long it had been open this time, with the air conditioning running overtime to keep up with the onslaught of humidity.

The rain and the chill were not what woke him from his light doze. There was a sound coming from the house that was loud enough to be heard clearly from where he was seated. It reverberated off the walls of the house and through the open door. There were two voices that were growing steadily louder, and he recognized both of them.

He pushed himself slowly to his feet, cringing at the strain that travelled up his spine, and crept to the open door. He blinked against the rain that flooded into his vision. The puddle was worse than he'd thought. The water had been hitting the top of the door before it curled around inside to drip over the floor.

"Your boyfriend walked out on you already, Ian." Mac's voice rose across the space. With all the hard flooring and minimal decorations, the sound travelled easily from the kitchen, which was tucked just around the corner.

"Why did I even call you, Mac?" Ian's voice cut in. "He's my husband, not my boyfriend, and he didn't walk out. He's just flying home."

Trent's heart swelled as Ian defended him, even when he didn't know he was there. His hand squeaked along the glass and he clenched it into a fist as he heard Mac's answering laugh. The pane sucked the remaining warmth from his fingers.

"Sounds pretty final to me," said Mac, his voice still trembling from laughter. "Maybe you should take the hint and leave him alone. He obviously doesn't want to be bothered by you." There was the scraping noise that sounded like chairs sliding over the tile floor, and the gentle thumps of two people sitting down.

"I don't get it," said Ian, sounding more upset with each word. "You are supposed to make me feel better. Don't drag me through the dirt when I've already been dropped in the mud."

"I just don't think he's the one for you, Ian. If he really loved you like you say he does, he wouldn't have left."

Trent clenched his hands so hard that his nails likely pressed lines into his palms. He knew Mac hated him, but hearing him say that, then hearing Ian's desolate sigh, was enough to gut him. A part of him wanted to punch Mac in the face, but only because what he said might be true. Why was he walking away? He loved Ian and wanted to spend the rest of his life with him. Wasn't that enough?

"Well, T was right about one thing," said Ian. "You hate him. Don't lie to me, Mac. Every time you talk about us, you're dragging him and me down. I thought you were just being an idiot, but I see now that there's more to it. Why do you hate him so much?" There was a pause before Ian's voice rose on the brink of a yell. "You're gonna tell me now or you can fucking leave."

There was a long pause, then mumbled words that were too quiet for Trent to hear. Shivering, he stepped through the door and pushed it closed behind him. His feet slipped in the puddle as he leaned back against the glass. The room was even colder than outside, and every hair on his body stood on end from the chill.

"What are you talking about?" Ian's voice came again, sounding like his rage was settling. "He didn't take me away from you, Mac. You're still my best friend and you always will be. Nothing is ever going to change that except you. Tell me the truth, because I can see that it's killing you."

There was a scraping sound followed closely by two thumps. The noises drew Trent across the floor, each step placed carefully so he didn't slip. He rounded the corner that held the row of kitchen cupboards that stretched from floor to ceiling.

The chairs had been tossed away from the island, with one leaning far against the countertop and the other turned over on its side. It looked like something out of a murder scene except for the two men in the room, who were very much alive. They were facing each other, so they didn't see Trent when he peeked around the corner, water pooling at his feet as it dribbled from his clothes. They were both wet as well, but only with a smattering of raindrops that glistened under the pot lights.

His chest tightened as he saw Ian again. He wanted nothing more than to cross the room and pull Ian close for a hug, but the sight in front of him had his limbs frozen solid. His hackles rose and every bit of his stiffness faded away to pure adrenalin. He clenched his fists, ready for a fight... Ready for murder.

Mac had Ian pushed against the refrigerator door with Ian's back pressed to the stainless-steel surface. The grip Mac had on Ian's shoulder dug deep into the muscle, painting a grimace across the edge of Ian's face. Both of Ian's hands were at his side, either in shock or in refusal to fight his best friend.

Although Mac was shorter, he was wiry and strong and he obviously knew how to centre his balance in order to push Ian around. Ian had told Trent about the scraps Mac would get into with much larger opponents, and how he managed to come out on top in every one. Trent had never been able to picture it, but here it was happening in front of him. Only the one Mac was pushing around now was Trent's husband.

Mac gripped Ian's shoulder violently as a snarl escaped his mouth. The singer's face had tinted pink and his eyes were narrowed, but Ian hardly reacted except for a single raised brow. Even as Ian's back struck the fridge again, shaking the meagre contents within, the drummer only grunted softly.

With a second snarl, Mac brought his other hand up and gripped the back of Ian's neck, pulling him down and crashing their lips together.

Ian started as if he'd been struck. His body flinched and he slapped his hands against the fridge door. Trent could see Ian trying to pull back, but Mac gripped harder on his neck, pushing into the sensitive nerves and making Ian let out a low keen. Every line in Ian's body went completely tense and his eyes bulged wide.

Mac loosened his grip on Ian's neck and he jerked away with a startled breath. Ian slid his hands along the door as his mouth opened and closed several times. They were both breathing heavily with their faces flushed, one in arousal and one in terror.

"Because I'm fucking in love with you," said Mac as he leaned up and pulled Ian back to him. The pull didn't look nearly as brutal this time, but Ian's eyes didn't slide shut. They stayed open, staring in what was obviously absolute disbelief.

Trent could almost hear the snap as his vision bled scarlet and he lost control of his anger. In five long strides he was across the kitchen. His feet slipped over the surface, but it was like he was immune to falling. He kept moving toward to the couple, clenching his fists tight enough to make his knuckles crack.

Ian noticed him first, his eyes going wider and gaping in shock. Mac took advantage of the suddenly open mouth and as he slid his tongue in with a deep moan. He flexed his hands on Ian, pushing closer until there was no room between them at all.

Trent gripped the back of Mac's neck like he would a stray cat and pulled. The thin column flexed under his hand and Mac let out a loud squeak as he was suddenly teetering off balance. A strength that Trent never known surged along his arms, until he was flinging Mac across the room.

He didn't make it to the cupboards on the other side but landed just past the island instead. When Mac hit, the impact had him half-sliding and half-rolling until he came to a stop on the hard tile. His eyes went wide and his lips were slick with saliva from the stolen kiss.

Trent rounded on him, putting his back to Ian as his husband clearly struggled to react. Mac was spluttering now too, but he didn't look scared. His eyes narrowed as he obviously realized who had scruffed him and flung him away like a mangy feline. There was still water clinging to his hair, making him dangerous and beautiful.

"Sorry to crash your coming-out party, but keep your hands off my husband." Trent didn't pause as he said the words, throwing himself at the singer with his fists raised.

His knees struck the unforgiving ground, but he barely felt the ache. He was too focused on wiping the dark smirk off Mac's face. This was the man who had tried to undermine everything that he had ever said to Ian, while stabbing Ian in the back at the same time. Mac was the one who'd given Ian such a hard time when he came out, while hiding himself beneath layers of disgust. This was the man with a wife and kid who he never saw.

Trent hit Mac's face with a sound that could never truly be reproduced by Hollywood. His knuckles cracked one by one as the cartilage in Mac's nose made an alarming wet sound. Mac let out a gasp at the impact, then a second one as his head flung back and hit the tile. He gurgled, groaned and screamed at the same time.

Trent didn't care that the impact resounded all the way up to his elbow, making his wrist ache. He was already pulling his arm back for a second blow. The second punch hit a few inches away from the first, squelching against Mac's eye. Mac's head didn't hit the ground this time, as the singer had braced for the impact. Trent's fingers felt as if they'd been broken against Mac's skull, but he couldn't stop. He pulled his arm back, so much slower than the first two times.

The third hit never made it.

Strong arms grabbed Trent from behind in a grip that was tight enough to make his eyes bulge as air caught in his throat. The smell of rain and that scent that was distinctly Ian engulfed him, but it didn't calm the burning rage in his gut. If anything, it made it worse.

Trent struggled hard as Ian shifted his grip low and used every bit of his strength to lift him off Mac. Trent gripped Ian's arm that was a band of steel over his chest and twisted his fingers into muscle and flesh, but it didn't deter Ian. Trent kicked out instead, and one of his feet managed to hit Mac's knee, sending him back to the ground as he tried to rise.

How could the singer recover so fast when there was blood dripping from his nose down the front of his shirt? Trent would still be lying there, maybe even for the rest of the day, before he had the will and ability to rise.

If Trent was a lion built on rage, then Mac was a viper, using every opportunity at hand to sink in his venom. Trent was nearly immobile in Ian's grip as he was pulled back against a solid chest with one arm trapped at his side, and the other trying to wrench Ian's hand away. Trent was so focused on getting free that he never saw the blow coming until it was stinging its way across his cheek. His head snapped back and to the side, completely out of his control, and his vision dimmed as his head struck Ian hard in the chin. He heard the click of Ian's teeth and smelled copper taint the air of Ian's breath.

Ian's grip didn't falter, apparently stunned by the blow to his chin, as Mac continued to advance. The singer was ignoring his injuries and the blood dripping from his nose with practiced ease. Trent could only lift one hand to try to protect himself as the hits rained down on his face faster than Ian or Trent could react. As the fourth one struck his cheek, sending his head back into Ian again, Mac wrapped a long-fingered hand around the column of his neck. Mac closed his hand and blood rushed to Trent's head in a whirling torrent.

Trent's vision was swimming by the time he felt Ian's grip finally falter. As his only support disappeared, Trent slid down and fell to one knee. The grip on his neck broke and the bludgeoning finally stopped just in time for him to keel forward into the tile. His face hit first, right at the line of his eyebrow, before the rest of his body caught up and he flopped onto the cold surface.

He heard yelling above him, then the smack of flesh against flesh, and he tried to rise, but his feet wouldn't cooperate. It was as if something in his brain had been switched off and he no longer had access to his body. He could still breathe in and out in a rhythm that made his throat burn.

Warm hands gripped his arm and he flinched hard at the contact, his body coming back to him all at once. He felt his leg twitch, and he kicked at whoever was standing above him. His ankle twinged as he struck bone, and he heard a curse above him. He wasn't going to take another pounding lying down. Not even Ian could hold him back this time.

"Ow, fuck. T, it's me." Ian's voice cut through the haze and his warm hands were back on him. Something was dripping down Trent's arm that was warmer than the rain that still clung to his skin. He remembered the way his head had snapped back to strike Ian's chin, and the awful sound that Ian had made deep in his throat.

"Are you okay?" Trent tried to ask, but his words were slow and slurred as if his lips were swollen to three times their size. Talking made his jaw ache, and his tongue too, strangely enough. His throat felt like he'd chugged boiling coffee just for the hell of it.

Ian's face sharpened into crystal focus before his eyes. His lip was split wide like a cut of raw beef, and blood poured from the wound. From there, the blood went everywhere. His chin was covered, as well as his neck and the front of his shirt. There was even a smear that looked like a handprint on his bicep. The cut looked like it was swelling fast, but the bleeding wasn't slowing in the least.

"I'm gonna fuck'n kill'm," said Trent as he gripped his husband's neck, trying to pull him down so he could get a better view. The blood was slippery under his hands, and something about that made his heart jackrabbit in his chest. He was breathing fast, but his lungs felt utterly empty.

The kitchen tilted violently as Ian tried to help him to his feet. His knees felt solid, but his ankles were like spinning tops on the slippery floor. He grabbed along his husband's neck, but Ian was so slick with blood that he couldn't stop from slipping and nearly falling. It was so red beneath the bright light, and it was all that Trent could taste, see and smell.

"Easy, T. Hold on to me. That's it." Ian's voice was low, as if he were trying to stay calm but failing miserably. "Don't try and stand. I'm gonna call an ambulance and we'll get to the hospital."

"I don't need a hospital," said Trent as he tried in vain to get his balance through the red haze. "I'm gonna fucking kill him, then you can take me straight to jail." He looked around the room, weaving as he searched for his target.

"He isn't here anymore. It's okay." Ian's voice broke.

When Trent looked up, he couldn't see anything but the blood on Ian's face. He sucked in another deep breath as his lungs burned. It was everywhere and so sticky that he knew it would never come off his hands.

"He hurts you then tries to force himself on you. Do you have a gun?" Trent asked as his vision flickered inexplicably. His hands were numb, like the worst pins and needles he'd ever felt, and the throbbing ache in his knuckles disappeared. Even if he found a gun, he didn't know if he'd be able to hold it, let alone take aim.

"T, calm down. I'm calling an ambulance now." Ian left him for just a second to grab for his phone, and it was enough for Trent to slide down to his knees. He grabbed the edge of the nearest cupboard and tried to pull himself back up, but his numb hands slipped away and he thudded onto his back. His vision darkened as his eyelids slid shut and he panted. He needed air, but it was like Mac's hand was still on his throat.

"I need an ambulance. There was a fight and my husband was hurt." Trent heard the distant voice and the trembling words, but they didn't mean much to him. His thoughts were a mantra that repeated over and over, and so much more important than the address that Ian said into the phone. "Yes, he's breathing and conscious, but he's not himself and he can't stand."

Ian's hands were on him again and Trent managed to pry his eyelids open, despite the aching itch. Ian's face had gone grey beneath the blood and was drawn tight with panic and something else Trent couldn't identify. Ian's lip was so swollen that it was making his words run together until they crowded around Trent's head like rush hour traffic. One thing was clear, though. Ian needed him.

"It's okay, Ian," said Trent between haggard breaths as he reached up to smooth the worry lines from between Ian's eyebrows. Ian moved closer, close enough that his smell washed over Trent and overwhelmed the acrid blood. "I love the way you smell, Ian," said Trent as he let his eyes fall shut again. They were too heavy to keep open any longer. "The first time I met you I thought it was cologne, and it made me so hard."

He rubbed his cheek over Ian's hand as it slid along his face, and Trent smiled at the memory. The man was so beautiful and so wonderful. It made him hard just thinking about it.

"Will you fuck me, Ian?" Trent said into Ian's ear as he leaned close, laughing as his husband's voice hitched. "Excited already?" He dipped his hand down Ian's chest, lingering on every hard surface before lowering to the front seam of his pants. Trent expected to find a tent there with flesh pressing against fabric, but instead he could just feel the outline of little Ian, soft and pliant. He panted harder, his lungs burning as things started to blur. Why were they in the kitchen?

"You okay?" Trent mumbled sleepily as he rubbed his palm in circles over the front of Ian's pants. He cracked his eyes open and saw the smear of blood everywhere he'd touched. His chest tightened until it was painful to even breathe.

"Fuck, T," said Ian, his voice going taut with worry. "It's gonna be okay." He wrapped one arm tight around Trent's chest, and suddenly he was leaning against Ian with the floor doing circles below him.

"Why are you crying?" Trent wasn't sure if he actually managed to ask the words, or if he only imagined their presence. His vision narrowed and he felt himself go limp as his body disconnected from his brain.

"T? Trent?"

He could hear Ian's voice, but he couldn't reply. Then there was nothing at all.

Chapter Ten

Trent slowly drifted awake. It was like coming out of one of his strange dreams about apocalyptic clowns armed with rocket launchers. There was a fizz of adrenalin just under his skin, but his body was slumped with the realization of the inevitable.

His eyelids refused to budge, as if they were crusted over and glued shut with his eyelashes acting as threads. There was a general ache that stretched from the left side of his jaw all the way up to his right eye, but it too felt like a dream.

He pushed against the fuzziness in his brain when he felt the rough sheets below him and smelled antiseptic mixed with stale blood. He tossed the dream aside and tugged his eyelids open with a sharp ache that sunk deep into his skull.

The sunshine was terrible, even with the unfamiliar floral curtains pulled shut and the silent fluorescent bulbs above his head. A headache racked his brain as the light rushed in, and his stomach flipped as his mouth watered alarmingly. He blinked at the unfamiliar walls, strange lights and ugly blue chair at the foot of the bed as his headache slowly dimmed to a manageable level.

The room was thankfully silent, but it was also empty of anyone except him. The bed was in the centre of the small room and it was just big enough that his toes didn't poke over the edge. The sheets were an off-white and rough, likely from repeated washings in unlike colours. The cushion below him was soft, but it was the softness of sleeping on a water bed. It squished in all the wrong places and made his back strain and long for something firm.

There were silver railings on each side of the bed that were clicked upright to keep him from falling. There was also a monitor beside his bed, but it was silent at the moment and its screen was black and dull. The single chair was empty, just like the IV pole next to the bed.

"Hello?" His voice was stronger than he expected, and he reached up to touch his neck. He remembered the fierce grip around his throat, and he could feel a layer of bruising under the skin, but his throat itself seemed fine. He looked around, but no one emerged from the bathroom or the other door, which presumably led into the hall.

He reached for the railing on the right side of his bed and lowered it flat. He recognized the place from when he had broken more than a few bones as a youngster. It didn't matter where the hospital was or who was managing it, they all looked and smelled the same. Everything was always outdated, except the equipment, and the smell was always a mix of antiseptic, death and sub-par food, all rolled into one.

His vision blurred and a throb pulsed beneath the shell of his skin as he dropped his legs over the side of the bed and pushed himself up into a hunched sitting position. The blows to his face felt as sharp as the memory of them, but the throb faded too after a few minutes of slow, deep breaths.

He waited one more minute, just to be sure, before he lifted himself to his feet and shuffled to the bathroom. The thin hospital gown, which certainly kept him aired out, fluttered around his legs as he made his way there. He pulled it down and back around to cover his exposed ass in case anyone happened to open the door.

His bladder was nearly ready to burst by the time he sat down and let it go. It wasn't a time to stand and pee. His pride would have to suffer.

His ankles peeked out of the gown, and there was a black bruise across one of them. He remembered kicking out and striking Ian by accident, thinking it was Mac coming back for more. He glanced back into the room through the door he hadn't remembered to shut. Ian still wasn't there, and there was no hint of his presence.

But there had been blood...so much blood. Ian was probably in his own room getting sewed up by the doctor. Rich people usually had hospital rooms to themselves, and that was definitely something he could see Ian doing—spending money for the sake of spending money.

The water from the tap was so hot that he gasped as he went to wash his hands. He drew back to see the bruises laced across his knuckles, still red and swollen as if the wounds were only hours old. It looked like very early morning from the dim light peaking in through the blue curtain in the bathroom, and he felt surprisingly well rested for just hyperventilating himself into unconsciousness.

His reflection in the mirror was so much worse than his swollen knuckles. He looked like he'd been in a rodeo where the bull had decided to make an example of him. Both of his eyes were swollen and black, with his left eye only able to open halfway before it simply stopped. There were two splits in the middle of his lip, and when he leaned closer to the mirror, he swore he saw a corner missing from one of his front teeth. The gum below the tooth had a line of dark blood around the root, and it ached worse than his knuckles when he touched it.

"Holy shit," he said as he looked at himself again, hardly recognizing his eyes looking back at him. It was strange seeing it and not feeling excruciating pain, though. He reached out and touched the corner of his eye, and let out a strangled yell as sensation suddenly rushed in. It hurt…a lot. The touch faded and the pain dimmed.

"Oh, there you are," said a female voice from behind him. He spun toward the woman, who was dressed in blue scrubs and carrying a small tray of food.

"It's good to see you awake and out of bed," she said in a soft voice, her weak smile pitying as she looked at his face. "Are you in pain?"

Trent looked down at himself and took stock of his injuries again. He felt almost normal except for the throbbing in his face, and even that hurt less than when he'd broken his arm. He knew he bruised easily, but Mac's hits had made his ears ring.

"Not really. Just sore." He dried his hands slowly on a paper towel and tossed it into the bin. "I thought I would feel a lot worse." He followed the nurse back into the room and sat down on the bed. He grasped the edges of his escaped gown and tucked them under himself. The movement made something in his wrist flare, and he winced before glancing at it. It looked fine too.

"You don't have a concussion, but you were very distressed when you arrived," said the nurse as she rolled a tray over and placed the small meal on top. There was a muffin, a bit of egg and a piece of white toast with a hint of butter on top. The eggs still looked warm and smelled delicious.

"Everyone displays their shock differently, and it was lucky that you just passed out on us." She pulled a plastic-covered fork from her pocket and placed it next to the steaming pile of eggs.

Meaning that he'd fainted... Like a shocked woman in 1889 who had done her corset up too tight. Fainted, then slept both the day and night away from the look of the light through the window.

She smiled and passed him a container of juice that had been in the top pocket of her shirt. A thin straw followed a moment later. He took them automatically and set them on the tray next to the eggs. His stomach grumbled as he took another steam-filled breath.

"Where's Ian?" Trent tried to ignore the breakfast, despite his hollow gut. There was no trace of his husband there and not even the lingering scent of his cologne. He'd never been there at all, perhaps.

"There are some officers here who would like to speak with you." Her face turned grim. "'I'll let them know you're up to seeing them now." There was sympathy in her gaze and it set Trent instantly on edge. Had something happened after he'd elegantly collapsed in his husband's arms after ranting about murdering his best friend? There was no way that Ian could have bled out from a split lip. But there had been so much blood.

He was near panic when the nurse returned with the two officers, before she excused herself from the room. Both the officers were women, and attractive, despite their bulky uniforms and intimidating weapons at their sides. Trent had a sudden longing for his best friend Candace. She would know exactly how to charm the women, even if they were straight.

The shorter of the two, with long brown hair twisted back into a bun, approached Trent and took the seat across the bed, hunching down until her elbows rested on her kneecaps. Her lips were etched into a tale of bad news, and there was sympathy in her eyes — the same sympathy he'd seen from the nurse.

His heart thudded in his chest as his palms leaked sweat on his thighs. He twisted the fabric in his fingertips, and the ache in his wrist hardened.

"How are you feeling?" she asked him. Her voice was light and kind, and so unlike the severe tone he'd been expecting out of such a heavily armed person.

"Okay, I guess, but I'd really like to see my husband," said Trent, shifting on the bed and pulling a blanket around himself so that little Trent didn't ruin the day for these women by making a sudden appearance out of the bottom of his gown.

She glanced back at her partner — just a brief twist of her head and a frown, but it was enough to make Trent's stomach plummet past the linoleum floor.

"Is he okay?" Oh God, how bad was he injured? Was he even conscious? They would have to let Trent see him. Some places might be homophobic, but Ian was his husband, and there was no one who could keep

Trent from his bedside. The gun at the woman's waist caught his attention as the second officer switched the lights on.

"What's the last thing you remember?" she asked him instead of answering his question. "It's okay if you need to take your time."

"I remember Ian calling an ambulance," said Trent, squinting painfully as he tried to recall the fuzzy details. What else had Ian been doing? And what had he looked like at that moment? He could only remember the blood, and how his lungs had been screaming for air.

"Okay, that's good. Thank you," she said before leaning back just a bit in her chair as if she was trying to keep herself from reaching out with a kind hand. "Has something like this happened before?"

Trent paused in confusion. He didn't know if she was talking about his trip to Miami, the fight with Mac or the ambulance call. The answer was the same to all three.

"No."

He saw her frown deepen after his long pause. "It's okay to tell us, sir. Anything you say here can be kept confidential unless you decide to press charges." Trent caught the sight of a taser strapped to her belt as well. He guessed if a bullet didn't work first, she could always shock someone into compliance.

"No, it hasn't," said Trent, shaking his head. She had to be talking about the fight with Mac. "I don't want to press charges. I mean, it was my fault anyway." The kiss hadn't been his fault—nope. But he had been the one to throw the first punch. His wrist ached as he gripped the sheets harder. They still hadn't told him where Ian was or if he was even okay.

Her face turned so sad at his words that he wondered where he could have misspoken. It was a simple question with a simple answer.

"How many times did he hit you?" she asked as her partner pulled out a notebook from her pocket. Trent looked between the two of them, feeling like he was on the outside of an inside joke.

"I don't know," said Trent. "I wasn't really expecting it, and it all happened so fast. A dozen maybe? It went kind of fuzzy after he tried to strangle me." Trent bit his tongue. He didn't want to get Mac in trouble, even after everything that had happened. Assault was one thing, but strangling sounded a lot like attempted murder.

"And after he hit you, what happened?" she asked, holding eye contact with him the entire time. Her eyes were deep brown, almost black, and there was kindness there despite the ammunition she was packing.

"He ran off, I guess? Ian said he left, but I don't know where he went. I mean, I'm pretty sure I broke his nose, so I don't know if he drove or called a taxi. I don't think you can drive with a broken nose? It's not against the law, I don't think, but your eyes would be watering like crazy." Trent's mouth opened and word garbage flowed out. With every word, the officer looked more confused, before she glanced at her partner again.

"But you stated that he stayed to call an ambulance," she said, referring to Trent's last vague memory. Trent thought back to what he had said, trying to figure out what the hell she wasn't saying.

"Ian stayed and called an ambulance. His friend took off," said Trent, his mouth dropping open in horror as he finally realized what they were not saying to him. "Wait! Did you arrest my husband?" The quiet and subtle way they'd approached him finally made sense. They thought this was some kind of domestic abuse case, and that Ian had pummelled the crap out of him.

"When we arrived on the scene, you were almost unconscious and obviously injured, and he was covered in blood. When we questioned your husband, he refused to make a statement, so he was placed in a holding cell pending charges." The second officer spoke up for the first time. "You're saying that he wasn't involved in the altercation?"

"No." Trent shook his head fast enough to make his vision swim. "He wouldn't hurt me." His heart pounded. Ian was in prison and it was his fault. What if the media found out and it ruined his career?

"What was the name of the third party who was involved?" The second officer's voice was like steel and left no room for a rebuttal.

This was what he had expected when they stepped into the room. His stomach clenched and his mouth went dry. His mouth opened, ready to spill Mac's name, but at the last second, he managed to bite down on his tongue.

"As I said, I'm not pressing charges. It was a misunderstanding that involved too much testosterone and got out of hand," said Trent. He could throw Mac under the bus right now and watch him get hit by all the tyres as he bounced around the pavement. It would be so satisfying to see him finally put in his place. But he wasn't going to do that to Ian's best friend, not if he wanted Ian to respect him ever again. Ian was loyal, more so than any dog that had ever lived. A betrayal like that would wound him more than it had already.

The officer closest to him let out a long sigh before she reached into her pocket and plucked out a thin white card. Her name was written on it in bold print, along with a phone number.

"Thank you, um, Beverly," he said as he took the card and glanced down at it. "I know you are just trying to do your job. Keep up the great work, by the way. Miami is a beautiful city. I hope you won't hear of any trouble from me again." A little bit of guilt lifted from his chest when she smiled at him. "Could you take me to the prison so I could pick up my husband?" he asked, looking around the room for his clothes. And if that wasn't the strangest sentence he'd ever said in his lifetime.

"He's not in prison, just at the station in a holding cell," said Beverly. She stood from the chair and took two steps back to her partner, who had her arms folded and whose lips were sealed in a tight line.

He found his clothes in a plastic bag looped over the end of the bed. "I can take a taxi if it's too much of a bother. I just don't know my way around town very well, and I don't even know where the station is."

"We can take you," said Beverly, passing the bag of clothes to him as he tried, and failed to reach it without flashing them. "The nurse said you were free to go when you're ready, as you only have superficial wounds. I wouldn't pass up on the breakfast, though." She quirked her eyebrows at the now-cold eggs and the plastic cup of juice covered in a foil wrapper. They still smelled so good and Trent's stomach gave an ominous rumble.

Trent didn't need to be told twice. The officers went to stand outside the door while he ate with one hand and dressed with the other. The eggs had congealed into an unrecognizable paste and the juice was very sweet, but he felt himself levelling off the moment it all passed his lips. His heart calmed and his lungs felt full for the first time since he'd seen Ian's blood. There was still a gaping hole in his heart where his husband's presence should have been.

The clothes were the same ones that he'd been wearing the day before, and they were slightly damp from sitting in a plastic bag overnight. There was also a smear of blood on the back of the shirt, shaped like a hand that was much larger than his own. He pulled it on regardless, forgoing the soggy boxers, but more than happy to leave the gown behind. Even with the dampness dragging heat away from his skin, it was still warmer than the gown.

He peeked his head out of the door, still chewing on the piece of toast, when a thought struck him.

"Um, do I have to pay somewhere or something?" asked Trent, feeling his swollen face flush with an extra throb. "At home we just kinda leave the hospital when we're better, but I know it's different here." He also knew that he had no way of covering the bill with his wallet at Ian's and his traveller's insurance inside it.

Beverly was waiting in the hall, looking extremely professional and not texting on her phone like Trent had imagined. Everyone texted while waiting in hallways, even when they were getting paid for it.

"I'll check with the nurse. Just wait here for me, please," she said and strode off down the hall. She turned down a stale corner as if she knew exactly where she was going.

Trent looked down at his feet. He'd found white slippers at the foot of the bed and had pushed them on. They looked cheap, and he hoped that they were for him, but he didn't have a choice except to nab them. His shoes were at home because he hadn't been wearing any when he'd fainted.

Fainted. The word still made him cringe.

"The nurse said you're all paid up and free to go," Beverly said when she returned less than a minute later. "Let's get you out of here."

He followed her through the maze of corridors that repeated themselves every fifty feet or so. Without signs, he never would've found his way to the elevator, let alone to the entrance where the squad car was idling. Beverley opened the back door for him and he paused, noting the bars on the windows and the lack of a handle on the inside.

"I'm not under arrest, right?" he asked. There was something about getting into the back of a cruiser of his own free will that just didn't sit right. She shook her head with a small chuckle before he slid into the seat.

He'd expected the smell of gunpowder and blood in the back seat of the cruiser, but it was way worse. It smelled like mixing a stagnant boardroom with the faint scent of that one guy in the office who always smelled, but no one knew him well enough to say anything. If he would just shower, then someone could get close enough to start a friendship and maybe offer hygiene advice.

"So, you're Canadian?" Beverley's partner asked from the front seat as she gripped the wheel and pulled away from the emergency entrance. "Are you enjoying your time in Miami?" Her eyes flickered to the rear-view mirror before she focused her attention back on the road.

Trent gripped the door as she launched her way into traffic, cutting between the lines expertly. "I'm not sure, to be honest. I mean, I can see the appeal, but I miss home too. Less drama." He shook his head as he thought back to his life back home. The last year had been nothing but drama. "Never mind... That's not true at all." He trailed off and looked out of the window through the thin gaps in the bars. The trees were still green, and the sky was so beautifully blue that it took his breath away—but it had changed. Maybe it was the bruises on his face or the absolute disaster of the last few days—he wasn't sure. Something about it had settled, though. It actually felt more like home than he was willing to admit.

The rest of the ride was thankfully silent and short, and soon he was being led into a brick building that looked nothing like a prison. The two officers disappeared into an actual office that smelled of burnt coffee and even stronger body odour. He sat in the middle seat of a row of chairs at the front desk, avoiding the stares of people who walked by. Phones were ringing in the background and there was the murmur of countless calls being transferred to distant cubicles.

An officer swept into the door and glanced his way, pausing as their eyebrows shot into their hairline. Trent tucked his chin down and kept his gaze on his slippers. They were either seeing a punk or a victim, and Trent was neither. He didn't even feel that bad, despite the persistent throb of his face. It was downright embarrassing. Since he looked the way he did, he should at least feel like shit too.

"T?" It was Ian's quiet voice and Trent snapped up his head. Ian was standing at the edge of the reception desk in an outfit that was definitely not his own. The fabric of his shirt hung off his shoulders and waist, and the cotton pants looked extremely tight and about three inches too short. His lower lip was swollen and black, matching the heavy circles under his eyes that only looked worse because of his pale face. The split on his lip was wide, nearly half as wide as Trent's pinkie finger, and it was bright red.

Beverly flanked him with a look that was more than a little judgemental. Trent knew what she saw in Ian — a big guy, a rock star, who was built like a tank and had tattoos to boot. Trent didn't even care to acknowledge her this time, which did make him feel a bit bad. She was just doing her job, after all.

"Ian!" said Trent, probably too loud for such a busy place. A grin split his face that was too painful to supress his wince. "Oh my God, are you okay? They told me you spent the whole night here." Trent stood, wanting nothing more than to wrap his arms around Ian, but he held himself back. He knew how Ian hated public displays, and one in a cop shop would probably be on the wrong side of the line.

"T, is that you, baby?" Ian sounded like he was about to keel over. There was a shiny redness in his eyes that only got worse when he suddenly lurched in recognition. His jaw worked, but no sound came from his lips.

"It's not as bad as it looks — "

Trent never finished what he was trying to say. Ian crossed the short distance in a few powerful strides and swept Trent up in an all-consuming hug. Beverley tensed, and her hand dropped to her weapon before he was swept up in the warmth and the smell that was all Ian.

"T, baby." Ian nuzzled against his neck as warm tears fluttered over the surface of Trent's skin. "They wouldn't tell me if you were okay. I thought—" He never finished. He turned his head, gently lifting Trent's chin until their lips met.

There was a piercing pain, and the shock of an ache that was too strong to ignore. Trent let out a whine as Ian's lips touched his abused flesh. It was like every nerve flared to life at the touch, only the nerves had been flayed alive. The feeling was gone in an instant as Ian pulled back, and Trent felt his face flush red with a throb.

"I'm so sorry, T, but I just needed to kiss you," said Ian with his eyes dark and red, and still spilling over the sides. The split on his lip looked just as painful as the bruises on Trent's flesh. He was hurting himself, just to show Trent his love.

"Be gentle, Ian. I'm not going anywhere." Trent leaned in and let Ian close the gap between them again. The touch was barely harder than the kiss of a butterfly, but it still sent a zing of shock up his lips and straight to his groin. Trent let out a small groan as the pain drifted away to pure happiness.

It was everything he'd ever wanted for Ian and himself—for Ian to be comfortable enough to hold Trent's hand in public, in front of the world and his fans. But Ian had skipped all the baby steps again and had gone straight to a kiss.

"I'm so sorry, Ian. All this was my fault," said Trent when they parted a second time. "I never should have threatened to leave. You're so good to me, and I just keep messing it up." He let his forehead press against Ian's, and the caress was completely pain free.

They were both crying and filthy from what they had been through, but Trent didn't care and Ian didn't seem to either. They stood there, breathing each other in, morning breath and all. Trent's fisted the front of Ian's borrowed shirt, and Ian settled his hands on Trent's waist. Neither of them were letting go for now.

"Don't apologise about this, T," said Ian. He pulled Trent in tighter for a warm hug.

"Excuse me, gentleman. I'm going to have to cut your reunion a bit short. This is a family-friendly area." Beverly's voice cut through their bubble like a cat-o-nine-tails. She still managed to sound sweet, even as she berated them.

"Sorry, Beverly." Trent leaned back a scant degree and gave her a small smile. He still didn't remove his hands from Ian's shirt, and Ian didn't feel as if he was pulling back any time soon either. "Could you call us a cab? Then we'll get out of your hair and be on our way."

"Already done, sir," she said, refusing the informality, but still giving him a small smile. She finally dropped her hand away from her side-arm and dipped her shoulders. He could almost see the thoughts written across her face as she looked between the two of them. It wasn't the homosexuality that bothered her but something different and almost visceral.

"Beverly, I promise you that Ian has never hurt me and will never do so. Ian's the best thing that has ever happened to me, and I don't regret him one bit. He would definitely hurt a fly or a spider, but he'd never hurt me," he said, hoping she could hear the honesty in his voice. Ian trembled against him and a sob caught in his throat. He pulled Ian tighter.

She must have believed him, because the last wrinkle between her brows disappeared and she gave a small nod. Trent wondered how many times she had heard those words before, thinking that it was a blatant lie.

"Ian, let's get you outside." Trent urged Ian to loosen his hold, and Ian finally released him, wiping the tears from his face with the corner of his sleeve. It wasn't until they were outside in the humid air that Ian finally spoke, his face tighter than Trent had ever seen it.

"Trent, what have you done?"

Chapter Eleven

"You're on a first-name basis with a cop, Trent, and suddenly I'm being released after sitting in there all night," said Ian, pulling back with horror dragging over his features. "What did you tell them?"

It was warm outside, as usual, and the sun was quickly making Trent's sticky clothes unbearable. The deserted street was quiet in the very early hour, despite the number of people who had already been hard at work on the other side of the station door. There were a few cars speckled against the concrete kerbs, but there was nothing to reflect Ian's hurtful words.

Trent had always tried to think the best of his husband, but there were times that he had failed. He'd failed the day that he thought Ian had cheated on him with a random chick in an elevator, but he'd been determined not to fail again. Their roles had never been reversed in such a way that Ian had failed him. Ian was his rock, his sail in a tumultuous sea and the only one he could ever really rely on. His accusation cut Trent to his absolute core.

"I told them the truth," said Trent, reaching for Ian, and wincing as his husband flinched away. Had the hug and the kiss moments before really meant nothing?

"How long is he going away for, Trent?" asked Ian, shaking his head and looking down at the bleached sidewalk. This time, Trent knew exactly who Ian was talking about, and it made his heart drop like a stone.

"Why would you even think that, Ian?" said Trent as he turned away and looked down the road for any sign of a cab. "I can't be that shitty of a person. I mean, I know I take things personally when I shouldn't and I complain a bit too much, but I thought I was still a decent guy."

"You are, Trent, but this isn't just about you. It's not about me either — or what happened, for that matter. There's a lot more riding on this than just a marriage." Ian's feet shuffled against the pavement as he spoke, a jittery move from his over-tired limbs.

"Just a marriage," Trent repeated as he looked back to his husband. "Wow, I'm so glad our commitment means so much to you." Ian didn't even have the decency to look apologetic.

Trent caught their reflections in the tinted-glass windows of the police station. With the two of them standing side by side looking bruised and bloody, it was a good thing that the street was deserted or Ian would probably already be on the news.

"You know that isn't what I meant," said Ian. He reached out, pulling Trent in close again on the bare sidewalk. His hands were still cold, probably from sitting in a jail cell alone, and the chill bit through the damp sweat on Trent's arms.

"I love you more than anything in the world." Ian kissed the side of his neck and a wave of warmth flowed through Trent's chest. His anger fluttered away on a sudden breeze, rising above to poke a hole in the atmosphere instead of his heart.

"Your heart is too big for just one person, and I know that," said Trent as he looked up at Ian's split lip. "That's why I'm never jealous of your friends. You can spend time with them, and love them, but I know that you will always come back to me. I love them too, Ian, even if one of them is a complete asshole. At least I know why now." He leaned up on his toes and placed a single kiss to the cut on Ian's lip. The flinch made him nod. *A fitting punishment.* "You've taught me to be loyal and a better person than I ever was. I didn't tell the cops anything, Ian. I told them what happened, kind of, but I said I wasn't pressing charges and I certainly didn't give them Mac's name. Your best friend is safe — and so are you."

"I don't deserve you," said Ian as he pulled Trent in for a kiss that was much too painful. Trent winced and pulled back, placing a hand in the middle of Ian's chest. He could feel Ian's heartbeat under his palm, so much stronger and steadier than his own.

"Yes, you do," he said, "but no more kissing until we get back to your place. I'm gonna take some acetaminophen, then I'm gonna go down on you, and there is nothing that's gonna stop me." He nodded to himself, completely committed to the plan. "Except maybe a shower first, then you can return the favour."

"Are you okay, though, T? I won't hurt you?" Ian pulled him back, his face going white as he raked his eyes over Trent's face again. "You look like—" He trailed off.

"Like shit, I know." Trent let out a small laugh. He remembered his reflection and doubted that it had improved much in the last hour. "At least I'm not the only one. I'm okay, though, just bruised as fuck, but I have a hard head, apparently. No concussion." He left out the fainting part and the fact that he'd slept through the night in the hospital bed. He didn't want to feel even more guilty than he already did about a good night's sleep.

The cab arrived with zero fanfare. It was a sleek black Chevy Cruze that had just enough leg room that they both felt like normal people when they slipped into the back seat. The driver took off after Ian rattled off his address.

"Hey," Ian called out to the driver, leaning forward until he was between the two front seats. "Do you care if we make out in the back seat or do you have some policy against that?" He asked it the same way he would ask the Trent to pass the salt at dinner—smooth, confident and one-hundred-percent sure of the answer.

Trent spluttered and felt his face flush painfully. He'd have to warn Ian to stop doing that. Blushing felt worse than getting goosebumps over a sunburn.

Ian snuck his hand back and squeezed Trent's uninjured wrist as the driver looked at them through the review mirror. The driver's face was blank and devoid of any recognition, which was probably the second biggest blessing of the day.

"Just no kinky shit." He eyed the bruises on Trent's face and Ian's lip. "And no cum anywhere. End of story." With that, he moved his eyes back to the road, flicking the blinker on to merge lanes.

"Nah, I'm not that quick, and we've only got about"—Ian looked out of the window—"ten minutes before we're at the front gate." He turned back to Trent, crowding into his space and lowering his voice. "This okay, T? I know it's one of your things, but I can't wait anymore. I'm worried that if I wait until we get home, I might never get to touch you. I'm not gonna let that happen this time."

Trent nodded, more than ready to break his own self-made rule just to have Ian again. He squeezed the seat as his stomach flopped in anticipation. And no cum meant that it wasn't really sex anyway. *Right?*

Ian's lips were on him, a painful sear within a burst of love. There was no embarrassment and no nervousness as the driver blatantly watched them in the mirror. Maybe it was because Trent knew their clothes were staying on — or maybe because they had permission to show their love behind the tinted windows. Either way, Ian was on board and Trent wasn't far behind.

Ian pressed his lips a touch harder as he cradled Trent's chin, and Trent let out a pained gasp. "Sorry... I just want to taste you," said Ian as he pulled back apologetically. Ian's eyes were already blown wide, still stained with red, but every trace of lethargy had faded away.

"Then taste me," said Trent, gripping the column of Ian's throat and smashing their lips together. It was probably the worst thing Trent could've done, despite how much he wanted Ian. It hurt like a motherfucker, and from Ian's grunt, Trent wasn't the only one who was feeling it.

"Sorry," said Trent as he pulled back with a pained smile. "I'll let you do your thing and I'll try to keep it in my pants until we get back." He was already hard and straining against his shorts. He'd skipped the damp underwear at the hospital, shoving them into his back pocket instead. It meant that the sensitive head of his cock was rubbing right against the zipper, and any moisture bled right through the metal teeth.

"At least I know you're on board with it." When Ian leaned back in, he dropped at the last second, and his lips fluttered along Trent's neck. Trent let out a small gasp, this time in pure pleasure with only a hint of pain as Ian skimmed the light bruises left by Mac's hand. Ian sucked the skin into his mouth and he raised his hand to tease Trent's pierced nipple through the fabric of his dirty shirt.

"I can still see his hands on you here," said Ian as he soothed the bruises with his tongue. "I was so fucking scared. I thought he was gonna kill you, T, and I just stood there and let him. I couldn't even move." He sucked a fresh bruise into the tender skin and Trent arched into the touch.

Trent hadn't realized that he had a bit of a pain kink. The tender kisses and possessive sucks along fresh bruises were definitely doing something for him. Then again, taking Ian's cock always smarted, and he loved that most of all. He should have known.

The walls of the cab faded away, and despite their uncomfortable position in the seats, Trent was getting into bedroom mode. His cock was leaking, his hips were jerking in the air and he was moaning like a penny whore.

"You sure we can't fuck back here?" he whispered into the air and giggled as he looked back to the cabbie. The driver was starting to look flustered, with a red blush across the bridge of his nose. If Trent was reading the signals right, the driver might even be on board with it.

"Not penetration," said Trent, shaking his head. That vulnerability was for them alone, "but maybe some grinding. I could definitely go for some hard grinding right now." He proved his point by releasing his seat belt, pulling himself into Ian's lap and dragging his groin along Ian's thigh, riding it despite the uncomfortable zipper.

"Only if you want your ass on the entertainment news," said Ian as he leaned up to bite at Trent's ear lobe. The car rolled to a stop and he moved away to glance around, huffing quietly. "We're home anyway." The word 'home' didn't sound quite as terrible coming from Ian's lips.

After leaving a generous tip and doing some serious adjusting, they got out of the car and into the early dawn. Trent tried not to look at the cabbie, who was hopelessly trying to cover his rather obvious erection. The man avoided looking at the picture of a beautiful woman clipped on the dash next to the radio too. *Talk about awkward.* He still didn't look like he recognized Ian, though, which was one more step toward avoiding a media disaster.

Ian punched the code into the gate, and Trent had a sense of déjà vu from their first morning in Miami. They were still the same people, but so much had changed since that early hour that felt so far away. He wished he could go back and smack some sense into himself, and hopefully avoid the disastrous days that had followed.

On the bright side, he was just as horny as that first morning, but this time he'd had a full night's sleep.

He adjusted himself again as they made their way up the walkway. The zipper was really starting to get uncomfortable, and he wouldn't be surprised if he had a welt on the head of his cock by the time they got inside. Luckily, the teeth weren't snagging on his piercing.

They were barely inside the grand entrance when Ian slammed the door and stepped into Trent's space. He was quick to grip Trent's shirt to keep him from escaping, as he leaned in to reignite the heat from the back seat of the cab. Trent stopped him with a firm hand on his chest.

"Shower first," said Trent. Ian's smirk dropped away into a pout as he hunched down. It looked as if Trent had dangled Ian's favourite candy in front of him before shoving it into his own mouth instead.

"But I want you *now*," said Ian, sounding closer to three than thirty and change. There were still black lines under his eyes that spoke of his fatigue, but they were wide and clear. He reeked, though, and so did Trent. And his morning breath was finally starting to take its toll.

"And I want your tongue all over my body," said Trent, moving in close. "I want you to dip it into my belly button, even though that makes me laugh. Then I want you to move down and flick it over my piercing until I'm begging you to stop. I want you to lick me open and push your way inside with nothing between us." He kissed Ian, slowly, gently and exactly how he wanted it, terrible breath be damned. "But I want to be clean too, and not swamp-assy from the hospital."

"You know," said Ian, pulling back. "You really know how to kill the mood with a phrase like 'swamp-assy'. What am I supposed to do while you're getting ready? I could cue up some porn and take the edge off while I wait." There was a television in the bedroom that Trent had assumed was exactly for that purpose.

And, of course, Ian would pay for the good porn instead of the free crap that Trent survived on.

"Or you could join me," said Trent. He tried to think of the nicest way to tell his husband that he stank too. "Then maybe I can do all the same things to you." Ian's eyes went dark, but there was also a flash of uncertainty. "Except that last part, baby. I know you don't like it and that's okay, but I'll warn you. One of these days you're gonna be begging me to take that ass, and I am going to take my time."

"Not today." Ian shook his head, his shoulders relaxing and his hands going limp against Trent's shirt.

"Nope, not today. Now come on, little drummer boy." Trent gripped Ian's hand and led him up the stairs and over to the bedroom. The sheets had been fixed in their absence and Trent's upended suitcase was set neatly on the ground once more. The sun was peeking through the skylight at the perfect angle, brightening up the crisp sheets like a beckoning rainbow.

Despite the temptation, Trent pulled Ian past the bed and through the door to the en suite. He pulled at the hem of his shirt, but Ian stopped him. Ian moved his strong, callused fingertips under Trent's shirt and over his belly, teasing at the skin, before slowly lifting the fabric over his head. Ian's shirt came next, followed by Trent's pants. Soon they were standing there naked with both of their cocks at attention.

Trent trailed his hand down Ian's chest until he met the brown stain that was still clinging to his few chest hairs.

"I don't think I've ever seen someone bleed that much." There was still a dried outline, even though most of the blood had flaked off. There were faint traces on the underside of Ian's scruffy chin too, and the faded puddle stretched all the way past his belly button.

"They took my clothes for evidence, but they didn't let me shower." Ian shook his head at the memory. His eyes went dark with something that wasn't arousal this time.

Trent could picture Ian sitting alone in a cold cell as the hours ticked by, and how no one had told him anything about his husband, who'd just collapsed in his arms — the threat of being charged looming over his head, and the fear of losing the people and the career that he loved most.

"Too bad. That was your favourite grey shirt and black pants," replied Trent, pulling Ian from his spiral before he could reach the bottom. He let out a small laugh as Ian's lips tugged upwards. "You might have to wear some colour. God forbid."

"Hey," said Ian, poking gently at Trent's solar plexus. His gaze dipped down, taking in every detail, from the bruise on Trent's knee to the dark stain on his shin.

"Come on." Trent grabbed Ian's hand before his husband's thoughts could grow dark again and led him under the heat of the shower. The spray was both wonderful and excruciating at the same time.

"I never thought I would curse great water pressure," Trent said, grimacing as the spray touched the edge of his sensitive face. Ian reached past him and adjusted the shower head. It was high on the wall and just out of Trent's reach, which was ridiculous for a man of six feet. A moment later, a gentle mist poured down on them instead of the pounding droplets.

Trent reached for the soap with a smile, but Ian was right behind him, pulling the bottle from his hand and crowding him under the spray.

"Let me," said Ian as he poured a dollop of shampoo into his palm. Trent gladly leaned his head back to give Ian better access, tilting his face so the water didn't go directly into his eyes.

One of the best things in the world was getting a massage from someone he trusted and desired. But even better than that was letting them bathe him. It wasn't the first time that Ian had done it, and Trent was actually starting to get a little bit addicted to the sensation of Ian getting him completely clean and ready. He also knew that, despite the huge turn-on it could be, it was something Ian needed at a visceral level. Ian needed to take care of someone, so he could pay his imaginary dues from his past life, and Trent was okay with indulging him every once in a while. He was also certain to return the favour with equal vigour, so he could tell Ian without words that he was a good man — and a good husband.

Ian swept his hands over Trent's body in deep circles that stripped the grime and sweat from the fight and hospital away. He dipped his fingers down to Trent's cock then back between his legs to get him completely ready for his mouth. He wasn't quite done when Trent whirled around to face Ian, reaching for the shampoo.

He'd learned something curious about Ian that he hadn't known until they'd first bathed each other in this way. Ian still liked to shampoo his head, even though he had no hair and hadn't had any in a while. It was a different kind of skin, he had complained, and shampoo just seemed to be the best for it.

It wasn't long before Trent was turning the shower off, dry-swallowing a handful of acetaminophen tablets and leading Ian back to their bedroom. He pushed him down until his back struck the mattress with his feet still dangling over the side. It was the perfect height for Trent as he lowered himself to his knees and took Ian into his mouth with no preamble. His knee smarted against the hard ground, so he grabbed one of the pillows and placed it underneath.

"I'm gonna see if my practice paid off," said Trent. He sucked at the tip of Ian's cock, then lowered himself down. He was careful to keep his lips away from Ian's cock to avoid the bruising, but it still wasn't completely pain-free. It meant that he had to take extra care to make sure that he didn't accidentally bite Ian or scrape him with his teeth. Leave it to Mac to ruin his blow-job skills as well.

Ian was so different from the way the toy had been. The toy was rigid and cold, but Ian was rock-hard and molten hot. He was also curved just a little bit more, and that sent him higher along the back of Trent's throat, tickling his gag reflex worse than he'd expected.

He pulled back and took a deep breath before he eyed up Ian's cock again. The angle just wasn't right, and the brief touch to the back of his throat had made his stomach churn. His knee was already aching too, even with the pillow beneath it.

"Change of plans," he said, slapping at Ian's thigh to get him to focus on anything but Trent's reddened lips. "You're going to stand up and fuck my mouth while I lie on the bed." He surprised himself when he didn't even blush.

"But, T, you're sore. I don't want to hurt you," said Ian as he sat up, but his cock twitched, even as he denied Trent.

"If it's too much, I'll tap your thigh twice, okay? If I'm ready for more, I'll just tap once. Abandon ship cause I'm gonna puke? I'll just keep tapping." Trent lowered himself onto the mattress and onto his back. He shuffled to the edge so that his head hung upside down off the bed and lined up perfectly with Ian's groin. There was a brief throb as blood rushed to his head, and his lips felt suddenly swollen, but after a moment of adjusting, things settled. The pills had already started to kick in and take the edge of his pain off.

"Please don't puke," said Ian, as he hesitantly moved in close. "That would literally ruin blow jobs for me for the rest of my life."

Well, that was one type of porn Trent would not be watching with Ian — not that he watched it that often. It was just that, every once in a while, he strayed from the 'wham, bam, thank you, ma'am,' to something a little less vanilla. Some things he would never try himself, like fisting, but it was interesting to watch.

Trent shrugged once and tapped Ian on his broad thigh. He took a breath, then Ian was pressing himself into Trent's mouth. It was strange at the new angle, but it was also easier. It opened him up enough that he could imagine Ian sliding all the way in with no resistance except Trent's own body. It also put him a little bit on edge to have his control completely taken away.

He took a deep breath through his nose to ground himself before he tapped Ian's thigh once and waited for the man to fuck his throat.

Ian rocked his hips, pushing himself about an inch farther inside Trent's mouth, before he drew back and pulled his cock from Trent's lips. He'd barely had three inches inside Trent's mouth, let alone his entire dick.

"Was that okay?" Ian asked, his voice low and concerned. Both of his hands were fisted tight and his entire body was a solid wall of tension.

"Ian, you aren't gonna break me with your cock. Now fuck my mouth already or I'm not gonna let you come." It was a terrible threat, and it worked every time.

Trent took another deep breath, then Ian was pushing back inside. Instead of pulling back this time, he kept pressing forward more and more, until he was at the back of Trent's throat and a little bit beyond. He pulled back and waited until Trent took another breath, before he thrust in even deeper.

If there was one thing Ian did better than drumming, it was fucking. He always seemed to know exactly what Trent could take and exactly how he wanted it. Even now, uncertain about hurting Trent, he was still able to push him to his limits and not a millimetre beyond.

He went deeper and deeper with each long stroke and hurried breath, until suddenly Trent felt a faint hint of pain as Ian's groin settled against his face. There was a moment of absolute astonishment when he realized that Ian was all the way inside him, his length throbbing in his throat as Ian shivered, trying to stay still.

"You okay?" Ian asked, his voice strained and low. He leaned forward and gripped the sheets next to Trent's head. His hand was trembling.

Trent tapped once against the strong thigh. He felt full, fuller than he ever had on this part of his body. And he was a little bit numb too, still astonished that he'd managed to pull it off.

Ian only trembled harder as he shifted back with steady control, letting Trent gasp a breath, before hilting himself again. He was so careful not to press too hard against Trent's face, and Trent would have thanked him if he didn't currently have his mouth full.

Trent couldn't swirl his tongue, suck or even hum to help Ian along. He could only lie there and be a vessel for Ian's pleasure, gasping in hurried breaths at every opportunity. It became a steady rhythm that was beating faster and faster like a racing metronome. His breaths became shorter as Ian's hips stuttered and he lost his grip on his control. Ian groaned loud, and his pace evened out again after a few shuddering strokes.

It was messy, with drool dripping down Ian's cock and smearing against Trent's face. It was loud, too, with a slurping gurgle as he was invaded, and the raspy breath when he finally got free. But it was also so fucking epic that Trent was rock hard and leaking down his shaft to his belly. If he wasn't focusing so intently, he could spare a hand, and he would be off with a single stroke.

"Shit, T, I'm gonna come." Ian rested deep inside, grinding just the tiniest bit before he withdrew.

Trent tapped his hand once on his husband's thigh, giving his consent and permission. The man above him shuddered as he lost himself. Ian let out a long groan before he buried himself deep one last time. His cock twitched and pulsed in Trent's throat like he'd swallowed something alive. He couldn't taste Ian's cum, but he could feel it flowing down inside him as a molten stream. His vision swam as Ian held himself deep just a moment too long, before he pulled back all at once.

Salty sweetness burned over Trent's tastebuds as the last bit of Ian's essence dribbled across his tongue. He sucked air through his nose and wrapped his sore lips around the head, sucking hard while reaching up to grip Ian's sac, which had gone rigid as it lifted. Ian choked, but Trent only sucked harder, not giving his husband any reprieve.

Finally, Ian pulled away, his eyes blown wide and his body shaking from the power of his orgasm. Trent couldn't help but smirk at the man that he had torn into pieces without even lifting a finger. Sometimes he could get more control just by giving it up.

"You have twenty minutes before you're gonna be inside me," said Trent, his voice deep and hoarse from the abuse. He watched as Ian's cock twitched, valiantly trying to rise but failing miserably.

"Fuck, T, I'm not twenty anymore." Ian laughed, but palmed himself gently anyway. His hand was noticeably tender on his cock, but he still winced from the overstimulation.

Trent rolled over onto his belly and ground down into the bedsheets, relieving some of the pressure that had built up. The sheets were so smooth and soft against his skin that he was on the edge immediately. He took a deep breath of the Ian-scented blankets and forced his hips to go still. He was so close. One little nudge and he would be done for.

"I figure that it'll be forty minutes for little Ian, but that's not our only option," said Trent. He watched as Ian went from confused to wide-eyed as he realized what Trent was saying. There was more than one thing in the house that was shaped like Ian's cock, even if the colour was off.

"Get your ass over here, T. You promised me a taste," said Ian as he gripped Trent's hips and pulled.

Trent yelped as the edge of the bed suddenly disappeared, and he scrambled for purchase on the floor. He knocked his sore ankle against the bed frame and let out a hiss. Ian kept on pulling until only Trent's chest and head were left on the bed, with his legs spread wide to balance on the ground. Only then did Ian lower himself and spread Trent wide.

There was always a moment of shame and embarrassment when his husband did this to him. He always worried what Ian would taste, no matter how clean Trent made sure he was. But then he would remember how many times Ian had done this, and how many times he had come back for more. It felt like Ian enjoyed rimming him, even more than Trent liked getting rimmed. And that was saying a lot.

"Do you think you can just come on my tongue with nothing else?" asked Ian as he bit down on one of Trent's cheeks before turning and licking a strip up the seam of his sac and along his perineum.

Answering was a physical impossibility when Ian licked a second time. But with Trent's hips pulled so far back away from the bed and his legs wide for balance, there was no way he could grind down on the bed. His hands were occupied holding his face just a little bit off the bed so he could avoid his bruises. If he could've said anything in that moment, it would've been a wicked curse against Ian and his devious plans.

Ian circled his rim with his tongue before he dipped in the slightest amount. It was so slick and soft that it was better than any finger or cock in the world. There was always a little bit of pain with penetration, but with a tongue, there was nothing but slickness and pleasure. And Ian definitely knew it.

He circled and prodded at the centre, repeating the same action until Trent was rolling his hips back to try to get Ian to go deeper. It was no use, though. Every time Trent rolled back, Ian would follow the movement or retreat altogether to mouth at one of Trent's cheeks. Trent's cock was throbbing between his legs to the beat of his heart, and it was getting stronger by the minute, but he couldn't come from this. There was just no way.

"Please, Ian." Trent finally snapped and his pride slipped away on the edge of the plea. He didn't even know exactly what he wanted — fingers, a cock or a plug. Anything would be better than this torture. He had waited so long already.

"I'm just getting started, T," said Ian, his voice deep and dark with lust. He pressed his face between Trent's cheeks again and sucked at the edge of his rim.

Trent didn't know if it was actually possible to get a hickey in such a sensitive area, but Ian seemed dedicated to proving it either way. His skin tingled under the onslaught and his nerves were suddenly overstimulated in the same way that they would feel after a hard fuck.

Only then did Ian finally push inside with his tongue, parting the swollen flesh with no resistance. It was a wonderful and terrible thing at the same time. Wonderful, because it lit up nerves that Trent hadn't even known he had before he'd met Ian. Terrible, because he was still no closer to coming, even though he so desperately needed to.

He was ready to offer his soul up to his husband to get a hand on his cock, when Ian stopped. Trent looked over his shoulder and shuddered at what he saw. Ian looked like he was the one who was getting fucked, with his eyes blown wide and his lips bright red. His face was sloppy with his own spit smeared over his cheeks and down to his rough chin that had scraped against Trent's sac in the most wonderful way.

"You okay?" Trent asked when Ian didn't move right away. Ian flicked his tongue over his lower lip a few times before he let out a sigh. Trent blinked when he realized that Ian's bright red lips were because of blood seeping from the split along his lower lip.

"Yeah, but I guess I can't do that right now," Ian sighed again before he smiled softly, wincing as the split opened wider. "At least, not up to my standards." He dabbed a finger against the seeping wound, and the tip came away watery red. The flesh around it was swollen too, with a layer of blue that faded to purple.

"It is a pretty high bar," said Trent with no little amount of disappointment. He didn't want Ian hurting himself, and it just added to the tally against Mac. *Blow jobs and rimming. Thank you very fucking much, Mac. What was next?*

"I could just fuck you on my fingers," said Ian with a shrug, scoffing as if it was a chore. He sucked the tip of his finger into his mouth, licking any traces of blood away from the surface and slicking them up at the same time.

"You can have me any way you like, on two conditions." Trent turned around and sat on the edge of the bed, leaning down to Ian's level. "I get to come soon, and you don't hurt yourself again." He kissed Ian's chin but pulled back when it sent a zing along his singed nerves.

"*Any* way I like," Ian repeated, and looked off to his side table. "That's a dangerous thing to say, T." He shuffled along the bed before opening the drawer and rifling through it. It sounded like there was a lot of stuff in the modest-sized compartment.

"I trust you." Trent crawled up the bed, right into the middle, and rolled over onto his back before he grabbed a pillow and pushed it under his head. The sky was slowly turning so blue above them that he could lose himself in the colour.

"Anything you really aren't into, T? I'm not talking heavy stuff, but I want to make sure I don't push you." Ian asked as he kneeled back on the bed, holding his arms behind him to conceal what he'd found. Trent made a mental note to look through that drawer when Ian wasn't there. Ian had raided Trent's beside drawer, after all.

"I'll try anything once, but just stop if I say 'red'," said Trent, shrugging as Ian's brows lifted. "I maybe read that in a book once, and it was totally hot, but I will never admit to reading it." Candace had been the one to recommend the book, and he'd been hard for days after he'd read it. Two days, three bars and five not-so-vanilla fucks later, he had finally got it out of his system.

"Works for me," said Ian. "We should probably have safewords anyway, just in case we ever get in over our heads with something. But it is good to know that you are up for new things every once in a while — not that we need anything to spice things up. It's just fun."

Trent nodded and settled farther into the sheets. His cock had calmed a bit as they'd spoken, but as he tried to picture what was behind Ian's back, he went ramrod straight again.

"I'd love to try a blindfold sometime, but I think it would hurt you too much right now. Can you keep your eyes closed for me instead?" asked Ian, moving closer and dropping something on the bed so he could skim one hand along the inside of Trent's thigh.

Trent closed his eyes and shifted his legs wider to give Ian better access, nodding his acceptance. He could feel every hair as they stood upright on his skin and the way Ian's breath danced across his flesh. The smell of Ian was so powerful, especially on the pillow where his head rested. This was truly Ian's home, and he could tell as soon as he closed his eyes. Even with the stark walls, the entire building was saturated with him.

Ian stopped his hand just below where his sac lay, before it disappeared off his skin. Trent strained as he listened for movement, but the room was still except for the sound of their breathing. When Ian's palm swept across his ribs unexpectedly, he couldn't stop from jumping.

"Just relax, T," said Ian, his voice much closer than he was expecting. He focused his breathing and slowed down, moving his thoughts inward and away from the panic he was starting to get trapped in. He trusted Ian more than anyone else in the world, and he knew this would be so much fun if he just let it happen.

"Sorry. I'm good now," he breathed out, his voice still hoarse. He wondered what his husband looked like at that moment, and if he was getting hard again as he teased him. He reached out, but his wrists were stopped by a tight grip. Something cool slid against the column of his wrist, then there was a click as it tightened. His other wrist was enclosed next, then they were both pulled above his head. There was another click, then he was trapped. The metal wasn't painful or tight, but it held him securely enough that he wouldn't be able to free himself without a struggle.

"Am I under arrest?" Trent snorted and let the last of his tension drain. He had asked that same question a few hours before, but this time his cock was throbbing, not wilted in damp clothing.

"The cuffs have a quick release, so let me know if they start to hurt," said Ian from somewhere above him, his voice serious but calm. "I don't want you to touch. I just want you to enjoy."

"Okay," said Trent. It was like a sparrow was fluttering its wings in his belly as nervousness bloomed. Ian sounded so confident, just like he always did. Trent had experience, but with Ian, everything felt fresh and new.

"Shh," said Ian, his finger gently resting against Trent's lower lip and caressing a small split. "No talking unless it's your safeword or if I ask you a question. You can make as much noise as you want — but no talking."

Trent nodded, clenching his jaw so he wouldn't be tempted to speak. His mouth always ran away with him at the best of times, and he knew he was in for a challenge. It was good that he was allowed to make noise, though, or maybe Ian knew that Trent had no way of holding back. He never could — not even in an aeroplane surrounded by two hundred or so strangers.

Ian's touch disappeared again and Trent heard shifting on the bed and the rustling of the sheets. When the hand touched his cock, he bucked up into the grip automatically. He groaned and bit back a curse as Ian stroked from base to tip before something cold slipped over the head of his cock. It wasn't the same cold as the cuffs, but more like the chill of a cup of coffee at room temperature. It slid down and down, a delicious pressure against his burning flesh, before it settled at the base. It was tighter than Ian's grip, and the blood in his cock throbbed in response to the pressure.

Trent let out a second groan when he realized what it was — a cock ring. He'd experimented in the past, but he'd always found it difficult to juggle a cock ring and a condom while fucking someone. When he had tried it, he'd lasted for nearly an hour before he had finally been able to come.

"Bend your knees and bring your feet up until they are under your cheeks. Good, T," said Ian, praising him as he followed the directions. "Now spread your legs a little bit wider. Perfect."

The praise sent a thrill up Trent's spine that he hadn't expected. He wasn't a dog that needed to be told that he was a good boy, but with Ian saying it, it was different. It made something in his brain click, like a puzzle piece that he hadn't known was missing in the first place. They were definitely doing this again.

Trent jolted when he felt something against his hole. It was slick and warm, but not quite like the cool lube he'd been expecting. After a moment, it tingled, lighting up his nerves in the strangest way. He groaned and arched his back, not sure if he wanted more or less of it. The cuffs held strong as he pulled against them, his hands useless above his head. He wanted to open his mouth and ask, but he didn't want to disappoint Ian. Not so soon.

"It's warming lube, T," said Ian as he answered Trent's unspoken question. The tingle grew harsher, from minty fresh into something molten.

Trent groaned as a finger dipped just inside him to spread the heated feeling past his rim. The burn was harsh until his body adapted, and the heat fizzled to a pleasant warmth. A tiny bit of it had dripped down between his cheeks, and even there, it lit a path of fire in its wake. His cock throbbed.

"Fuck, you're always so tight for me. You must do Kegels or something." Ian's voice was strong and confident, and not the quivering mess that Trent felt like.

Trent's laugh was cut off when Ian suddenly plunged two fingers knuckle deep. The shock of it was good, and only skittering along the edge of pain as Ian curled his fingers and went straight for his prostate.

"I think I've teased you long enough, though," said Ian, whispering into Trent's ear. The fingers shifted again, prodding harder than Ian usually would against the sensitive bundle. "You can come right now, T. You don't have to hold back." He prodded again, harder still, and a third finger slid in with the rest.

Trent reached for his cock, only to be stopped by the jingling cuffs. He wanted to come so bad, and his dick was twitching and leaking, but it wasn't enough. He needed something on his cock to cross that final line. Even a bit of fabric would do. He let out a whimper. This was torture.

"Please," said Trent, unable to hold back any longer. To hell with Ian's rules. He had to speak, and he had to come *now*. He curled his hips up, seeking a hand, but there was only air. When he flopped back to the mattress, it drove Ian deeper and harder against his spot.

"Go ahead, T. Come for me right now, baby. You look so fucking hot all spread wide and ready for me. You're gripping me just perfect, like you never want me to stop. I could do anything to you right now, couldn't I? You can answer." Ian swirled his fingers inside and pushed Trent beyond anything before, but still he couldn't come.

"Anything, please just let me come," said Trent, bucking his hips up again. His cock swung around in the air, then slapped against his belly. It wasn't enough.

"Here you go. I'll make you come," said Ian.

Ian withdrew all at once and Trent cried out at the loss. He throbbed and his hole clenched at the sudden emptiness, but before he could beg for more, something else started to push into him. It was broad and felt like it could be Ian's cock, but the temperature was off. It was just a little bit too soft and a little bit too cold. The ridges and veins felt familiar, though, and he knew it wasn't the first time he'd taken it inside him. This time was so much better with Ian in control.

"You take that so good inside. Fuck, look at you swallow it up," said Ian, his voice going harsh. There was a snap of a cap, then warm lube spread around Trent's rim.

The toy went deeper and deeper until he wondered if he would break. It was the same width and length as Ian, but every time seemed like the first time with his husband. He could never be stretched quite enough to take all of him inside without a little bit of an ache. The warming lube seemed to be doing its job, though, and the ache was dimmer than it normally would be, fading behind a curtain of tingling.

The toy rubbed against his sweet spot with purposeful strokes, but the ring around his cock held him back from the edge. He was so close that heat burst in his gut and his toes curled, but it wasn't enough. There was a sloppy mess of pre-cum on his belly that dribbled from him every time his prostate was stroked, but it had none of the satisfaction of an actual orgasm.

"So good for me, T."

Ian's voice grounded him through his closed eyes and vibrating skin. His husband had moved again, his voice no longer against his ear but coming from closer to his chest instead. Suddenly something pulled at his pierced nipple, harsh and unrelenting.

"Ian, I need—" The words poured from Trent's lips as he started to break. His cheeks were damp, but he couldn't remember when he had started to cry. It was just so much.

"I know what you need, and it's exactly what you are gonna get," said Ian, his voice calm and deep.

The words were an ominous promise that had the hair standing up on Trent's body. When Ian sounded like that, there was always something hiding just around the corner. Ian loved giving surprises almost as much as Trent grudgingly accepted them.

Trent heard a click, and suddenly everything was dialled to the max as the toy jumped to life. It wasn't just vibration either. Yes, it hummed against his prostate and made him see stars behind his closed eyelids, but it also moved. It twisted and writhed like it was alive and thrusting inside him like an unleashed beast. It was almost too much as it nailed against his bundle of nerves, buzzing harshly, before stroking his sensitive walls.

Trent didn't moan. He screamed in both ecstasy and overstimulation. Then a hand was at his cock, the ring slid off him and every ounce of blood rushed to and from his cock like a tidal wave. He was coming before it was all the way off, spurting all over himself as his hips jerked.

The toy withdrew and flopped against the floor, still thudding and buzzing. Ian's warm, rigid cock replaced it as Trent's walls continued to clamp down, his orgasm lasting too long to count. His eyes opened of their own accord as Ian's hips settled against him. Ian grabbed his legs and tossed them over his broad shoulders as if Trent weighed nothing.

Ian looked almost wild with a sheen of sweat glistening on his head and his eyes blown so wide that they were black. His lip was still bleeding, and his teeth gnawed at the red flesh as he pistoned his hips at a rapid pace. The lines of his neck bulged as he put every ounce of effort into slamming inside Trent.

Trent took it all in a mindless haze where a continual wail was pushed through his lips. He wasn't sure if it felt good or hurt, but he'd never felt anything quite like it. It was like he was losing himself, and all that was left was the cum dribbling from him and the cock slamming deep.

Ian gripped his hips hard and pushed all the way inside one last time as he came inside. Ian released a groan that was practically obscene before he collapsed down onto Trent.

Trent let out a whine as the air was pushed from his lungs and his back twinged harshly as he was bent nearly in half. The metal on his wrists tugged at him, reminding him that there was no escaping the weight. They pulled tight, too tight, as Ian pressed him into the bed. The last of his breath was squished from his lungs as Ian's full weight hit him.

"Red," said Trent, his words barely a gasp.

Chapter Twelve

Ian pulled back as if he'd been burned, morphing from collapsed teddy bear into a startled deer at that one word. His cock tugged painfully from within Trent, slipping out with what felt like a substantial amount of cum and lube that dribbled down on the bed below them. Trent heaved in a breath, filling his aching lungs, and shifted up so that the metal cuffs were no longer threatening to break his wrists.

"T, are you okay?" Ian's voice was peaked and frantic as he darted his blue eyes over Trent. "Oh my God, I hurt you, I'm so sorry. You just looked so good and, fuck, you felt so good that I couldn't stop myself." Ian fought with the cuffs, and they were off Trent in a moment. Trent dropped his hands back to the bed, because suddenly they were impossible to lift.

"S'okay, Ian, you're just heavy," said Trent, his voice slightly slurred. His orgasm had caught up with him with the force of a 747 jet and had drained every bit of energy from his bones. "I've never come that hard before and it hit me." That was the understatement of the day. "You can do it again, but just give me a few."

With each breath, his head cleared and Ian's frantic face came into sharper focus. Ian was moving his hands up and down Trent's heaving chest to the rhythm of his pounding heart.

"C'mere," said Trent, looping an arm around Ian's neck and pulling him down for a kiss. Ian was stiff, until Trent licked into his mouth with a sluggish tongue. Only then did he relax, dropping his shoulders as he leaned into the contact. Trent looped one leg around Ian and used the other man's surprise to flip them over so that Ian's back was pressed into the crumpled sheets.

"I love that your bed is big enough to do that without falling off the edge," said Trent as he pressed Ian into the mattress. He ground down and Ian's cock brushed against his loose hole. Reaching back, he slid Ian inside. He was still firm, but on his way to softening, and Trent could tell he was sensitive from the way he gasped.

Trent rocked back, letting Ian slip in and out just an inch, not wanting to be empty quite yet. Ian gripped his hips, clenching and unclenching his hands as if he was trying to push himself deeper and pull Trent off him at the same time.

"You're insatiable," said Ian. His face was flushed red from exertion and a few beads of sweat dripped along his forehead and fell back to the pillow. "There's no way, T. Twice is already pushing my daily quota." Even as he said it, he ground his hips up, his softening cock almost slipping out of Trent.

"What if we decide to have a threesome some day? Or a foursome? I have to keep you in prime shape for that," said Trent, smirking as Ian's eyes went wide. He jerked his hips a little, relishing the tug, then dropped to push Ian back where he belonged.

"Would you really? Want to do that, I mean?" asked Ian, his jaw dropping as Trent nodded shyly. His softened flesh gave a valiant twitch, still trying to rise despite its exhaustion.

"I've had threesomes before. Did I tell you that?" asked Trent as he continued to roll his hips. He braced his palms on Ian's chest for better traction, tangling his fingers in the soft hair there. "One was with Candace and a guy I was dating at the time. He told us that he thought he might be bi and wanted to explore it." Trent shook his head at the memory that had finally lost its edge.

"You had sex with a chick? Candace? What the fuck, T? You've been holding out on me all this time," said Ian, laughing and bucking up. He squeezed Trent's hips, pressing into the bruises that he'd carved during their lovemaking.

"I didn't get anywhere near her twinkle cave. Not happening *ever*. I did touch her tits, though, and that was just weird." Trent shook his head and moaned as Ian gripped tighter, deepening the possessive marks on his hips. "I felt kinda bad in the end, though. The guy, I think his name was Scott or something, realized that he was definitely straight, and Candace realized that she only wanted women."

"I thought you said that you're good in the sack," said Ian, laughing harder as Trent smacked his chest.

"I'll have you know that I am fantastic. Go a little deeper, yeah." Trent's eyes rolled back as he was momentarily distracted. "Thought you couldn't get hard again."

"Well, now that a threesome is on the table, I have something to prove." Ian snapped his hips up and buried his half-hard cock as deep as he could.

"I once made this guy come four times before I even fucked him. I didn't even know that was possible." His soft cock dribbled as the tip of Ian's cock pushed against his prostate. He didn't think he could come again either, but rutting like this was fun all the same. "I'm pretty sure he was high, but I'm still taking credit. I worked hard for that record."

"I made a chick come six times once." Ian slowed his humping to a gentle roll as his cock refused to harden any further. "That's like fucking rocket science, and I wasn't even into it all that much."

"Fake." Trent shook his head. "I betcha fifty bucks that at least five of them were fake. Candace told me that like eighty percent of her orgasms were fake, and that all chicks were like that." He paused for a second, simply riding Ian's waves without making any of his own. "Do you still like chicks sometimes, though, or is it only guys now?" It was a question that had always been a bit hazy in his mind. He knew Ian had done both, but he'd also been drunk out of his mind for a lot of them.

"Uh, sometimes, I guess," Ian shrugged, flexing as he lifted Trent a few inches. "Like, I might see some chick and think about it, but at the same time, I would probably prefer her boyfriend. When it comes to porn, though, I prefer straight porn. I couldn't tell you why."

"I get it," said Trent, nodding along in time with his hips. "I watch straight porn all the time. The guys can be so hot in them sometimes, and they don't hold back as much compared to some of the gay porn I've seen." He loved to watch someone lose control. It was one hundred percent his biggest turn on. He dropped his head back and looked through the skylight. The warm Miami sky looked right back at him. It was perfect and clear like it always seemed to be.

"So, how did this thing work with you and Candace?" said Ian. "If she was gay and he was straight, where the hell did things go?"

Trent laughed, pausing to wipe a line of sweat from his forehead. His thighs were burning from repetitive motion, but he wasn't ready to stop yet. A gush of cum slipped from his hole and dripped down Ian's cock. It was a little bit gross, but it felt good too.

"She was on her back, with him inside her, and I was behind him, going to town." The memory was clearer than he would have thought.

"At least, we were like that for a bit," said Trent. "He went down on me before that while Candace got him ready for me." He shrugged at Ian's incredulous look. "That's what friends are for."

"You guys are so fucking weird." Ian laughed and jerked his hips up suddenly. "Is that the kinkiest thing you've ever done then? I never thought you had it in you."

"Oh. Um. No." Trent flushed and lifted one leg over Ian's hips. Ian's cock slipped out and Trent lay down next to him, curling into his side and throwing one arm over his middle. "Not even close, actually. I didn't have anyone steady until you, so I jumped around a lot. Some of the guys I was with were into some pretty fucked-up stuff. I didn't mind, though, not as long as we had a safeword and it was consensual."

"Like what?" Ian asked, turning over to face Trent and drawing a line from his shoulder to his hip. "Come on. You can't leave me in suspense like that." Ian nudged Trent's shoulder as Trent flushed brighter and looked away.

He wasn't sure how he felt talking about his past. There was a lot there — like, a lot. But at the same time, Ian had been so open and honest with him about the most painful of his demons. Trent could be strong enough to admit he had been a bit of a slut.

"Fine. Jeez." Trent shoved at Ian's arm and rolled onto his back. His husband followed him, refusing to let up. "So, I met this guy in a club and we were grinding. I could tell something wasn't really right. He felt rock hard against my leg, but really fucking small. I shrugged it off. It didn't really matter how small he was, if I was the one topping — which I always was."

Trent took a breath, hoping he didn't somehow offend Ian by saying that. His husband was just watching him with wide-open eyes, waiting for the next line.

"I tell him we should get out of there and go back to his place. He leads me over to the bar where his guy is waiting for him. I thought I was gonna get punched in the face. I mean, this guy was taller than me and looked like he spent eight hours a day in the gym. But he just nods at me, then we're getting in their car." It had been one of the most terrifying car rides of Trent's life. He had spent the whole time looking out of the window and trying to memorize the surroundings so he would know where he was when he woke up without a kidney.

"The short guy I was dancing with, he'd been twitching and sweating the whole time we were driving. I thought he was on something, but his eyes were fine. He just wouldn't stop moving. He leaned over and started going down on me. I prepared to be crucified, but his man didn't even look up in the rear-view mirror. The little guy just thanked me when he swallowed and tucked me back into my pants. Then his man looked back and asked me if I was up for more."

"Were you?" asked Ian, his voice strangely quiet. His face had drawn together, the arching seam between his brows more defined. He looked so tired.

"Yes." Trent stopped and looked at his husband. "You okay? I'm not offending you or anything, am I?" These were the moments when Trent wished he had a filter so he didn't dig a hole in the first place.

"I just didn't think you were like that. That's all," said Ian, his hand going lax where it rested against Trent's hip. "I just know I was your first top, and in my mind…" Ian didn't finish.

"You thought I was a blushing virgin when you rolled through town. I kinda was. I had never trusted anyone enough for that before you, Ian," said Trent. "I had opportunities, lots of them, but I always managed to come out on top. No pun intended." He laughed at his own little joke but trailed off when he realized that he was the only one laughing.

"Do you think less of me knowing that I've had lots of men before? Because I don't care how many people you've been with, Ian. I know where your heart is, and I know you'll always be loyal to me." Trent watched and waited for his husband to say something, but Ian only shrank down on himself the more Trent spoke. Trent's heart sank.

"Here," said Trent as he reached for the phone on the side stand. Slick and lube slipped between his cheeks, now uncomfortable and awkward. He should've thought to clean up before he dove into a conversation.

"I need you to make a phone call." He passed the phone to Ian, and the drummer put his password in automatically. Trent settled down on his belly, resting his head on his hands. The touch hurt, burning every bruise on his face, but the call was going to hurt so much worse.

"Who am I calling?" he asked, his forehead furrowing in confusion. His gaze flickered between the phone and Trent's face, and confusion turned into worry.

"You know who, Ian," said Trent, rubbing his hand over his face, cursing when the bruising flared to life. "I know you love him. You can't hide something like that from me."

Chapter Thirteen

Trent forced Ian to make eye contact, grasping his hand as Ian's expression shuttered. There were only a handful of times that Ian had closed off to him completely. It was like taking the kindest soul and burying him under cold concrete until nothing remained, not even the crinkle of laugh lines at the corner of his eyes. It was so similar to his stage face and the stoic man that his fans could never touch.

"It's okay. I understand," said Trent. He took a deep breath and tried to keep the worry and heartbreak off his face. Ian was frozen between shock and terror, but there was no denial. It was true, that Ian did love Mac, and it was more than the love of friendship.

Trent never would have guessed that the feelings were reciprocated when he'd first met Mac in an expensive hotel room, but he saw it clear as day on Ian's face. The man would do anything for his best friend, no matter what was thrown his way. Only love could make him that blind to a person's faults.

"Is this some kind of trick?" Ian snarled, his face twisting as he pushed himself out of bed and tossed his phone onto the covers. "Why the hell would you say something like that? You're my goddamn husband." He clenched his fists along his sides, and every line in his naked body pulled taut.

"Remember who you're talking to, Ian." Trent pulled himself up to his knees and the sheets tangled in his legs. "Don't try to lie to me, because I know you're better than that. I know you love me, Ian, and I know that you aren't going to up and leave me. If that were the case, you never would've married me when you were already in love with another man. You would've waited for him forever." He lowered his voice as he noticed the shimmer in Ian's eyes from held-back tears. "I'm not afraid of him and he's not a threat to me, even if I have to kick his ass to prove it to him. I don't need to prove it to you or myself." He didn't mention that he was definitely the ass that would be getting kicked and not the one that did the kicking.

"What do you want me to do?" Ian slumped back onto the bed, his shoulders shaking with suppressed sobs. "I don't know what to do, T. You must hate me. I love you so much, but..." He trailed off as the first tears dripped down his face. Ian was handsome, even when he cried, and he didn't go bright red and puffy after the first drop.

"You have a big heart, Ian, and I know there's room in it for more than just me." Trent wrapped his arms around Ian's shoulders and leaned heavily onto him, needing the support just as much as Ian did. He knew Ian's heart was big, but he wasn't so sure that his own heart would be as flexible. It certainly didn't help that he absolutely detested Mac. He didn't want to add another point to Mac's tally, though. He couldn't lose Ian completely.

"So, I think you should call Mac and invite him over for dinner. I can stay with you, or I can go out for a while. Either way, I'm coming home to you, Ian. I could never hate you. I love you more than anything in the world and I just want to make you happy." Trent leaned his forehead into Ian's shoulder and kissed the naked expanse. It was damp and cold under his sore lips, and he imagined his skin felt the same. The mess between his cheeks was now dry and tacky, and he definitely needed another shower.

"Why did you say you were going to leave then?" Bloodshot eyes turned on him and pulled a piece of his essence out of his soul.

"I didn't think you wanted me here," Trent admitted, looking away when he couldn't bear to look at Ian any longer. "I didn't want to interfere, and I know your work is important to you. Your work was making you happy, and I...wasn't." Trent shrugged. It might've been a bit of an overreaction, but he always did things in full-blown cups and not measly smidges.

"Oh." Ian wiped his eyes on the back of his arm and took a shuddering breath. "You're wrong, though. You do make me happy, even when you have no taste in clothing."

"I knew it!" Trent smacked Ian gently as the man let out a low chuckle. "I looked like a farmer boy ready for a night out at the drive-in. You are such a brat." He laughed as Ian nodded and his chuckle turned warm. The concrete wall was crumbling, and Trent could almost see his husband again. He looked lonely and terrified, but Trent wasn't going to make him do this alone.

"Will you call?" Trent looked at the innocent phone between the sheets. Ian nodded as he followed Trent's gaze. Trent's heart clenched in his chest and his stomach twisted into a knot that would probably never untangle. His husband was in love with another man, and the other man loved him back.

"Did you want me to crash at Brian's or something? That guy is a hoot and I'm sure he wouldn't mind. I would love to hear a few more childhood stories about you," said Trent, even though he knew that if he went to Brian's, he would probably never return to this house. Once Ian saw what life could be without him, why would he ever ask Trent to come back? Mac was everything that Trent could never be—gorgeous, fit, talented and rich. *God knows, he probably has a massive cock too.*

Ian shook his head, giving Trent hope with that simple action. "I think I need you to stay, T. I have to get my mind wrapped around this, and I think I might need your help to do that."

"Okay," said Trent as he kissed the top of Ian's head. "I'll get the Kevlar and the brass knuckles just in case."

Ian made the call while Trent quickly washed with a warm cloth, then pulled on a casual pair of shorts and a T-shirt. He pulled the door shut just in time to hear Ian murmur into the phone, sounding calm and even, despite his obvious nervousness. Trent wished he could have his husband's strength of will and level head, but he knew there wasn't much chance of it.

He made his way to the kitchen, pausing at the entrance as memories flooded forth of the last time he'd been in the room. His face throbbed, despite the way the swelling had gone down.

The shower and sex had done him wonders. He would've looked completely normal to anyone who was colour-blind. He could open his eyes completely, and his split lip had shrunk in size. The only things left to disappear were the massive array of blue, black, purple, yellow and green bruises across his face.

The sneaky maid had struck again. The pool of blood had been cleared from the floor, leaving only a sparkling shine, and the only hint that there had been an altercation was the tiny dent in the stainless-steel fridge.

Trent slid a hand along the dented surface. It was the place where Ian's back had hit as Mac pushed him. He could imagine how much force it would've taken for a blow to make that impression — more than anyone should ever use on a friend or a lover.

"I won't let him hurt you." Trent shook his head and pulled open the fridge door. He would do anything to keep Ian from getting hurt both physically and mentally, even if it sacrificed his own wellbeing.

The fridge was a monstrosity that Trent would never have been able to afford on his own. It was massively wide and had both cold water and ice available at a single touch. The shelves were clear glass and polished delicately by loving hands. Despite the beauty of it, it was nearly empty. There was a carton of milk and of orange juice that were both dangerously close to expiring. There was also a container of leftover Chinese food that Ian had ordered in. Every one of their meals had been take-out or at a restaurant, leaving Trent craving a home-cooked meal. He didn't know how Ian managed it.

He slipped back into the en suite bathroom without disturbing Ian, who had fallen asleep amongst the pillows. The worry lines had smoothed on Ian's brow, and his mouth was open in a soft snore as Trent snuck by. It was so tempting to get naked and snuggle into Ian's warmth, but he also had a mission.

One of the first things he had done on his days alone in the house had been to open almost every single drawer in every single room. He'd missed the side drawer in the bedroom, but by the time he'd been done the rest, he'd found out a few interesting things about his husband. It wasn't snooping if nobody caught him.

He'd stumbled upon a drawer that was almost full of different kinds of makeup. At first, he thought he'd discovered one of Ian's secrets — the longing to prance around as a woman. It made him harder than he cared to admit. But after laying out all the makeup out, he'd discovered that every tube, gloss and powder, were skin-toned coverup.

It made sense that Ian would need coverup if he didn't want to be caught out and photographed with a stubborn zit on the side of his face. It also came in handy now that Trent needed to conceal literally his entire face. He would never curse Candace again for testing out makeup on him.

Looking nearly normal, if not a little bit more tanned than usual, he grabbed a set of car keys and took off in the red rocket, as he had affectionately named her. And, of course, the BMW was a her. It was, in fact, the only lady he ever wanted to be inside. And, man, did she feel good.

He pulled up to a grocery store with his cock soft in his pants, which was an absolute blessing. Ian must've taken a harder toll on him than he'd thought — or he was finally catching up to his age.

The store had a name he'd never heard before in his life. It had looked like a market when he'd driven by earlier in the week, and through the windows he could see the layers of fresh produce, stacked ornately like an obsessive compulsive's dream.

The prices had him hesitating inside the door before he remembered Ian's card in his wallet. He shrugged to himself and grabbed a cart then started down the first aisle. Ian would probably be the one to eat most of it anyway. And leaving a store empty-handed, especially when he'd already grabbed a cart, was almost sacrilege.

A menu sprang up in his mind as he tossed things into his cart that was quickly becoming over-full. Avocados — three of them would cover anything from burger toppings to straight-up guac. He wasn't quite sure what lemongrass was, but it smelled divine. And he added some sort of fruit that didn't look like anything he'd ever eaten before.

The lady behind the till did a double take when he pulled up with two carts that were filled to the brim with everything and anything that had caught his eye. Luckily, his flush was hidden beneath ten layers of makeup as her eyebrows practically hit her hairline.

"Having a party?" she asked with a smooth accent that sounded like a brook over silk. Her grey hair was twisted into a bun, but most of it had escaped, giving her a halo of frazzled silver. Her eyes were blue and kind as she took in the mismatched array.

"Starving husband," he replied with a shrug. She nodded and gave him a soft smile and a brief glance before she started to type each thing into an ancient computer. Two people appeared from nowhere and started packing things into bags so everything was perfectly sorted and stacked. It wasn't like his store back home, where they thought that tomatoes and pie should go underneath the canned beans.

"Your total is — "

"Wait!" Trent nearly yelled. The last thing disappeared from the cart and into a paper bag that was etched with dark designs. There was a lot there, and the prices had been so steep. He pointedly turned his head away from the computer where the glaring red total reflected back at him.

"Please don't tell me. Just take the card." He passed her the card from the side, with his head still pointed away. She took it with a soft laugh, running it through a machine and waiting for the beep before handing it back. Ian's daily limit must've been massive if there had been no flags or complaints.

"Did you want me to burn the receipt?" she asked with a chuckle. Her long nails gripped the receipt tape that was larger than it had any right to be, ready to tear it to pieces for him.

"Hide it in the bottom of one of the bags. He'll find out eventually anyway." She tucked the too-long list between trays of chicken breast and gave a sigh of relief. "Thank you so much. The cupboards were bare, and I've got the dinner date of a lifetime to prepare for."

The crew of three were even nice enough to pile the bags into the tiny trunk, the back seat and the passenger seat of the BMW. He waved at them as they stepped back into the store, the woman shaking her head with a smile on her face. A can of tuna slid from the bag on the passenger side and struck the stick shift before rolling beneath his feet.

"Oh, close call." It was lucky that he hadn't started the car yet, because he probably would've ended up wrapped around a tree if it had got stuck under the brake. He fished the can off the floor and tossed it into the glove box, snapping it shut with a sigh. Finally, everything fit.

He drove back to Ian's a bit faster than he probably should have, the car purring beneath him as he shifted seamlessly. It was already well after lunch and into afternoon, and his stomach was eating itself in place of his missed lunch. It also gave him less time than he'd hoped to make dinner.

He hit the code for the gate and screeched into the garage, using the parking brake to avoid hitting the solid back wall. He ran to the door that led into the house and threw it open on its hinges.

"Ian, help me," he shouted into the house before turning back and grabbing as many bags as he could lift while still being able to twist the doorknob. Ian appeared at the door a moment later, red-faced and out of breath.

"I heard you screaming. Are you okay?" His gaze snapped up and down Trent's body as if he was looking for new bruises. "Are you wearing makeup?"

"Bags. Inside. Please help me carry them." Trent turned so he could make it past Ian without whacking him with the bag of tomatoes. He tossed it all on the island before he opened the fridge and a half-dozen cupboards and got to work. He stocked dry goods, canned goods, perishables and snacks. He even had one cupboard that was completely dedicated to different flavours of crackers that he'd never heard of before.

"What the hell did you buy?" Ian asked as he came in with the third trip of bags. His arms were covered in lines from carrying too many bags and he was slightly out of breath. He didn't look angry, and the short nap had done wonders at returning the colour to his face.

"Groceries?" Trent paused, feeling unsure for the first time. Maybe he should've stopped at one steak instead of buying seven, but they'd been on sale. And the chicken breasts…? Well, there were probably about two dozen, but there was so much he could do with them.

Ian peeked into one bag that contained about ten pounds of ground beef. "What the fuck are you doing with all this meat?" He grabbed another bag and pulled out a tin, squinting at it as he tried to read the label. "And what is this? Do people actually eat this stuff?"

"It's coconut milk, and yes, they do," said Trent as he snatched the can from Ian's grasp and added it to his stash of canned goods. "In that paper bag there's some fried chicken for lunch. I was gonna do salads, but it smelled so good." Trent grabbed the new box of freezer bags and started to divide the ground beef up into one-pound portions before he slid it into the freezer.

"You spent a thousand dollars on groceries?" Ian's asked, his voice eerily calm.

Trent spun around as fear spread through his belly. He thought it would've been three hundred, maybe three fifty since he'd splurged a bit. But a thousand? *Holy fuck.*

Ian had ignored the fried chicken that Trent had pointed out and had continued to pull everything out of bags instead, including the chicken breasts. A slightly damp receipt hung from his limp fingertips and one eyebrow was cocked, but his lips were pulled up on one side in a smirk.

"I didn't think you had it in you, T." Ian laughed and shoved the receipt back into the bag, crumpling the paper and shaking his head.

"I'm so sorry, Ian. You didn't have anything I needed to make dinner, and I think I got a little carried away." Trent slumped against the counter and kicked at a lower cupboard that was still open. He could probably return some of the canned goods, but not the meat. Grocery stores could get really picky about that kind of thing.

Ian peered over Trent's shoulder to the crackers that Trent had organized by box size and colour. "It's good that you finally realize that it's okay to spend our money."

"Oh," said Trent, flushing. He scrubbed a hand gently over his face, wincing at the bruising and frowning when his hand came away caked with beige. "And thank you for letting me use your make up too. I had enough of the looks yesterday."

"You did a good job on it," said Ian as he reached for a box of crackers and inspected the label. "I can hardly tell." He hummed at the package and pulled it open, then crunched one between his teeth.

Trent tossed the beef wrappers into the garbage and washed his hands in the sink. A wall of heat hovered against his back and there was a brief press of lips against his neck.

"Thank you," said Ian, kissing him one more time before pulling back and continuing to unload and munch on crackers.

They ate quickly and Ian disappeared from the room when Trent banished him. Trent heard the distant, muffled sounds of drums before a door slammed them into silence. He grabbed his phone and pulled up a few recipes that he couldn't quite remember, while starting on another few he did. When Ian returned a few hours later, Trent was dripping sweat in the overheated kitchen with four burners and the oven going simultaneously.

"You need another stove," said Trent as he smiled over his shoulder and wiped the sweat from his forehead with the back of his hand. He'd washed the makeup off, but his face still felt slimy and thick. "All this space and only four burners." He grabbed one of the spoons and stirred a pot, hoping that the slurry inside would thicken soon.

"I'll get you another one, baby," said Ian as he moved in close. "Can I try it?" He slid his hand along Trent's arm, before grasping the spoon and bringing it to his lips. "Holy fuck, that's good." He went to dip the spoon back in the pot for a second bite but Trent grabbed it, tossing it into the sink where a precarious pile of dishes was already waiting.

"Don't double dip, not when we're expecting company," said Trent, nuzzling his forehead into Ian's shoulder. The man was fresh from the shower and smelled fantastic, and the wave of heat from his skin only made it that much better.

"Do you want me to babysit these so you can go get ready?" Ian grabbed another spoon from the drawer and dipped it back into the pot.

"Give me a minute. It's almost done, actually." Trent grabbed the spoon before it made its way back to the pot a second time, and he reached for the oven mitts. He pulled a piecrust out of the oven—something that had taken him three tries and a slight mental breakdown to get right—and set it on a pad on the counter.

He poured the mixture inside, scraping the bottom of the pot then sliding it back into the oven, cranking the heat way down. He switched two burners off and left the third one to simmer slowly before he put a freshly coated spoon in his mouth and twisted back to Ian, who had taken a seat at the island to watch him, looking even better than he had a few hours prior.

Trent sucked along the edges of the spoon, using his tongue to lick every last delicious drop from the metal surface. Then he leaned in and placed an open-mouthed kiss on Ian, thrusting his tongue straight inside the man's mouth. Ian groaned, sucking Trent's tongue and getting every drop of the sauce. A part of Trent was a little grossed out at the thought of Ian swallowing him like that, but another part, the part in his pants that mattered, was definitely on board.

"You taste like lemons," said Ian, pulling back with one last lick into Trent's mouth. "But I guess that would explain the three bags of lemons that you bought." He licked his way back into Trent's mouth and pulled him close between his splayed legs.

"How much time do we have?" asked Trent, suddenly wishing that he had spent the afternoon in bed instead of the kitchen. He moved his hands along Ian's shoulders, feeling the stiff muscles there that were still hot from hours of drumming.

"About ten minutes," said Ian, dropping his mouth to Trent's neck and licking a line of sweat from him.

"Are you kidding me?" Trent looked at the clock in alarm, before looking down at himself. His shirt had a hole right near his belly button and there was an alarming number of stains down the front. His wedding ring was caked with flour and he was pretty sure there was butter in his hair.

"Just go shower, T. I'll keep an eye on the food for you," Ian offered, as if he wasn't the same person who had almost burned Trent's house down when he had tried to make breakfast.

"Just don't touch anything…at all." Trent glared over his shoulder before running back, turning off the last burner then darting out of the room.

He was naked before he hit the bedroom and under the water before it had even warmed. He shivered distantly as he shampooed with one hand and grabbed his loofah with the other. Ian might make fun of him for using the thing, but it did a really good job.

When he was just on the right side of clean, he turned off the water and darted back into the bedroom, completely forgoing a towel.

Flapping his arms like a bird to air-dry faster, he darted over to his bag and grabbed the exact outfit that he had meant to wear the night he'd met Ian's friends. Farmer boy or not, he was going to fucking rock it. He stumbled over the buttons, deciding to ignore the missing one at the top, but the jeans were a real problem. They were already tight, but with his damp skin, they were next to impossible to get up. It led him to do something that he usually didn't consider.

Free-balling was dangerous. He'd tried it a few times in college, as guys had always seemed to be turned on by it, and it made for easy access. It had taken one drunken night in a bathroom when he'd zipped a little too quick, before he had vowed never to do it again.

He'd already taken a risk that morning at the hospital, as his boxers hadn't been wearable, but his shorts had been super loose then. He'd been careful too.

But now, with his piercing just another thing to get caught on the teeth and pants so tight that he would need butter to get out of them, the idea of it was downright terrifying. He was out of time, though, and Mac was probably already there. Ian definitely wouldn't have listened to him and had touched the stove by now, mixing and matching his perfectly organized spoons and mingling the flavours of each pot.

With an expectant flinch, he zipped. He looked down, seeing that he hadn't accidentally castrated himself, and gave a sigh of relief. It was still uncomfortable, and his piercing was getting tugged in the most alluring way as he rushed down the stairs, but it would have to do.

He hit the bottom of the stairs at a dead run and slowed when he heard raised voices. He forced himself to take a deep breath when he heard Mac's voice, bright, clear and coming from the kitchen.

"I will not kill him — not unless I have to." Trent repeated it like a mantra, hoping that he could follow through. He paused at the kitchen entrance when he heard Ian's reply.

"That's not what you came here for, Mac," said Ian, his voice dark, and sounding like he just managed to get the words past gritted teeth.

"You're trying to tell me that he convinced you that he didn't sell me out?" Mac's voice cut through the kitchen sharper than a smoke alarm. "I came because you asked me here as your best friend. What do you mean it was his idea all along?"

Trent rounded the corner before things could get out of hand. Ian was standing in front of the stove, adjusting dials as Trent knew he would be. Mac was on the other side of the room with his arms crossed and every line taut in his smaller body.

"Hello, Mac. Thank you for coming." Trent tried to sound sincere, he really did, but there was still an edge to his voice. He looked at Mac's face and couldn't supress the tiny bit of satisfaction when he saw the dark smudges under both of Mac's eyes and a band across the bridge of his nose.

Trent rushed to the stove, sniffing for smoke but finding none. "Can you grab bowls and drinks and set them up on the island, please, Ian?" The man nodded, looking relieved to be able to do something without confronting his best friend.

"What the hell is this, Ian?" Mac seethed from the corner of the room, taking a step back and clenching his jaw as he glared at Trent.

Trent whirled to face the other man, done with the utter bullshit that Mac had put him through. He took four steps toward Mac and watched as he pulled himself up, his hands raised so he was ready for a fight. Trent didn't blame him. He had half a mind to smack the man right in his broken nose, but that wouldn't get them anywhere.

"This is an attempt at making amends," said Trent after he took a deep breath. He held out his hand, offering to shake on it. "I'm not going to apologise for breaking your nose. And I'm definitely not going to apologise for marrying Ian. He is the best thing that's ever happened to me — and to you, I think." He glanced over at Ian, where the man stood frozen with a bowl in each hand. "We are going to sit and eat dinner like adults, and we're going to talk about what happened and what we're going to do about it." He dropped his hand that still hung in the air, not really expecting Mac to shake it, but offering the gesture nonetheless.

"I'm not talking about anything with you," Mac hissed at Trent like a feral cat that had been caught in a garbage can.

"Then talk to Ian," said Trent with a shrug, turning his back on Mac and grabbing the bowls from Ian. He reached for a third bowl before filling them with two scoops of rice each, then a ladle of thick curry. The steam curled into the air, carrying the spiced scent into his nose and making his mouth water.

Trent tried to ignore the silence as he placed the bowls on three different sides of the island, making his seat at the head of the table so Ian and Mac could sit across from each other. He followed with utensils, then three glasses of water before he slid into his chair. Glancing at each of the frozen men in turn, he brought a forkful of curry up to his lips.

"I don't know about you guys, but I'm starving." As he took the first bite, it seemed to snap Ian out of whatever daze he'd been trapped in. Ian slid into his spot, grabbing his fork and looking expectantly at Mac.

"I'm not eating at the same table as him," said Mac, shaking his head and scowling. He leaned back against the wall of cupboards, glaring at Ian and refusing to even look Trent's way.

"Sit the fuck down, Mac, or you'll never hear from either of us again," said Ian, leaning over the island and pointing his fork at his friend. "I don't think you realize how close I am to leaving right now. Sit down—or we're done and the band is done." Ian stabbed his fork into the bowl and brought another mouthful to his lips. He looked like he was trying to appear relaxed, but

Trent could see the anger simmering just below the surface.

Mac had gone from furious to deathly pale as Ian spoke. He shuffled to the table, pulling out his stool and lowering himself onto it. He grimaced as he looked at the bowl, before he grabbed the fork and tentatively pushed a small bite into his mouth.

"It's delicious," said Mac, his brows rising into his hairline as if it was the last thing he'd expected. He took another bite, then another, barely pausing to chew in between. He glanced at Trent, scowled and slowed his pace.

"Ian said it was your favourite," Trent said into the bowl. He was instantly glad that he'd spent a ridiculous amount of money on getting fresh produce for the curry. He could only imagine what would have happened if he'd screwed up dinner.

"I don't remember that," said Ian, locking startled eyes with Trent. "It's true, but I didn't think you knew his favourite food."

Trent just shrugged, uncomfortable with two sets of eyes on him. "It was before we got married. You said we needed a restaurant in town, and I called dibs on Thai. You mentioned that you could invite Mac to visit because coconut curry was his favourite food." He remembered that, and so many other conversations about Mac. He hadn't minded at the time, but sitting where they were now, he wondered if he should've.

"What did you want to talk about?" Mac cut off the tale as his fork clattered to the table. His bowl was empty, nearly scraped clean as well. He was looking straight at Ian as if he could completely push Trent from the room if he just ignored him long enough.

Ian's mouth gaped and closed a few times like a drowning fish that had been caught unaware in a powerful tide. He fisted the paper napkin and his eyes dropped to the tabletop.

Trent saw the struggle and Ian's walls coming up like a brick fortress. This was Ian's chance to be happy, and he couldn't let his presence be the deterrent. He took a deep breath, swallowed a curry burp and looked at Mac.

"Ian's in love with you."

Chapter Fourteen

There was nothing quite like pulling off a Band-Aid at high speed. It didn't end up feeling any better at all, despite the desire to just get it over with. Instead of the slow sting of each individual hair tug, there was a startling burn that swarmed from the spot like a bee sting. Sometimes he would lose a chunk of hair or a patch of skin would peel off with the bandage. Either way, looking at the two men, perhaps he should've taken a slower approach.

"T, what the hell?" Ian rocked back on his stool as if he'd been struck, his face pale and his eyes wide. His fork clattered to the table before bouncing once and skipping onto the ground. Rice and curry splattered onto the lower cupboard, painting it yellow and white.

"It's true," said Trent with a shrug. He glanced over at Mac. The man was completely frozen, his mouth half-open and his eyes flitting between Ian and Trent. At least the declaration had finally made the singer acknowledge that Trent was in the room.

"So here's the problem, Mac. I love Ian, and I'm not gonna let him go—not for anyone or anything." Mac narrowed his eyes and Trent could see the gears clicking in his brain. He was probably thinking of the most efficient way to get rid of Trent and where best to hide the body. "But that doesn't mean that I never learned to share," said Trent, lowering his fork and preparing himself for whatever would come. His gut was a solid ball of twine that had rolled under the table in a knitter's haven. It wasn't going to unravel anytime soon.

"What?"

"What the fuck?"

The two men spoke almost simultaneously, but Ian was the one who stood, throwing his stool back and advancing on Trent like a lion on a baby gazelle. "What are you saying, Trent?" His voice was low and dangerous, but Trent could see the pain in his eyes. "You really think that it won't bother you if Mac and I are together?" Ian dropped down to his knees and grasped Trent's hands in his own. They were cold and layered with a sheen of sweat that made Trent want to wrap his husband in a hug.

"Of course it would bother me," said Trent in a low whisper that he knew Mac would be able to hear. "But I love you, Ian, and I'd do anything to make you happy. I meant what I said earlier. If being with Mac makes you happy, then be with him." He brought Ian's hand to his lips and placed a kiss on the broad, callused palm.

"But I want to be with you, T. Don't you know that?" Ian's voice caught and his eyes shone with unshed tears, but he didn't break down. He was so much stronger than Trent could ever be. Trent was ready to bawl and squeal like a child or dig himself a hole where he'd never have to see daylight again. Ian was steady.

"Then be with me too. I told you that I would always wait for you to come back to me, Ian, and that's the truth." He looked away from his kneeling husband to the intruder in Ian's home. The breathtakingly handsome singer was cruel and vicious from a lifetime of lies and suppression.

"Mac?" Trent asked. Mac still hadn't moved, but something had changed in him. It was the first real peek that Trent had of the man that Ian loved. There was no misplaced anger that would turn his face into an ugly frown or false disgust at something he really desired. He was just a man—a terrified man, who was the closest he'd ever come to being happy.

"I don't know what to say," said Mac. Not for the first time, Trent noticed how beautiful Mac's voice actually was. Even when he was speaking in a low, scared voice, there was a melody to it.

Trent looked back to his husband and squeezed his hand once before nodding. Ian rose, still looking like he was walking through an alternative reality. Their hands slipped apart, then Ian was going to Mac.

Mac surged forward, gripping Ian's neck like Trent had so many times before. There was no hesitance in Ian this time. He followed through with the touch like a man who had been locked away for years. He wrapped his arms around Mac and pulled him up, pressing them together from chest to pelvis.

Their lips met and Trent could almost feel the heat of the kiss from across the room. Their mouths opened to each other and the kiss deepened as Ian tightened his grip and pulled Mac up. Even on the tips of his toes, Mac could hardly reach Ian's lips without straining, and Ian was so used to kissing Trent, who was that much taller than Mac, that it looked like he hadn't been quite prepared for the difference.

A minute into one of the most passionate kisses that Trent had ever seen, something completely unexpected happened. Trent had been bracing himself for pure jealousy and rage, while being completely determined to keep it under wraps. He wouldn't go back on his word, no matter how many pieces his heart ended up in.

There was still a spark of jealousy when he saw the raw passion in front of him, but then he remembered that it was the same passion between Ian and himself. It wasn't something more that shadowed their marriage like a black cloud, nor was it a false mirage of feeling. It looked exactly the way that Ian kissed him, and exactly how Trent liked to be kissed.

At the first groan from Mac's lips, heat stirred in Trent's groin. His cock twitched in its confines, just enough to drag his piercing along the inside of his zipper. It sent a bolt of sensation up his cock that had him letting out a groan of his own. He was quiet enough that he didn't interrupt the two men — *and thank God for that*.

Ian dipped his hands beneath the hem of Mac's shirt, running along the naked seam of flesh. Mac let out a soft cry as Ian nipped at his lower lip, his head going back as Ian sank lower to kiss along his jaw and neck. Ian was so careful to place tentative kisses so that he didn't touch anywhere Mac might be bruised or reopen his own split lip.

Fuck. Trent went rock hard, leaning one elbow against the table for balance as he palmed himself. The restriction of his jeans was too much for little Trent, and it was starting to get painful. He flicked the button open without a second thought and carefully pulled down his zipper. He was lucky that he kept himself so neatly trimmed, as pubes caught in a zipper would be worse than a leg wax.

He was throbbing when he skimmed his hand down his shaft for the first time. He gripped the base, holding himself a touch too hard as he willed himself to calm. But the sight in front of him was doing nothing to help his problem. The thump remained rhythmic against his hand.

Ian pulled at Mac's shirt and lifted it over his head. The singer may have been on the shorter and slimmer side, but he was ripped. It was a wonder that Trent didn't have a massive concussion from the strength that was so clearly etched in every line and muscle. Mac had a goddamn six pack, for Christ's sake. Even Ian didn't have a six pack.

It could only mean one thing. Mac had held back when he'd punched Trent in the face. Even through the anger and the rage, he had still held back.

"Is this okay?" Ian's voice travelled through the kitchen. He waited for Mac's nod before his hands began to roam. The question was intended for Mac, but it still made Trent's toes curl. There was something about Ian and the way he was always checking in that was just too sexy to name. His partner always came first, whether it was his husband or his best friend.

Trent let out a loud groan as he fisted himself. He was never any good at keeping quiet at the best of times, and there was no holding back right now. How could he have ever thought that he would be jealous of this? This was his own personal porno starring the man of his dreams and the man of his nightmares.

Ian's gaze snapped to him, his pupils blowing wide as he looked at Trent's lap. He'd probably been expecting the same thing Trent had—jealousy and regret.

"Enjoying the view, T?" Ian quirked his lips as he ran his hands up Mac's torso, pausing to pinch at a peaked nipple. Mac let out a gasp, his eyes flying wide and meeting Trent's across the room. He gripped Ian's shirt as if the thin fabric was the only thing that was keeping him upright. Knowing how those hands felt, it probably was.

No matter how much of an asshole Mac was, he was still beautiful. His eyes were exotic, and his cropped hair was the perfect shade of brown. With his lips kiss-swollen and his face flushed, he pushed that line from beautiful into epic. He was exactly the type of man that Trent would've picked up in a bar during his former life.

Mac looked him up and down and his gaze settled on Trent's piercing. His eyes went wide before a smile spread across his face. It was so similar to Ian's smirk, but there was an inherent cockiness to it as well. It made Trent want to blow Mac's mind and turn that smirk into a shout of ecstasy.

"Join us?" Mac's voice cut through the haze and went straight to Trent's cock. He was stumbling off the stool and tripping over his pants before Mac had even finished speaking. The curry was forgotten, and the pie would just have to wait in the cool stove until morning. Frankly, he didn't care if every bit of food went to waste at this point.

"Bedroom?" Ian asked a moment later. The idea was brilliant. Trent nodded, then all three of them were moving up the stairs in a single file. It would have made a strange view for anyone who cared to peek their head through the front door. Ian was in the lead, fully dressed and looking back over his shoulder every few steps as if he couldn't believe who was following him. Then there was Mac, flushed rosy red and shirtless, with his swagger stumbling into a nervous shuffle that he couldn't quite hide. Trailing behind was Trent, still fighting to get his pants off one leg and giving his best effort to avoid falling on his bruised face.

Trent paused, watching Mac's ass as it swayed back and forth as he stepped up the stairs. His jeans left very little to the imagination, and fuck, it looked good. It was tight and high, with the perfect-sized cheeks for Trent to fit into his hands and squeeze. He hardly remembered getting to the bedroom with that view filling his sight.

"Any rules to lay down?" asked Trent as he came through the door, throwing his pants in the general direction of his suitcase. "With this many hands and cocks, things go down quick sometimes, but I'm fine switching, just so we're clear. Ian, I assume you are gonna stick with top only."

Ian lowered himself to sit on the bed and nodded once before he tilted his head to the side and looked Trent up and down. His cock was tenting his pants in an obscene arch that strained the fabric more than it was ever designed for, but somehow, Ian was able to ignore it.

"How many three-ways have you been in again?" He didn't look upset this time, just turned on.

"I didn't say how many," said Trent as he lifted his shirt over his head, happy to be the first one naked one in the room. He may not have been streamlined or powerful like the other two men, but he was comfortable with himself.

"Four? Ish. Once with more than three." He shrugged and flushed as Ian's eyes widened and Mac spun to look at him. They faced each other, with Ian beside them on the bed, with a full view of everything going on.

Mac's gaze dropped to his chest and Trent's nipples peaked under the scrutiny. They were close enough that Trent could feel the heat of Mac's skin and see the fine dark hairs sparsely dusted over his chest. He was about half a head shorter than Trent, but he held himself upright, as if he could be just as tall if he only tried harder.

"My first time with Ian was the first time anyone had ever been inside me," said Trent quietly, his eyes flickering down to Mac's lips. "He took such good care of me, Mac. I would've married him that day if he would've proposed. But he's big, a lot bigger than any of the other ones I've seen up close and personal. He's gonna take such good care of you."

Mac nodded, looking more like a terrified virgin than the cocky man Trent knew him to be. But he also looked like he was ready to jump in ass first. Mac raised his trembling hand up to Trent's chest with a tentative touch, and Trent gasped when Mac brushed against his pierced nipple, sending a bolt of sensation straight to his gut.

"He likes it when you pinch it hard. The rougher the better," said Ian, watching from the bed as he palmed himself. His eyes were dark, and Trent's past life was forgotten again when both of the beautiful men focused on him.

Mac pinched harder, his gaze never leaving the glinting barbell. His hands were warm against Trent's cold skin as the air conditioning caressed his naked flesh. The pinch was enough to make Trent's toes curl and he let out a small gasp, but it was still softer than he was used to — softer than he liked it.

"Harder." Ian's voice was a command more than a suggestion. The button on Ian's pants had come undone and his hand had disappeared into his boxers.

Mac took a breath, his eyes flickering to Trent's face as he ran his fingertip over the bud before he pinched — hard. Trent let out a gasp that turned into a whine as the sensation hovered between pain and pleasure. His nipples had always been sensitive, but since the piercing, it was like one had a direct line to his cock. Mac must've taken the sound for pain, though, because he pulled back.

Trent remembered what Ian had said to him when they'd first fallen into bed together. How he'd tried to play with the piercings through a woman's nipples and she had told him to stop because it hurt her too much. Ian had had experience with men before meeting Trent, but Mac had nothing. He probably couldn't even fathom what Trent could take.

"Don't stop," said Trent, ready to beg if he had to. Mac lifted his hand back to its place and moved in closer, feeling his way along Trent's chest. Mac's tongue dragged along his lower lip in determination, and something in Trent snapped at the sight.

He cupped Mac's chin, tilting his head slightly to avoid Mac's broken nose, before he leaned in for a tentative kiss. His lips were still tender, but not as bad as they had been. The amount of pleasure thrumming through his body seemed to dull the pain, mixing up the signals and firing them all to his cock.

The kiss felt like nothing short of touching an electric fence to his bare cock. It was the ache of his lips and every single thing that this man had ever said against him, but it was also the heat and warmth of forgiveness. The heat made him want to sink in and lose himself against the singer — and pull so many sounds from Mac's lips that weren't curses and dark thoughts. He wanted to show Mac how good it felt to be with a man and how much better it could feel when it was a man that he loved.

Trent was careful not to brush against Mac's nose, and he kept the kiss loose so their breaths lingered in each other's mouths. When he dipped his tongue inside Mac's mouth, he tasted the curry they'd had for dinner, along with something deeper that threatened to drag him in. Their tongues twined and Mac sucked at him, pushing their lips closer until they could scarcely breathe.

When Trent pulled back, they were both panting and flushed. Mac had moved his hands from Trent's chest to his lower back, where he was gripping hard and digging into the layers of muscle. Mac had transformed, with kiss-swollen lips and blown brown eyes, into a true siren. Trent could jerk off to the image in front of him and be completely satisfied.

From the corner of his eye, he could see Ian on the bed with his cock in his hand. Ian's cock was leaking over his palm as he slipped his thumb over the wet head and smeared his pre-cum down his cock. Only part of him was peeking from his lowered zipper, but he already looked huge and completely proportionate to the rest of his body.

"I think Ian likes what he sees. Should we give him a show?" said Trent, mouthing along Mac's ear so that only he could hear. A tremble went through the singer, and Trent gripped his earlobe with his teeth to keep Mac from looking to the bed. If Mac looked, he would be as lost and in love as Trent already was, but Trent needed his attention.

"I need you to tell me you're okay with this. I know you hate me, and I don't want to force you to do anything that you aren't up for. I can still leave if you need me to." He kept his voice low and soothing as he nibbled at the sensitive spot beneath Mac's ear. He could jerk off in the hallway behind the closed door if he had to.

Mac pulled back, looking at him with wide eyes and shaking his head.

Trent dropped his hands, taking a step back so they were no longer touching. Oh God, he had pushed too far and now he'd ruined everything. His stomach sank, even as his cock continued to throb between his legs, nearly slapping his belly with the force.

"I don't hate you," said Mac, the corners of his lips lifting.

Trent did a double-take, crossing his arms and taking a second step back. Ian had said the same thing, but Trent couldn't exactly trust his opinion on the subject. And Mac could be lying. He had to be lying... Right?

"Are you sure? Because it definitely feels like it," said Trent, shuffling his legs closer together so he felt a tiny bit less exposed. He looked at his shirt that was on the floor and just out of reach. His pants were too far down the stairs to go for, but the shirt might hang low enough to offer him a tiny bit of decency.

"I don't," said Mac, shaking his head and reaching for Trent with an aborted gesture. "You're beautiful and so sexy. Every time Ian told me about you, it made me want to strangle you and picture you naked at the same time." His smile widened and he took half a step forward.

"That's kind of concerning," said Ian quietly from the bed.

Mac rolled his eyes and cut him off. "You are everything I want to be but can't. You were there for Ian when I wasn't, and of course he fell in love with you. Who wouldn't? You're fucking perfect, and that made me so fucking mad." His reached out and pinched Trent's pierced nipple with steady fingers. "Then you gave me Ian, like it's not even a hardship. I kissed him like I've always wanted to, and I looked over at you and see this." He tugged harder as his gaze dropped to Trent's pierced cock. "And I realized that my imagination didn't do you justice."

Trent was gone, and he wasn't checking in any time soon. Both of these men could be on the covers of magazines... Hell, they probably had been. And they thought *he* was beautiful? Ian had said it too many times to count, but Mac was different. Mac didn't owe him anything, but he still said it.

"In your fantasies, was Ian fucking me or were you?" Trent asked without a hint of shame. He could picture Mac alone at night in his big bed or on his bunk on the bus with his hand on his cock and his lips bitten red from trying to keep quiet.

"Ian would fuck me, then you would shove your cock down my throat and make me take it." Mac looked him dead in the eye. "Then, sometimes, you'd switch places."

"Shit," said Trent as he grabbed his cock at the base. He'd always had a weakness for dirty talk, and Mac seemed to have the same talent for it as Ian did. Ian groaned and saw his husband stroke himself from base to tip. Ass-to-mouth wasn't exactly his thing, but it sure made for a pretty picture, especially when he was already so close. It also gave Trent a view of exactly where Mac had been doing his research.

"Then let me return the favour." Trent dropped to his knees hard enough to make them ache, and he let the pain ground him in the moment.

He loved to suck cock, and he was fucking good at it. He enjoyed the strong taste of his partner as he took them as far as he could and the way his jaw would ache. He appreciated the heaviness against his tongue and the salty sweetness of pre-cum. But mostly, he revelled in the feeling of someone coming apart from his mouth alone.

He worked the button of Mac's pants then the zipper before he nuzzled at the thin briefs that hugged Mac's package. He was already standing as a proud arch that strained against the fabric, and Trent's mouth watered as he took it in. He wasn't prepared to tease right now or take his time. He wanted his cake and he was damn sure he would get to eat it too.

"You clean, Mac?" asked Ian from the bed. He hadn't moved anything except his hand, and he was watching them with pure intent. He was more than eye candy, watching them fully clothed. He was melted chocolate and caramel drizzled over ice cream.

Trent balked at the question. He'd been with Ian long enough that he hadn't thought to worry about asking for protection. Thank God for Ian and his ability to keep his wits about him.

"Yeah, I got tested six weeks ago. It has been about two months since I've been with anyone. Carol and I, we divorced, and I've been careful with anyone else." Mac stuttered out his response, his gaze dropping to the floor next to Trent.

"Shit, Mac, why didn't you tell me?" Ian finally stood and wrapped his arms around Mac from behind.

"Doesn't matter, just fuck me," said Mac, rolling his hips and leaning back into Ian.

Trent met Ian's gaze and knew that the conversation definitely wasn't over, but it was not the time or the place to talk about exes. It also made the last of Trent's guilt disappear. Part of him had wondered about Mac cheating on his wife, and where that left his kid that he never saw.

He pulled Mac's pants and briefs down with one solid tug, letting the singer step out of them before he grasped Mac's cock to steady it. It really was a thing of beauty, just like the rest of him, and was nestled in dark, trimmed curls that had been mostly waxed or lasered away. He was just above average, but narrow and long, which was the best kind of cock in Trent's opinion. It curved gently up and jutted out completely straight instead of leaning off to one side. The shaft was decorated with narrow veins and peaked with the mushroom head of a cut cock. At least Trent wouldn't have to think about calamari when he was going down.

Before Mac could say a word, Trent sucked the head into his mouth and took it down to the root. It slid easily past the back of his throat and his gag reflex before it settled deep. It was nothing to Ian's cock, which had carved a literal spot for itself in Trent's throat. Mac had a cock that was made for deep-throating, and Trent hoped to give a repeat performance as many times as he could bear.

He swallowed around it and hummed in a way that he knew would feel amazing. Mac flexed his hips under his hands, but they barely nudged against his face before something stopped them. When he looked up, Ian was looming behind Mac, holding the singer's hips in a tight grip to keep him from thrusting too deep. Mac's head fell back to rest on Ian's shoulder as he gently gripped Trent's hair.

Trent pulled back, locking eyes with Ian and licking the drool from his lips. "Let him fuck my mouth. I can take it."

The two men groaned at the same time, then Mac was thrusting fast and deep and Trent was doing everything he could to keep up. He sucked in hurried breaths every time Mac pulled back, only to have them catch in his throat when the singer slammed forward. He was wild and brutal with a varied rhythm that Trent couldn't follow. It was nothing like Ian's even and powerful strokes, and Trent was wholly unprepared for it.

"I'm going to come," said Mac through gritted teeth as he pulled Trent's hair. The pull was good, but it was just a little too far on the side of pain for it to be perfect. Mac had obviously been expecting to fuck a porn star, but it was Trent's job to remind him who was really in control.

Trent looked up at him through watering eyes and gripped the base of Mac's cock hard enough that it throbbed in his hand, and Mac winced above him as he drew back until his ass settled against Ian. Trent took a deep breath and wiped his mouth on the back of his arm, refusing to let Mac go, even as he groaned.

"If you try that again, you can find someone else to fuck and you can pay them for it," said Trent, waiting another moment until the cock in his hand was nearly purple and his chest didn't ache quite as badly. Ian was looking at him, his face drawn and his lips pressed into a frown. He looked like he was ready to put an end to it all, but Trent just shook his head, coughing once to clear his throat. Mac, at least, was failing to hold back a whimper with his legs pushed tight together as his cock, no doubt, ached to the point of real pain.

A sigh cut the air as Trent released his grip and dropped back down on the cock before him. This time, Mac stayed almost still, bucking his hips gently like a lapping wave. To show his approval, Trent hummed and moved his hand between Mac's legs, just behind his balls. He pressed in just the right spot, massaging Mac's prostate from the outside at the same time as he forced Mac back against Ian's solid body and took him all the way down his throat. He could show Mac things that would blow his mind, but he would do them on his terms.

Mac's grip in his hair tightened as the cock in his mouth twitched. Trent jerked his head back, scraping his teeth over the head of Mac's cock in a real warning. *Pull my hair that hard, and you'll need a prosthetic.*

Whether it was the jolt from Trent's teeth or the touch on his prostate, Mac came with a gasp. He was salty — saltier than Ian ever was, and there was a touch of something wild, almost gamey, to his taste. It wasn't bad enough that Trent didn't suck at the tip and take everything Mac had to offer and more.

"Ah, fuck." Mac's voice went high as Trent continued his assault, pushing him beyond his body's limits. He massaged Mac's prostate hard, getting every last drop, before he finally pulled away when Mac sounded like he was on the edge of a scream.

Trent knew the feeling. Ian did it all the time to him, just to see him squirm. It was the best and worst kind of stimulation that made a guy wish he had a clitoris so he could come six times in a row. He hoped that Mac's recovery time was better than Ian's, who sometimes wasn't ready again until he'd had a full-blown nap.

Mac went boneless against Ian, as if his soul had been sucked out of his dick. Ian caught his weight, lifting him from the ground as if he weighed nothing and laying him out on the bed. The demonstration of strength made Trent moan, and he followed them with a slight wobble to his numb knees, slumping onto the bed and giving his cock one pull to ease the ache.

The singer took a heaving breath, his eyes half-closed and his legs splayed wide. His cock was still swollen and red, but it was quickly softening with each breath through parted, bright-red lips. Ian lay down beside him, eclipsing him with the size of his body and reverently brushing over each inch of exposed skin.

Pristine was the best way to describe Mac. It was as if he were carved out of an image of raw strength, and there was nothing to pollute that. His body hair was groomed to a dainty layer of dark fuzz over his chest and a neat triangle on his groin. His balls were smooth and hair-free, and his chin was shaved close enough that it was baby-smooth. There were no tattoos, no piercings and not a single scar, despite the fights. He was a blank canvas, ready to bruise with teeth and tongue.

Trent crawled up the bed and hovered over Mac's body, pushing Mac's legs wide so they straddled his waist, and lowering himself onto the prone man. It had been so long since he'd had someone beneath him who had no intent of topping him, and it brought back every dirty trick he'd ever learned.

He never stopped as he kissed, licked and bit every inch of available skin, marking it up in a way that would last for a week. Mac was a mewling mess and his cock was half-hard again by the time Ian grabbed Trent by his chin and pulled him in for a kiss that was all teeth and tongue. There were smooth hands on his cock and his chest, while others grabbed his ass and squeezed tight. Things were starting to blur as the three of them moved in sync, taking and giving exactly what they needed. Mac was learning so quickly, following their lead instead of trying to forcibly take it.

"Lick him open for me, so I can fuck him," Trent said into Ian's ear, nipping at the shell before soothing it with his tongue. He hoped that Ian had healed enough to be able to do it.

Ian gripped Mac's hips, flipped him onto his stomach and dove between his cheeks like a starving man. The final touch was tentative, though, and Ian curled back his lower lip, forcing his nose down into Mac's crack so he could be at the right angle and still avoid pushing against his sore lip.

Mac cried out, lost and surprised by the sudden assault. His back bowed, but then Trent was there, pulling him up so Ian was forced to flip onto his back to reach his goal. It made the angle so much easier for Ian and kept his injured lip back from the fray.

"It's almost like a woman, isn't it?" said Trent, bracing his hands against Mac's hips to help keep him aloft. "No hair at all back there, just smooth skin." Like Trent would know. He let out a little snort. It would be

240

nice to not have to pull stray pubes from his tongue once he got his turn, though.

Mac looked like he had barely heard Trent at all. His eyes were rolled back, with the lids fluttering and his lashes dancing against his cheeks. His hips strained against Trent's hands as if he was unsure whether he wanted to thrust back into Ian or pull away. Trent brought one hand to Mac's chin, curling under it and bringing the singer up into a kiss.

"Sorry," said Trent pulling back and readjusting after he accidentally brushed against Mac's sensitive nose. Mac's eyes were watering as he blinked back tears, but he didn't look any worse for wear, so Trent dove back in, putting his mind to one task, and that was taking this man apart piece by piece.

He felt the groan against his lips and looked down to see one of Ian's hands disappearing between Mac's legs. Ian's forearm flexed and Mac's cock jerked into full hardness again, already dripping a pearl of white fluid from the tip.

"Is he fingering you open, Mac?" asked Trent, already knowing the answer. Heat flared up his spine as Mac nodded, closing his eyes and tilting his head back in bliss. "He's going to take his time to get you ready for me. He'll rub your sweet spot so good until you beg for my cock. Or did you want him for your first time? Do you want him to split you open and push in to the hilt until you're so full that you can hardly breathe?"

Mac's hips stuttered as he bit his lower lip, his forehead furrowing as he looked over his shoulder to Ian's shaft. His eyes grew wide. Then he looked back to Trent, dropping his gaze to the pierced head that was glistening in the low light. Trent wasn't small, but he was at least closer to average than Ian.

"I don't want it to hurt." Mac cried out as Ian flexed again, completely oblivious to Mac's struggle. He lifted his hands to grip Trent's neck, bringing their heads close together until their breaths mingled.

"Do you want me to fuck you first? I'll go real slow, Mac, and get you stretched out so you can take him. Or I can fuck you, and Ian can fuck me at the same time. Every time he pushes himself deep, it will push me inside you a little bit more." That was if Trent even made it that far. He was about one small touch away from coming and ruining all his plans. He took a few deep breaths, focusing on the small hole in the wall where he wondered if a picture used to hang.

"That. Fuck...do that." Mac ground down into Ian as the man thrust three fingers home and spread them wide. He was still holding himself up and forward so Ian could breathe and his lips were free. Trent nodded his approval and gripped Mac's ass in both hands, pulling him wide and squeezing the tender flesh.

Trent retreated long enough to grab a condom and lube before he rolled it down onto his cock and spread a generous amount of lube down his length. He sat on the bed facing Mac, his heels digging into his ass as he tried to get his position just right. He wanted it to be seamless, and he wanted Mac to know exactly what to expect. It would be like nothing he'd seen before on a glowing computer screen.

"You ready?" asked Trent, brushing his hands down Mac's flank as he rocked back into Ian. He waited until Mac nodded, then gripped the singer's hips, lifting him off Ian's face and directly onto his cock. There was only a moment before Ian withdrew his fingers as he caught on and the head of Trent's cock pushed against Mac's ring of muscle.

It was loose and stretched from Ian's tongue and fingers, but it still felt so tight as Trent pressed against Mac's entrance. No one had ever been inside Mac before, and Trent knew personally how tight that would make him. The stretch wouldn't be too painful for Mac, not with Ian's devoted attention.

He ground against it a few times before he lowered Mac's hips just enough so the head of his cock slipped inside. Instant pressure wrapped around Trent as Mac clamped down with a strangled moan. Fuck, it was so tight and so good. It had been so long since he'd been inside someone, and he hadn't realized how much he'd missed it.

Ian was there, whispering into Mac's ear and kissing the line of his throat, as the singer relaxed and Trent's cock sank deeper inside the unrelenting heat. Every inch squeezed him so tight that Trent had to reach down and grip himself at the base to stave off his orgasm. Now would be the perfect time for the cock ring that Ian had hidden in his drawer, but there was no way he was lifting Mac off to reach for it.

With a soft sigh, Trent moved his hand to brace against Mac's hip to guide him the rest of the way down. Mac's brows were drawn together in obvious discomfort, but every time he started to tighten up around Trent to the point of pain, Ian would whisper into his ear and rub up and down his sides. It was so intimate and open and exactly how it was supposed to be, and it struck Trent to his very core. He wanted to do this again, more times than he cared to count. It wasn't even about Mac at this point, but the feeling that was binding all three of them together.

He waited until the lines on Mac's face relaxed and his bruised eyes fluttered open before he rolled his hips. He didn't pull out at all but ground himself deep inside in a way that would push his cock directly against Mac's prostate. He was rewarded with a soft groan, and Mac reached out to his chest to grip the dusting of hair there. Trent rolled harder, determined to get this man to scream for him.

He lifted Mac up an inch before he dropped him and curled his hips at the same time. He knew he would hit Mac's prostate dead on, but the singer seemed to be less sensitive than him.

He was rewarded with a slightly louder groan and a dribble from Mac's cock, which hadn't softened in the least. Trent took the groan as implicit permission to take him apart.

He rocked his hips hard, using the momentum to lift Mac higher before slamming him down. It was hard to learn how to ride someone in this position, and Mac just hung on. Trent was still determined to make it an amazing ride, though — without bucking the man off, of course.

It took a few thrusts before Mac started to catch up, rolling his hips to meet Trent's, and stuttering to a stop as he lost his rhythm. One thing was for sure... Ian could keep a beat in his sleep, but Mac was hopeless.

Trent sat up, clinging to Mac's hips as he flipped them, so Mac's back was pressed into the covers. He pushed Mac's thin, wiry legs up and out as far as he could until he felt them fight back against him from the stretch. It wasn't much to work with, but it would have to do. Trent would've been able to fold almost in half for Ian, but Mac could barely go halfway before it looked like his muscles were starting to strain.

"We gotta stretch you out so I can fuck you properly, Mac." Trent ran a hand along the back of Mac's thigh to the muscle that was practically bulging from the stretch. With his other hand, he reached for two pillows and jammed them under Mac's hips to help with the angle. "That's better." He slid to the base before pulling back and slamming deep while curling up at the same time. He glanced over his shoulder at Ian, who was watching the two of them with obvious quaking awe. His cock was nearly purple and dripping steadily onto the messy sheets.

Mac let out a sound that was halfway between a shout and a scream as Trent nailed his prostate hard enough to make his cock spurt. The singer gripped the headboard and clawed at it as he tried to grind up into Trent.

"Do you think I can make him come from just my cock, Ian? Help me, won't you?" He could feel Ian looming behind him. Trent turned his head to the side, seeking and finding Ian's lips in a hungry kiss. He groaned as fingers found his entrance, which was still slightly loose from their earlier activities. It wouldn't be enough for Ian to thrust in now, though. Trent was always tight, as if he'd never taken anyone inside, and Ian always had to stretch him.

Three fingers pressed into him with enough lube that it dripped down between his cheeks and onto his thighs. His groan turned high at the wide stretch, and Ian skimmed over his bundle of nerves.

Very suddenly, it was too much. With Mac around him, and Ian inside him, he was not going to last. He stilled his hips and gripped himself hard to stop his impending orgasm, managing to catch it just as his balls drew up tight.

"Fuck," cursed Trent. It was good, so fucking good that it made him ache. It was edging in its purest and most terrible form. "Fuck, give me the cock ring or I'm not gonna last until you get inside me."

Ian pulled out as he launched himself at the drawer, rifling around for the ring then tossing it at Trent as he scrambled back. Trent eased out slowly, gripping the condom carefully, before he slid the ring on with another layer of lube. When he breached Mac again, the slide was easier, and, despite the throb of his groin, he wasn't at risk of ending it before he even started.

Ian came back, rough and insistent as he spread lube inside and out. His cock was pressing in almost as soon as Trent pushed, and he was in to the root, naked and massive as always.

He cursed and gripped Mac's hips as Ian pushed himself to the base in one long thrust. The stretch and burn were so good, but completely overwhelming at the same time. As Ian brushed against his bundle of nerves, he thanked the cock ring that held him tight.

"Fuck, you're so tight, T. Always so fucking tight for me. How does Mac feel around you? Is he squeezing you just perfect as he tries to make you come?"

Trent could only nod. He was torn by the desire to roll his hips deep into Mac and melting against Ian and letting him have his way. It was his present and past selves warring with each other, and he wasn't sure which one would come out on top.

Ian made the decision for him as he pulled back then thrust ahead hard. It was a bit rougher than Trent was used to, but it was also enough to drive him deep into Mac. He rocked his hips at the last minute, making sure to nail Mac's prostate. The movement made Ian flex inside him and drag against his own sensitive bundle.

"Fuck, Ian. Fuck us both and make us come," Trent groaned and let his head fall back so he could see the skylight above. It was dark outside, and a few of the brightest stars were shining through the perpetual city lights.

Ian gripped Trent's hips and proceeded to do just that. He held Trent still as he pulled back, dragging him along the last few inches so Trent's cock pulled from Mac. Then he slammed forward, burying himself and Trent brutally deep. With every thrust, Ian went harder and faster as he started to lose control. Trent could only grip Mac's hips and bring him up to meet every thrust.

Mac was the first to come, with his long cock spurting all over his belly in creamy streaks. He clamped down on Trent and nearly screamed as Trent's cock continued to piston inside, driven by Ian's steady thrusts.

Ian gripped Trent and hauled him back so his cock pulled from Mac's entrance. Trent nearly lost his breath as Ian bent him over, pushed his face into Mac's spend and thrust brutally into him from behind, pulling Trent's hips back to meet every stroke.

Trent clawed at the bed and arched his back, desperate to come but unable to with the ring still on his cock. He tried to reach for it, but his hands were occupied holding his sore face above Mac's toned belly.

Ian came in him with a rush of heat, and his cock seemed to swell even further as it hardened, stretching Trent to his maximum. He pulled out before he even finished coming and flipped Trent over as if he weighed nothing. Trent landed on his back, his legs going wide to give Ian better access as the condom and cock ring were ripped from his body and tossed across the room. He heard the ping of metal as it struck the wall.

Ian sucked him down to the root, then Trent was shooting. He gripped the sheets and gasped as his orgasm stole his breath away. Lips pressed against his own, too rough to be Ian's, but so good that he didn't care about the bruising along his lips. His chest burned for air, but the lips were persistent, delving deep and taking more than he had to offer.

His vision was starting to flutter by the time Mac pulled back, turning to Ian and pulling him in for the same brutal kiss. Trent groaned when Mac shared his essence with Ian. If he could have come again, he would have.

Ian winced and tried to pull back, but Mac grabbed the back of his neck, pushing his tongue deep into Ian's mouth as if he were trying to get every bit of Trent's taste. Trent's stomach sank and his vision snapped into place with sudden clarity.

He grabbed Mac's arm, gripping tight enough to bruise, before he pulled him away from Ian. If pain was the only thing that Mac understood, then that was exactly what he was going to get. The move pulled Mac off balance, and he tumbled from Ian's arms and onto the bed. He whirled as he landed, turning on Trent with one hand already clenched into a fist. He looked like a viper that was ready to strike out without any notice at all. He was always ready.

"Don't hurt him. Can't you see that you were hurting him?" Trent asked softly as he tried to calm the rage that was suddenly directed at him. Mac was worse than a landmine, and just as destructive. How would they ever survive him?

Mac paused, his body going tight as he turned back to his best friend. Ian's tongue was already out and tracing along his lower lip that was bright with fresh blood. He brought a finger to his lip and it came away red. Trent's lips throbbed in sympathy.

"I'm sorry, Ian. I just got carried away." Mac shook his head and shrugged, his hands settling loosely by his sides. There was no remorse in his gaze, just dismissal. It was the same dismissal that Trent had seen directed at Ian before, and the same that had nearly crushed his husband.

Trent reached for Mac, grabbing his arm in the exact same spot and digging into the forming bruises. "That's not good enough, Mac. If you are a part of this, you don't fucking hurt him — ever. They'll never find your fucking body if you do. You can't get carried away with something like this."

"T—" Ian started, but Trent cut him off.

"No, Ian," said Trent shaking his head and glaring at Mac. He tugged on the singer's arm, forcing him to meet his gaze. "I'm serious, Mac. You can let yourself go, but never get carried away again. Never hurt him."

"I get it," said Mac, tugging his arm free from Trent's grip much more easily than Trent would've thought. The singer moved to sit back on the bed but winced as his ass came into contact with the mattress.

"Speaking of not getting carried away," said Mac, reaching back to touch his loosened muscle and wincing again when he did. "Does it always hurt this much after?"

Trent shrugged, not about to apologise for giving the man everything he'd asked for. "You get used to it. I kinda like it now, actually. It reminds me how well I got fucked." He let his anger slip away and relished as

Mac winced again. Perhaps the hard fuck would humble the man just a bit.

He moved in close enough to touch Mac's lower abdomen, which was still sticky with cum and sweat. He followed the bump of the raised abdominal muscle, going lower to the strong cut of his groin.

"Ian's a lot bigger than I am, and if he'd fucked you, you'd feel it here too." He pushed on the spot on Mac's belly that mirrored the ache in his own. "I like that the best. When you can feel how deep inside he was and it makes you ache for days."

"Fuck, T," said Ian, kissing the back of Trent's neck and sliding a hand down Trent's abdomen to that same spot. "Can you really feel me there after?" He pushed harder against the spot and Trent let out a soft whimper as he nodded. He always felt so empty after Ian pulled out, and when he pushed against that spot, the sensation peaked and he could feel bursts behind his eyelids as they slid closed.

"And if you fuck me again while it still aches, sometimes I get so sore that I can't even sit straight in my chair," said Trent, stretching up to loop one arm over Ian's neck and pressing Ian's hand even harder to his belly. "If you fuck me just right, I can feel you there under my hand."

"Fuck," said Ian, humping against Trent's ass with his cock that was somehow still half-hard. "I don't want to hurt you, T." He eased his touch on Trent's belly and rubbed as if he could soothe the deep ache.

"I love it, Ian. I wish I could feel it every day. The harder you fuck me, the longer I feel it. And trust me, I want to feel it for days." Trent rocked back against Ian's cock as it brushed against his slick entrance. He could feel Mac's interested eyes on them, but Trent's focus was solely on Ian this time.

With one thrust, Ian was back inside him. Even though he wasn't fully hard yet, he still felt massive inside his walls that tightened so quickly. Trent clenched down harder as he rocked his hips back against Ian, doing everything he could to bring the man to full mast. He needed to show Ian what he did to him, and he needed Mac to watch. No matter what he said, he knew Ian would never push him too far and never hurt him. Mac needed to see that too.

His instinct was to fall forward so he was on his hands and knees, rolling back to each thrust as Ian gave it. But this time, he stretched up high against Ian, so his body looked longer and leaner than it actually was. He tilted his hips back to take Ian in as deep as possible and sucked in his stomach so his fine layer of softness disappeared.

Ian's hand was still on his belly, holding him tight, so Trent grabbed it and pushed it hard into his stomach. Low down, just above his pelvis, he could feel the very tip of Ian moving under his skin. When Ian drew back and Trent was left empty, the pressure disappeared under their hands. But as he thrust himself deep, he bumped against his own palm that was stretched across Trent's belly.

"Fuck, T, holy shit," said Ian as he rocked deep a few more times, just so he could feel himself. Trent tried to hold himself taut, but the position was terrible for both his hips and his back.

Trent let himself relax and flopped down to his elbows, looking over his shoulder to his husband. "Make me come, Ian."

He did.

Chapter Fifteen

Trent woke up much too warm for his liking and so tired that he could barely move. It was as if his limbs knew that it hadn't yet hit three o'clock in the morning, and they had no intention of waking up any time soon. It was dark too, with nothing but a dim glow through his closed eyelids.

He didn't even open his eyes, just grabbed the edge of his blanket and tossed it from his shoulders. The chill of the air conditioning struck his skin immediately, and he let out a sigh before turning over onto his side.

He was just on the edge of sleep, where he wasn't quite sure what was a figment of his imagination and what was real. There was a soft moan and he felt the blankets move over his hip, then down farther until they were at his knees. His limbs were so heavy, and the heat fluttered away, turning him stiff.

Now he was too cold, and the covers were out of reach of his fingertips. He tried to grab them with his toes, but the movement pushed them even farther down until they were past his calves. Goosebumps prickled along his skin as he tried to sink into the mattress and absorb the heat from it alone.

He snapped his eyes open at the sound of a second moan, deeper and louder than the first. It was definitely real, and the fog of his dream was getting farther and farther away. He blinked in the darkness, the only light a dim nightlight across the hall that Ian had installed after Trent had lost his way on a midnight trip to the bathroom. It gave off enough, though, that he could see the outline of the two other people in the bed with him.

It was no wonder that he had overheated. Ian and Mac were moving together in a steady rhythm with Ian on top as he thrust down onto the singer. Their lips smacked softly as they kissed, their arms entwined around each other in a passionate embrace. Mac leaned up into the kiss so delicately, looking as if he was finally taking every precaution to keep from harming Ian.

The sight had Trent smiling sleepily from ear to ear. The two of them were beautiful together. They were both powerful, but one was raw and wild, while the other was controlled and utterly dominant. They were also two of the sexiest men that Trent had ever met.

He reached out for Ian and skimmed a hand along his lower back. He was hot and damp with sweat and his muscles bunch under Trent's palm.

"T?" Ian's voice cut through the darkness as his hips stuttered to a stop. The light of two sets of dark eyes turned to him, so wide and alert in the wee hours.

"Mm-m," said Trent, too tired to form actual words. He ran his hand down and cupped one of Ian's cheeks, squeezing it in his weak grip. The globe flexed, a solid firmness built from endless days of swimming and drumming.

"You wanna join?" asked Ian, his voice clear and without a hint of sleepiness. Trent could tell how hard he was, just from the tone of his voice. He was close to coming — with a few more thrusts, the drummer would lose himself.

"Schleepy," said Trent, slurring his words as his eyes started to drift. He could see the smile on Mac's lips and hear the little laugh before his lids closed completely. The dream in the back of his mind snagged his thoughts and pulled him closer to sleep.

"He always this cute?" asked Mac, laughing again as Trent let out a small grunt.

"Just wait until you see him in the morning. He gets all ruffled the morning after a good fuck," said Ian.

The ass cheek under Trent's palm tensed as Ian started to move again and grind their cocks together. Trent squeezed once more before he slipped down to the mattress. He drifted off to the sounds of his lovers and the gentle rock of the bed.

* * * *

The next time he woke, the skylight was just starting to tint grey from the early hours of actual dawn. He was freezing cold, and without a single blanket over his entire body. He glanced around to see the entire ensemble of two sheets and a comforter pulled over the two sleeping men beside him, leaving him with nothing more than a pointed corner.

He pulled his legs up to his chest, stifling a grumble as the aches in his body made themselves known. He hadn't been exaggerating to Ian, and he would definitely be feeling the man for days, but there was more soreness in the rest of his body than usual. He poked at a muscle on the inside of his leg when it protested as he tried to stand from the bed. That part of him hadn't been sore in years.

"Crap," he said quietly, running his hands down his arms when they throbbed. "One gym membership, please. I need to get back in shape to improve my topping ability," he mumbled to himself as he slowly crossed the room and pulled on a pair of pyjama pants. He left his shirt off, ignoring the smear of dried cum on his belly, determined to deal with it later. There was a lot of scrubbing to be done, but he was also starving. Sex made him want to eat a ham sandwich. Good sex made him want to eat half of the pig.

He paused at the bedroom door and looked back at the two sleeping men. They weren't curled around each other like he'd expected, but sprawled wide, and barely touching on the huge mattress. Ian was on his front with his face buried in the pillow and the blanket pulled up to his neck. Mac, however, was on his side with his arm inverted and thrown over his face in a pose that looked anything but comfortable. Trent could see Mac's legs through the blankets, spread wide and stretched across the bed, and taking up more than his fair third of it.

Trent was expecting a mess when he came into the kitchen. He'd left a pot of curry on the stove and a lemon pie in the oven, along with several other back-up dishes, but everything had mysteriously disappeared. The bowls, the island and the dishes in the sink had magically been cleared, emptied and washed.

He eventually found the pie wrapped neatly in the fridge, looking only a touch drier than it should've — but still salvageable. To the side he saw a container of curry that had condensation under the lid. Someone had put it away when it was still warm from the stove.

He made a mental note to ask Ian if his house was cleaned by an actual ghost or if there was some kind of alarm system that told the cleaner when no one was around. Someone had been in the kitchen cleaning when he was fucking and getting fucked, and that bothered him more than just a bit. It also made him feel terrible for leaving such a huge mess for someone else.

"Rule number two," he said to himself as he searched for a frying pan, "dishes first, then sex. Nothing like Palmolive to get you in the mood." He searched through the fridge for ideas to make for breakfast, hoping he had enough for three people instead of just two. A thousand dollars' worth of groceries but still only a dozen eggs... He settled on something greasy and easy. It was dangerous to cook without a shirt, but one-hundred-percent necessary after the workout from the night before.

He paused, flicking off the burners as he heard a knock at the front door. It was the last sound he'd expected, especially so early in the morning. People here just tended to walk through the door without even announcing themselves. And everyone in town seemed to sleep until at least ten in the morning anyway.

He padded to the front door just as the knock came a second time, loud enough to rock it slightly on its solid hinges. He flicked the lock, grabbed the handle and pulled it open, looking over his shoulder at the same time to see if there was any movement on the staircase. Hopefully, the other men would continue to sleep, or they would be in for one hell of a sex hangover.

"What?" came a strangled gasp from the illuminated figure on the front porch.

Humid air swept over Trent's skin, reminding him that he was shirtless and absolutely filthy. There were at least two separate shots of cum splattered over his belly and clinging to the trail of hair leading down to his groin. The pyjama pants he'd chosen were loose and comfy but displayed every single love bite above his groin and the one in the hollow of his hip.

Brian's face came into view as Trent's eyes adjusted to the lower light. His mouth was hanging open and his eyes were wide as he looked Trent up and down. His gaze stopped at Trent's face, and the shock morphed into something else.

"You look like a hamburger patty, Trent," said Brian as he took a step forward into the light. He reached out, his hand hanging in the air for a moment before it dropped back down. The man looked like he hadn't seen his bed in the last twenty-four hours. His long hair hung limp and there were dark shadows under his eyes. "Who did this to you?"

"Um," said Trent, taking a step back so the doorway was clear. The air was thick outside, and he could feel the cold air from the house rushing past him. Brian stayed frozen on the porch, ignoring the welcoming gesture.

Trent didn't know how to answer that question. He didn't want to get Mac in trouble…period—not with the cops and not with his band mates. He also really didn't want to explain the copious amount of love bites, the bruised handprint on his hip or the flakes of dried cum on his belly. He'd already scarred Brian for life. He didn't want to send the man to therapy too.

"Trent, you don't have to take this," said Brian, his face going pale in the dim light. "I had no idea. Is he drinking again? Shit, I should have seen something like this coming. I'm so sorry." He shook his head, his greasy locks fluttering around his shoulders.

"Brian, it's not what you think," said Trent as he stepped back under the light. Why hadn't he grabbed a housecoat? There were probably twelve of them in Ian's closet. From the look on Brian's face, he knew he had said the wrong thing.

"You can't make excuses for him, Trent." Brian took a step forward and his hand touched Trent's naked shoulder. His gaze snapped down, as he finally noticed the filth that still clung to Trent's belly. "Shit, did he…? What else did he do to you, Trent?" His gaze was serious and the grip on Trent's shoulder turned tight.

"Brian, just come inside. Ian didn't hit me. I don't think he would, even if he was drunk," said Trent, letting out a long sigh. The hand dropped from his shoulder and he stepped back, letting Brian through and closing the door. He touched his hand to his face. It actually didn't even feel that bad anymore, but from his reflection in the glass, he really did look like a piece of hamburger — if it had been left out of the fridge well past its expiry. "He hasn't drunk anything since I've known him, and I think it will stay that way. He's trying, Brian, he really is, and he's a good man. The best person I know, actually." Trent turned away and started to walk to the kitchen. "I'm making breakfast if you wanted to join me."

"Don't lie for him, Trent," said Brian, following right behind him like a tiny but powerful wall. "You are the victim here, not him. Don't twist this and blame yourself. He beat you, then he rapes you and you're what? Up early making breakfast for him?" His voice grew louder with each step, echoing through the hall and the rest of the house.

"Brian, shut up," said Trent putting a finger to his lips, and glancing up the stairs to where the bedroom lay beyond. "You're not listening to me." The hall was still dark, and there was no movement above the stairs.

"Trent, you can come stay with me and we'll get this figured out." Brian reached for Trent's shoulder again, but this time Trent shrugged him off. His limited morning patience had just evaporated.

"Brian, you're a nice guy but fuck off." Trent crossed his arms as he tried to hide some of his body from view. It wasn't the love bites or the bruises that bothered him, but the fact that Brian was the second person to assume that Ian was in the wrong. Brian was supposed to be Ian's friend.

"Trent, you're a victim here and I can't trust what you say," said Brian, his voice echoing along the kitchen cupboards.

Trent ground his teeth together with a squeak, as he tried to keep a handle on his patience. He knew Brian was only trying to be a good guy, but combined with his helpless ignorance, it was annoying and frustrating. If his knuckles hadn't been so sore, Trent might've actually considered punching him.

Trent let out a sigh when he saw Ian stumble through the entrance to the kitchen, still rubbing sleep from his eyes like an adorable giant. He was at least wearing a shirt and pants, but he had the languid movement of the recently laid.

"What the hell, Brian? Why are you making so much noise?" asked Ian as he rubbed his hand over his face before dropping it to his side. His eyes were bloodshot and his split lip had cracked in his sleep so it was lined with thick red blood and swollen to twice its normal size. It would take forever for it to heal with two men kissing him now.

"He thinks you beat the shit out of me," said Trent as he leaned back against the counter and gripped the cold surface in his hands. Brian slid between them as if he could protect Trent from Ian.

"At least he got a hit in," said Brian, taking a step back until his back was almost against Trent. Trent held his ground and refused to budge as the man bumped against him. The scent of unwashed hair was overpowering.

"I explained to him that you didn't hit me or do anything else that I didn't want, but apparently, he's deaf." Trent rolled his eyes and pulled himself out from behind the shorter man. Brian bristled like a cat, his shoulders coming up around his ears as he glared at both of them. Trent couldn't help but feel a little bit guilty.

"Well, if it wasn't Ian, then who was it? And who hit you, Ian?" Brian took another step back until he was pressed against the countertop. For trying to protect Trent, he was doing a pretty pathetic job. Granted, he wouldn't survive that fight.

"Technically, I did that," said Trent as he strode up to Ian, placing a finger gently against the cut. "Does it hurt this morning, or is it okay?" The swelling looked worse than the previous day, but the cut itself was smaller, despite the repeated trauma.

"S'fine, T," said Ian shortly, glaring right back at Brian. He was calm but also ready for the fight that would inevitably break out.

"Have I ever told you that your friends are kinda assholes?" Trent asked loud enough for Brian to hear. "It's a good thing you are loyal, because they would all be out on their asses if you weren't." Trent shook his head and reached into the fridge, pulling out the eggs and a few onions.

"He's just looking out for you, T," said Ian, speaking as if Brian wasn't right in the room with them. "Right, Brian?" His voice was tight, leaving no room for argument. It was honestly terrifying for Trent to watch. He could imagine Ian with a few too many drinks, and that same calm, unyielding voice. No one would ever be able to say no. And if they did…? Well…

Brian paled under the look and shifted against the cupboards. Trent could see his mind whirling behind his poorly constructed mask of bravado. It looked like Brian wasn't about to give in, but he also didn't want to end up with the same decorations as Trent.

"Who hurt him?" asked Brian, his gaze dropping as he scuffed his feet against the floor. He was still in his running shoes, and bits of dirt were spreading across the kitchen tile. *Just another mess for the invisible maid.*

"I did," said Mac as he appeared at the doorway. His eyes were even more bloodshot than Ian's, and the dark bruises under them looked that much worse against his pale skin. The bruises had started to heal, and the green and purple stains made him look perpetually nauseated. He was wearing one of Ian's hoodies that practically dwarfed him, and a pair of Trent's sleep pants that were too wide and too long for his legs.

Brian choked as his gaze went from the massive hickey on Mac's neck to Trent's ensemble, then to Ian, who had flushed bright red as soon as Mac had appeared. His eyebrows hit his hairline as relief carved across his face.

"Well, I actually came to find you, Mac. You were supposed to call me yesterday with the tour dates, but

I never heard back. I see now that you were busy." His eyebrows went higher as he took in the three of them again. "I'm glad you finally worked your shit out. This romcom has been a long time coming. I didn't realize it would have a bonus feature too."

Trent snorted and turned the stove back on as Brian started to leave the kitchen. "Brian, wait," Trent called across the room. The man paused, his limp hair swinging about his shoulders. "Do me a favour and never work with victims. You would just scare the shit out of them."

Chapter Sixteen

"When does the tour start up again, Mac?" Trent asked as he handed off a pile of eggs heaped over hash browns. Mac was the manager, after all, on top of being the singer and the front man of the band. They'd released their latest album a month before Ian and Trent's wedding, which had been right on the heels of their last tour. They were one of the hardest-working bands that Trent had ever heard of.

He grabbed the syrup out of the fridge and cringed at the bottle. "You'll have to deal with this crapola on top. I couldn't find real maple syrup anywhere." There were a few ingredients listed that he couldn't pronounce, but the main ones were liquid sugar, water and artificial flavours... Yum.

"That *is* maple syrup," said Ian, grabbing the bottle and pouring a generous squirt over the heap of food on his plate. He handed the bottle to Mac, who set it in the middle of the table before he dug into the pile of breakfast.

"I thought I taught you better than that, Ian," said Trent, shaking his head. "There's a reason that my French toast is literally heaven on earth, and that's because it's topped with actual maple syrup that came from a tree. I'm gonna have to smuggle some down here, because I cannot deal with this stuff." He grabbed the bottle and took a sniff before setting it back down. It smelled like corn syrup with a hint of maple flavouring—and was definitely not a part of his complete breakfast.

"Ketchup will have to do. I'm glad you have that, even if you don't have ketchup chips or all dressed. I'll just bring one suitcase of food next time." Trent grabbed the ketchup out of the fridge and squirted a dollop on top before he passed the bottle to Mac. It ended up in the middle of the table next to the syrup.

"It's good," said Mac as he dug in without looking up. He curled his arm around the plate and hunched his shoulders protectively over it. Ian's fork shot out a second later and grabbed a stray piece of egg from Mac's plate before he plopped it into his mouth.

"It's better with the syrup," said Ian, smiling as Mac smacked away his fork and curled farther over his plate. Ian's fork jabbed at Trent's ketchup-covered array next, and the drummer hummed as he sucked it from his fork.

"So, I know it's early, but we should probably talk about last night," said Trent, glancing around the table, and still very aware of how truly defiled he looked in front of the other two. He was definitely the one who'd got the most sleep, but he knew he would back out if they didn't have this conversation now.

Ian kept eating, but Mac had paused his fork on the plate, twirling a hash brown through the yellow yolk.

It was runny, pale and tasteless, and nothing like the rich eggs from Trent's backyard hens.

"You think it was a mistake?" asked Mac, as he avoided their gazes. His broken nose looked worse from this angle, with the entire bridge black and blue. Trent couldn't help but feel the tiniest bit guilty about it. A *very* tiny bit.

"Do you?" asked Trent, reflecting the question right back. Mac was an enigma to him, and he needed to know what the other man was thinking. One moment Mac would be wild and untameable, where the next he was professional and considerate. There didn't seem to be a middle ground.

"I don't know how you think this is going to work," said Mac, moving his food over to the right side of his plate. "You and Ian are married, and I know I'm just a third wheel. I don't want to ruin what you guys have, but I don't want to give this up, either. Maybe it was a mistake, but it was a good one."

"You're not a third wheel, Mac," said Ian, reaching out to squeeze Mac's shoulder. The singer finally looked up, meeting Trent's gaze with bloodshot eyes.

"If anyone should feel like a third wheel, it's me," said Trent, turning and locking eyes with Ian as he spoke. "I know you love me, Ian, but I don't know if I can make you happy." The drummer drew back, looking startled, but Trent ploughed on, not willing to stop until he was finished. "I mean, where are we supposed to live? And what happens when you go back on tour? I can't keep getting in the way of your life and career, and I can't stay in this huge house with only myself and the ghost maid. Mac can be with you when you're on tour, though, and when you come back too. He can be there for you when I can't, and when a phone

call just isn't good enough. He can take care of your..."
Trent took a deep breath. "Your needs. I think what
happened last night was the best thing that could've
happened for you, and I think you should embrace it."

Silence settled on the kitchen, and even Trent's
heartbeat seemed quiet in his ears. A tension settled
over them as he waited for his heart to break forever,
knowing that he loved this man more than anything in
the world, but maybe they just weren't meant to be
together. Could he live without Ian? Yes, he could. But
that didn't mean that he wanted to.

The strain snapped as Ian stood from his chair,
pushing it so hard that it clattered back to the floor from
the force. Trent found himself standing and even taking
a step back as a furious Ian strode to him, gripping his
arms hard enough that he let out a gasp.

"Brian was right, T," said Ian, his voice low and
dangerous. "I'm gonna beat the crap out of you. If you
keep talking like that, like you mean nothing to me,
then I'm gonna have to smack some sense into you. I
love you. Don't you get that? I fucking love you, no
matter where you are in the world or what you are
doing."

"I should go," said Mac, suddenly lifting himself
from his chair, his breakfast forgotten and cooling on
the plate.

"You sit the fuck down. I'm not done with you
either," said Ian as he finally started to lose control of
his rage. Trent could feel it in the strength of the man's
hands on him and the tremble in his arms. His eyes
were wet, though, and he looked like Trent had
betrayed him beyond consolation.

"The three of us are staying together and that's final.
Mac, I know you're attracted to Trent, and I also know

that you won't be able to stop yourself from loving him a little more every day. Trent, I know you think you're trying to do what's best, but you are an idiot and you're thinking with your head and not your heart."

"Okay," said Trent, dropping the façade that he had been trying his best to hold on to. He broke out into a grin that was so broad that it actually hurt. "I'm so glad to hear you say that."

"Wait." Ian pulled back and dropped his hands, his forehead furrowing as he looked at Trent's joyous face. "Was this some kind of test?"

"Yep," said Trent with his smile going even broader as Mac let out a weak chuckle.

"You're an asshole," said Ian as he let out a huff, breaking out in a grin of his own. His entire body relaxed, his shoulders slumping and the wrinkle between his brows smoothing out.

"Yep," Trent replied, "but I do have one thing to add. I've been thinking about it over the last few days and I think I do want to stay here." He put his hand up as Ian gasped. "Not all the time, but half the year. If I stay six months here and six months in Canada, I can keep my citizenship, then you can tour in the off-months." He looked to Mac.

"If you let me know ahead of time, I can work around your schedule and be here when you're here. I was already looking around for a job, and there are a few places that look like they would take me seasonally." The help-wanted sign in the seafood restaurant had started his mind on a train that just couldn't be derailed.

He paused when he realized that the other two were still staring him with utter disbelief. "Is that okay?" He wasn't really sure what to think with the oppressive silence, but his stomach started to wind up tighter.

"Ian said you were cute in the morning, but I was thinking more along the lines of grumpy and ruffled, not chipper and revolutionary," said Mac as he shook his head.

"I do *not* get grumpy," said Trent, defensively crossing his arms. "I get pissed at the world before ten a.m., but the world has been really good to me for the last twenty-four hours and I thought I would return the favour."

"I want to ask you something, and don't punch me again," said Mac. He ran a finger along his nose, wincing when he lightly touched the bruises. "What happens when Ian fucks me at a hotel in Vegas? Are you going to break my legs?" There was a small smile that tugged at the edges of his lips as he asked, as if Trent could actually do that to him. Both of them knew Trent didn't stand a chance in a fight if he didn't have the element of surprise.

Trent looked at Ian, really looked at him for the first time that morning. As long as he'd known Ian, there had been a crease between his eyes that spoke of the stress hiding just beneath the surface of his skin. For the first time, his face was smooth and completely relaxed. He knew that this was how things were meant to be.

"If you would've asked me three days ago, I would've told you that your broken legs would be the least of your problems, but I'm not sure now." Trent paused and searched every inch of himself for jealousy or concern. He imagined the two of them together, grinding and fucking in a hotel while he sat at home alone under a foot and a half of snow. It didn't hurt as much as it made loneliness seep in like the frost on the walls of his house.

"I don't think it would bother me knowing that you were together, as long as you didn't hurt Ian in any way. I think it might get lonely at home, though, knowing that you are together and I'm so far away." A stab went through his chest as he thought of six months without Ian...and Mac—but mostly Ian, if he was completely honest with himself. Mac was attractive, and Trent could see himself falling for the singer, but only if Mac could pull his head out of his ass.

"I guess I don't know what to do," said Trent, "not really anyway. I just wanted to at least try to make this work. I can deal with being alone for six months." Could he actually, though? He wasn't so sure he would be able to follow through without some kind of breakdown. At least he would have Candace and his family to fall back on when he was at his lowest point.

"The only thing I'm afraid of is that you'll come back from six months together and you'll figure out that you don't need me anymore." He put up his hand again before Ian could speak. "What you have is new and exciting, but our relationship is new, too. Don't leave me in the mud, okay? I'll never be able to find my way out again."

"We won't," said Mac, staring at Ian and Trent as he stood and moved around the table. He put an arm around Trent's neck and pulled him up into a kiss. The first touch was fierce and wild, and much harder than it should've been, but then Mac seemed to remember himself. His lips softened against Trent's, and he relaxed his arm so the touch was soft and almost gentle, probably as gentle as Mac was capable of.

"I'll make you a deal," said Mac as he pulled back and took a breath. "While we're away, we can only do things that we've done with the three of us together. Nothing new while the third person isn't present, so we can share each step. That way no one gets left behind." He kissed Trent again, deeper and longer, until Trent's lungs were screaming for air.

"Do I get any say in this?" asked Ian. His husband had been silent up until that point, but Trent knew better than to think he wouldn't make his wishes known. Sometimes Ian took his time to reply, but when he did, he expected everyone to listen — which they always seemed to do.

"Nah, we've got it covered," Mac joked, letting out a small laugh as Ian frowned. Okay, so maybe Mac wasn't much of a listener. Trent poked the singer in the ribs, silencing him.

"I had something to say but looking at the two of you together… Well, now it's gone." Ian broke out into a smile, coming close and placing a sweet kiss on Trent's, then Mac's lips. "But having you both here with me sounds like the best thing in the world."

"As long as we don't kill each other," said Trent, smirking as Mac subconsciously touched his nose. Mac reached up and gently poked the bruise beneath Trent's eye in retaliation. It was still sensitive to the touch, but not the hair-splitting ache that had made him near-delirious before.

"Truce?" asked Mac, putting his hand up.

Trent nodded, ready to jump in with both feet and a blindfold. Ian was worth it, after all, and Mac might just be as well.

"Truce."

Want to see more from this author? Here's a taster for you to enjoy!

Karma's Kiss
M.C. Roth

Excerpt

"No. No. No," said Zack as he pushed the gas pedal all the way to the floor. The ancient car responded sluggishly, a full second passing before the engine vibrated with a purr that made his foot go numb. The bald tyres spun, trapped in a sheen of ice and snow that coated the road and the lone vehicle.

The storm sagged against the windshield as the wipers tired lethargically to keep up, leaving large, frosted streaks with every swipe. With each pass, the ice crystals grew denser, coating the wipers with budding globes of ice.

Another burst of wind battered the side of the car, fluttering against the door and buffeting the tiny cracks in the vehicle. A trickle of cold air brushed against his chilled knuckles, and a shiver cascaded though his body.

The vehicle lurched closer to the ditch that had disappeared into the blizzard's cloud. The tyres caught, edging sideways in a frozen rut. He jerked at the steering wheel, but there was no response as he was buried deeper in the drifts.

Zack's heart pounded as he lost control of the wheel and the engine sputtered. But he barely noticed as the car lurched into a stall or as the air got even colder through the flimsy heating vents. The storm was the furthest thing from his mind.

It had happened again. And, of course, *it* had chosen the moment when the biggest snowstorm of the decade was blowing its way across the lakes. The radar had probably gone from red to purple then black while he'd driven with no destination in mind.

The roads had been relatively clear a few hours before, when he had fled to his car, putting it straight into second gear before he even had his seat belt on. He had hit the highway, flipping a virtual coin to choose the exit he'd take before the heavy flakes had started drifting down from the grey sky.

He shuddered. His darkness — his curse — the thing had haunted him for as long as he could remember... It always seemed to choose the worst moments to rear its ugly, jealous head. This had to be one of the top five, though.

He had tried to keep moving. He'd tried to leave before he could put anyone else at risk.

But he'd been sucked in by another pair of sweet blue eyes and a soft voice that had promised him a good night. That night had turned into a stream of great weeks and gentle touches that had him coming more consistently than he ever had.

The sex had been fantastic, if not a little bit soft, more often ending in their mouth or his hand — and not somewhere better, tighter and hotter. His nights hadn't been cold in an empty hotel bed or on a couch that he had claimed during a stranger's party. He had started to look forward to waking up in the morning and seeing someone other than himself in his bed.

But then it had all gone wrong. One word and a spurned rejection, and his past had caught up with him with the force of a starving tiger. He'd staggered as he'd felt the blood drain from his face.

He had fled before anything could happen to the man who he had almost started to like. If he'd had the opportunity, he could have developed full-blown feelings, which were more dangerous than his curse.

He'd grabbed everything in sight that belonged to him, leaving more behind than he'd taken. His socks and underwear were lost beneath the bed and in the basket of laundry, but he hadn't had the time to retrieve them. They weren't the worst things that he'd ever left behind.

He'd had run to his ancient Honda, breathing hard by the time he had tugged the door open. As he sped away, he'd left another chunk of his past behind him, the sweet memories tainted by his bitter curse. The traffic had steadily thinned, until he was the only car in the midst of a forest that seconded as a snowy hell.

His trusty Honda was only five years younger than him and had more problems than he did, which was saying a lot. Its most recent issue was that it apparently couldn't drive through more than two centimetres of fresh snow.

He fumbled with the key, glancing out into the bleak stretch of swirling snow as he tried to start the engine yet again. Stomping on the gas, he waited for the RPMs to climb into the red zone before popping the clutch and putting the car directly into second gear. First gear didn't exactly work, and on ice, it was its own death trap.

There was a shuddering jerk that had relief flooding his gut, until the car rocked once and stalled into silence. The dials dropped and the fuzzy radio station faded until the barest hint of the country song vanished under the sound of the wind.

"Shit," he said as he slammed his hand against the steering wheel. It shuddered, barely holding on to its rigging after his repeated abuse. He could imagine the wheel finally tumbling off as he merged lanes on a highway doing one-hundred-and-thirty-five kilometres per hour. *I'm lucky like that.*

His palm ached from the hit and the cold that was steadily seeping into the car, but it didn't stop him from slamming the wheel a second time. His thumb caught the edge of the horn, but the blaring sound was swept away on the wind.

The inside of the car noticeably dropped another few degrees, and his breath turned into a misty fog that coated everything it touched. The car's heater was lukewarm at best, and without a working defrost, ice had started to crust on even the inside of the windshield.

He turned the key again as he popped the car back into neutral and pushed the clutch to the floor. He shivered as another gust of wind cut into the Honda. His thin jacket was best suited for balmy fall days, but it was the only one that had been in sight as he'd scrambled to leave. His toes were numb in his sneakers, and his hands? Well, he was afraid to look at them, because he wouldn't be surprised if a few fingers were missing. His gloves had been one of the many things that he had left behind, and his hands had been aching since the snow had started.

The car key turned under his hand, jingling with the other attached keys and mementos that he had picked up in his travels. There was a tiny metal sandal that he'd picked up in a beach town and an iron sun from a gift shop that he'd found in the middle of nowhere. The rest were worn, their edges smooth from their constant motion. He kept them close, so he wouldn't have to look back and remember.

The key turned, with the promise of escape and a hint of heat. *Silence*. Not even a putter from the flooded engine. His gut churned as a shiver racked his body. It was so freaking cold, and according to the last clear announcement on the radio, the storm was just getting started.

He grappled with the horn, pushing the button as hard as he could. There had to be someone close by who would come to his rescue if they heard him honking. People in the city might not have looked twice, but he was pretty far into the wilderness, on the only road that probably ever saw a plow in winter. People were different out here — lonelier.

The button clicked under his palm as the battery finally gave out. The same battery had lasted him twenty years. Of course, it would choose to fail him when he was about to lose his toes.

Zack took a shuddering breath as his vision blurred and his heart sank. He wrapped his arms around himself, trying to keep the warmth from escaping. Perhaps everything was finally catching up with him. Freezing to death wouldn't be the worst way to go. He'd seen worse before — so much worse. His stomach clenched as memories fluttered to the surface of his mind. He tried to push them away before he could retch.

"Look at the snow. Just look at the snow," he said, holding himself tighter as he tried to focus on an individual flake in the whirling mass — anything to leave the flashes of his past behind.

Beyond the window he could see bits of the forest through the gaps in the gathering ice on the windshield. The road was nearly invisible, with no tyre tracks except his own behind him. Even those were almost gone now.

A green bough fluttered in the wind, dumping its heavy load onto the ground below it. A bird fluttered from the branch, battling against the wind as it took off. For a moment, it looked like it would lose the fight and be tossed into the nearest trunk. It pumped its wings faster, finally triumphing over the storm.

There were no hydro lines along the road or lamp posts that would guide a traveller along at night. It was a tourist's nightmare. He cursed himself, wondering if he should've taken the other fork in the road that had probably led along a path that was closer to the city.

A smudge of colour caught his eye as it flashed along the very edge of the trees. The trunks grew close together, dark and foreboding within the mass, and their limbs danced and swayed in the wind, dumping the snow back to the earth with each pass. There was so much movement that he wondered if he had imagined the blur.

He squinted and leaned closer to the window, trying to make sense of it through the fluttering snow. It could have been a deer. He'd already seen a few along the way, looking ready to jump out at his car and double his insurance. Or it could have been a bear with how far he'd come, although he'd only ever seen them on television. The dark beacon had looked too small to be the creature he'd seen on *Planet Earth*.

He spotted it again as the wind stilled and the blizzard cleared for a moment. It moved through the snow with a fluid grace that could only belong to an animal who could survive a harsh winter. Nothing battered or beaten could survive this cold, and no predator could live without hunting in the perpetual storm that was February.

It grew closer with every loping step, until it seemed larger than what he imagined a bear would be. It was fast, too, cutting through the drifts as if it weighed nothing. Zack knew how hard it was to walk through snow that deep, which was why he usually avoided it at all costs. That, and he really didn't want to get his too-tight jeans wet.

Zack scrubbed the inside of the window with his fingernails, bits of ice stinging his numb fingertips. His breath frosted it over again, until everything blurred.

It could have been a dog with how dark the colouring was, but he'd never seen a dog that big. A bear would definitely make more sense, but according to the television, bears hibernated in the winter.

The ice on the window thickened into an opaque crystal as he pressed his forehead against it, desperate to see what was coming. It was running at a pace that was hardly possible over the covered ground, gliding over the snow without seeming to disturb it at all.

A bubble of fear simmered in his gut as he pictured a bear breaking through his window with its massive, clawed paws. He was small enough that he wouldn't be able to put up much of a fight, but there was still enough meat on him to make a decent meal, he supposed.

He took a deep breath, closing his eyes to try to ground himself. The wind around him paused, the car going suddenly still and silent. He snapped his eyes back open, looking through the tiny gaps from his fingertips. There was nothing but the dark tree trunks capped with pure white.

The seat creaked as he freed himself from the seatbelt and lifted himself to his knees, pressing against a strip of clear glass. He blinked, rubbing his eyes to clear the imagined fog, but nothing appeared. The snow was undisturbed, except for the partially covered ruts from his own tyres. There were no footprints, and no animal was out in the wind.

I'm officially losing my mind.

A loud knock sounded directly behind him, pushing a small scream through his lips. He slapped his hand over his mouth, muffling the noise as it battered his ears in the small space. He whirled around in his seat, his heart pounding as he spied something on the other side of the car. Whatever it was, it blocked the entire passenger-side window with its bulk.

The knock came again, a booming slam against the fragile window. It sent a shiver up his spine and straight to his core. How had anyone found him so fast? The road was deserted, and no one should have been able to hear the scream of his horn over the wind.

It could still be a bear. They were probably smart enough to knock. They could outsmart bees, for Christ's sake.

After a third knock, he stretched over the centre console to move closer, folding his legs up to his chest one by one so he could slide into the opposite seat. A muscle in his side twinged from the stretch, worse than any awkward position he'd been manhandled into.

The ice was thinner on this side, and he could see the outline of a dark shape but no details through the crystalized fog. It could have been anyone, or anything, but the knock was too loud and too annoying to ignore.

The handle was stiff as he pulled it, bracing against the wind as it surged again. The gust curled around door, ripping it from his grasp and flinging it wide with a crunch of metal. The shadow stepped back as the squall cut into the car with the strength of an iceberg, stealing the breath from his lips and sucking the remaining warmth from his limbs.

The shadow moved back into view, leaning down to peer at his prone body. It was nearly as wide as it was tall and took up the entire doorway, thankfully blocking the majority of the cruel wind.

Zack was able to get his first real look. It was completely covered in thick, dark fur, the strands clumped together with clinging snow and ice. He couldn't see a face, but his imagination created one for him, with snarling teeth that were whiter than the snow.

Zack's heart raced. It had to be a bear. *Why did I open the door for* that?

He took a deep breath, choking on the scent of wet fur, so similar to that of his childhood dog Max when he'd wandered out into the rain. It also brought him a strange sense of calm that he hadn't expected. It, at least, was familiar.

He gasped as gold eyes pinned him. They weren't yellow, or jaundiced, but a glowing gold that almost seemed to resonate as they stared at him, unblinking.

He swallowed, his mouth dry and his throat clicking. It wasn't a bear at all—or even an animal. It was a man. He was covered in furs like some sort of reincarnated caveman, and his face was shadowed beneath a thick hood. His eyes were the only thing Zack could see through the gloom.

"Are you okay?" the stranger asked as he leaned into the car, blocking more of the wind with his bulk. His eyes weren't just gold, they were molten, drawing Zack in and stealing his breath. The scent of pine and woodsmoke clung to him, beneath the film of wet dog. His hands were wrapped in rough-looking leather that was cracked from either age or overuse, but the rest of him was hidden beneath the dark furs.

"I'm fine," said Zack trying to keep his voice even. His heart was still thundering, but he could breathe again. An alarm was blaring in his head, and he suppressed the urge to reach for his keys. The car wouldn't start anyway.

He gripped his hands into fists to resist pushing the stranger away. He had to get out of there. He didn't want anyone else to get hurt.

A glint of white caught the light as the stranger pulled his lips back over his teeth and a low chuckle reverberated from his broad chest. "You don't look okay. This storm is going to last for a few days, and it'll take even longer than that to get the roads cleared. You shouldn't be out here in the first place. Are you an idiot, or are you just trying to get yourself killed?"

The gold eyes narrowed and Zack's heart beat so hard that his vision swam. The insult didn't matter to him, even though it made the hair stand on the back of his neck. It didn't matter to *him*, but it would matter to his curse.

The last time someone had called him an idiot, they'd ended up with two broken wrists. Zack had started running shortly after — once every offhand and cruel remark threatened the people close to him.

Zack tried to look past the man's bulk, to the threats that could be looming from outside the car. The man could freeze in the storm, or a tree could collapse on top of him. It would seem like an accident...or a coincidence. It was always something that could happen to anyone that was unlucky enough.

He clenched his eyes shut and gripped the seat, waiting for the man to be maimed or injured. He knew it would happen quickly and without mercy. It always did.

He took one breath, then two, sinking deep into his core until he could hardly feel the cold. The shivering that racked his body ceased, and the ache drained from his fingers. Maybe his curse would take him this time, too, and put him out of his misery.

"Okay, now I know you aren't okay." The stranger's voice came again, so low and quiet against the rumble of the wind. Zack opened his eyes and met the glaring gold. He was watching Zack as if there were no storm around them at all — as if it were just the two of them in the world and they had nothing to fear.

Zack looked down at his trembling hands, the ache rushing back into them as he stared in disbelief.

The stranger was still alive. *How is he still here, looking at me like I have three heads?* He should be on the ground, twisted in some unimaginable way for the simple crime of calling Zack an idiot.

Zack reached for the stranger, tangling his fingers in the rough furs. They were stiff and coarse beneath his frozen nerves and so cold that it made him shudder. A clump of ice crumbled in his hand, and the pieces slipped down the sleeve of his jacket like tiny razor blades.

"How?" The word caught in Zack's throat as a sob tore from his chest. His vision blurred and his breath caught. *It isn't possible.*

"Here… Let me help you. I won't hurt you," said the stranger, speaking slowly as if Zack would try to run at any moment. His bulk blocked the rest of the wind, and the scent of pine, smoke and something else peaking as he leaned close. He wrapped his arms around Zack's waist and half-lifted, half-dragged him from the seat.

The fury of the storm beat at Zack's face, blinding him and bludgeoning his ears in a whirling roar. He tried to cry out as the needles of ice sharpened on his skin, but the sound was torn away. He could hardly breathe, even as his lungs begged for air.

He could never have imagined that winter could be like this. Winter for him meant sitting by a baseboard heater and looking through the glass window, complaining about the snow and the cold. It was about wearing so many layers that he looked like he had indulged in too many Tim Tam Slams, and it was about a perpetual howling wind that cut through the naked trees and narrow buildings.

This wasn't winter. It was an icy hell.

Zack's feet sank into the snow as the stranger tried to right him, and cold spilled over his old sneakers that had seen too many days. The tight green laces did nothing to protect him from the slithering crystals that slid up his pants and along his ankles, making his bones throb in protest. His feet were soaked in seconds.

The stranger's grip disappeared, and Zack fell against the Honda's unforgiving frame. It was the lightest shade of blue that would meld with the sky as he drove along on a fresh summer's day. Now, the same blue looked as frigid as his fingertips.

His face thudded against the roof as he lost his balance, his feet slipping on snow and ice as the taste of copper burst over his tongue, deep and rich, like sweet pennies. He thudded back into a drift, a spurt of fluff rising as he landed.

"Shit. Okay then," said the stranger as he hauled Zack back onto his feet before lifting him from the ground. He didn't even grunt or show any strain at all. He simply lifted him as if Zack weighed nothing, as if Zack were a child and not a man.

The man turned and started to walk, each step taking them farther from Zack's car and his only real safe-haven. No matter what had gone down in the world, he'd always had his car to get away. Leaving it behind was like leaving his best friend, but he couldn't say anything, not when he was trembling so hard.

The man's feet glided over the snow, hardly sinking into the crunching powder and barely leaving a mark between the blowing drifts. His breath was silent, only a whisper of fog that filtered from his hood before it was swept away.

Zack had never been swept off his feet before, but now that the danger had seemed to pass, he was definitely on board. The stranger's body was hard and strong, his hands large and firm where they gripped under his legs and around his shoulders. Zack wasn't quite sure where to put *his* hands, or if he could even grip them with how numb they felt, so he held them against his chest.

They moved down an unploughed road that had drifts that looked like they would be up to his waist. There was barely enough room for a small car, and every side was blocked by impenetrable forest. The trees themselves were thick with curled bark that was wounded from age. It was no wonder that he hadn't even noticed the lane. It didn't look like it had been travelled for the entire winter.

Zack's eyelids sagged as his adrenalin finally started to fade, causing him to relax into the stranger's chest. There had to be something different about the man. He was the only person Zack had ever met who had been able to resist the power of his curse.

He snuggled into the warmth of the furs, shielding himself from the blowing snow that covered the man's footprints almost as fast as he could make them. Hopefully, he could still find the lane when it came time to leave. But right now, he just wanted to be warm again.

A tiny and haphazard-looking log cabin appeared out of the haze. It was a small and simple one-story that had been carved out of logs stripped of their life and their bark. It was nothing like the beautiful identical logs that made up the cabins he'd seen before in magazines. This was rugged, like someone with no construction experience had attempted their first DIY and had managed to pull it off.

Smoke rose from the rough chimney, tossing the sweet smell of burning wood around the tiny clearing. It was the same scent that clung to the furs that were pressed against his cheek. The porch was unshoveled and heaped with snow, and the windows were dark and ominous.

It was unlike anything Zack had seen during his travels. He'd also never been half-kidnapped by someone in a snowstorm. Why couldn't it have been a billionaire who had happened upon him on the road? *Probably because they would have mobile data and weather reports, so they wouldn't be out in the first place.*

They crossed the threshold like a married couple, and Zack half-expected to be tossed on a bed and ravaged. He wouldn't have even minded at the moment. It would get him dry and so much warmer than he was now, and his standards weren't exactly high after looking for new places to stay for years. The stranger had beautiful eyes and was strong as hell. Those were two out of the three boxes that Zack wanted checked for a good lay. Most days, he only required one.

A wave of heat engulfed him as the stranger stepped inside the cabin and closed the thick wooden door, locking a latch that rattled harshly in the wind. Prickling struck Zack's face first, before singeing his fingers and toes. The snow that had gathered on his hair melted and poured over his face to drip on the scraped wood floor beneath them.

The cabin was simple on the inside too, almost shockingly so. Zack had lived in small places before, if rent prices had run too high to cover with the odd jobs he took to avoid touching his trust fund. But he had never had to subject himself to something this depressing. Even the nights that he'd slept in stranger's homes hadn't been quite so bad, because he knew that at some point he would be sleeping in a real bed again.

There was only one room — one perfectly square room that encased everything that someone needed to *survive*. The walls were stark wood logs that had something stuffed between them, keeping the wind and light at bay. The roaring fire flickered in an open hearth that had no barrier between itself and the rest of the room. It looked like the biggest fire hazard Zack had ever seen.

To the left of that, there was a kitchen that would have fit in a tiny home catalogue, with a single silver sink and a cupboard above and below it. Beyond that was a bed that was little more than a box spring and mattress on the floor, covered with a single fur blanket that looked similar to what the stranger was wearing.

But beside the bed was the worst part of it all. There was a toilet and a small shower only feet from the front door and the bed. There were no walls separating them from the rest of the cabin — and certainly no door. The shower didn't even have a curtain. It was just an expanse of white over a tiled slab floor that had a drain in the centre. *And is that a watering can hanging from a hook at the top where a showerhead should be?*

"It'll be best if you take your clothes off before you sit in front of the fire. Everything is soaked from the storm, and there's still a chance of hypothermia if you sit around in something wet." The stranger made it sound like it was the most natural thing, to strip down naked in front of someone he didn't know. *This isn't a club or a frat party.*

Maybe it *was* natural for a man who was missing the 'room' in bathroom?

"I…" Zack paused, not sure what to say as he was lowered slowly to his feet. He dropped his hands when he realized that he was still holding onto the furs. He wasn't sure if he should thank the man, slap him or follow his directions.

"There should be some clothes by the bed that are clean. They won't fit you, but they'll be dry," said the stranger, cutting off Zack's whirling thoughts.

His feet were truly aching now and starting to throb in time with his heart. The idea of getting naked sounded better with every chunk of snow that melted and wicked into his jacket. It's not like he was bad off in the looks department, but he was very cold. He looked down at his groin. There wouldn't be much there to look at if the stranger watched him undress.

He looked around the cabin once more, searching for anyplace he could hide his dignity. Even a curtain would do, since there wasn't a door in sight except for the one that led outside. The windows hung bare. There wasn't even a rod above them.

Who the hell is this guy? Even preppers have curtains.

He looked up from his internal debate as the door swung open again, snagging the heat from the room and chilling the water that had started to warm on his skin. The stranger took two steps out of the door, looking back over his shoulder with his eyes flashing in the blinding storm.

"I'll get your car off the road so it doesn't get wrecked by the next plough."

The door slammed and the storm retreated to the warmth of a crackling fire and the freezing dampness of his clothing. His shivering started again, and his teeth chattered so hard that he thought he might chip one.

He looked at the door, staring after the stranger and trying desperately to understand. Under the layers of sodden clothing and shivering skin, something bloomed in his chest that he hadn't dared feel since he had been a small boy with ambitions of taking on the world.

Hope.

PUBLISHING

Sign up for our newsletter and find out about all our romance book releases, eBook sales and promotions, sneak peeks and FREE romance books!

About the Author

M.C. Roth lives in Canada and loves every season, even the dreaded Canadian winter. She graduated with honours from the Associate Diploma Program in Veterinary Technology at the University of Guelph before choosing a different career path.

Between caring for her young son, spending time with her husband, and feeding treats to her menagerie of animals, she still spends every spare second devoted to her passion for writing.

She loves growing peppers that are hot enough to make grown men cry, but she doesn't like spicy food herself. Her favourite thing, other than writing of course, is to find a quiet place in the wilderness and listen to the birds while dreaming about the gorgeous men in her head.

M.C. Roth loves to hear from readers. You can find her contact information, website details and author profile page at https://www.pride-publishing.com

www.ingramcontent.com/pod-product-compliance
Lightning Source LLC
Chambersburg PA
CBHW020604260626
47157CB00003B/854